STARSHIP GALATEA

Also by James Swearingen

Fiction

Black Sheep (2011)

The Prodigals (2013)

In the Hollow of Time, Galatea Saga, I (2021)

History of a Dying Planet, Galatea Saga, III (2021)

7 Maladies of the Soul (forthcoming)

Nonfiction

Reflexivity in Tristram Shandy (Yale, 1977)

STARSHIP GALATEA
A SACRED AND PROFANE TIME MACHINE

THE GALATEA SAGA, II

A Chronicle by I. Kahn

Cover layout and Interior Design: Creative Publishing Book Design
Cover designs inspired by Michael Rooks and Jeffrey Cassens

ISBN Paperback: 978-1-7373376-2-1
ISBN eBook: 978-1-7373376-3-8

Printed in the United States of America

THE ORIGIN OF THE END

"OUR SITUATION IN SPACE has just changed forever. Yesterday at 18:03h we received the last signal we're likely ever to get from Planet Ulro. For two Ulro centuries signals from Ground Control have been streaming toward us without interruption, until suddenly the signal broke off in the middle of a transmission. We have no way of knowing what happened. We've sent an urgent message, of course, but it will take more than a human lifetime to reach Ground Control, if it ever does, and as long again for us to get a reply. So we're alone in space!"

This news was delivered by Galatea Commander Alison Rawls in person. She had burst into the Chamber of the Council of Elders uninvited and unannounced, come to a halt at the head of the long oval table, glared down at us without a by-your-leave, and delivered this curt message.

I can tell you it sent a shock wave through the room, first startling, then leaving us amazed. As you might expect of a starship commander, Rawls is an imposing presence. Tall, slender, very attractive in a strict, official sort of way. The short blond hair that sweeps back from her face is an emblem of order and efficiency. Very feminine in the uniform that hugs her figure, yet a femininity that conveys an unrelentingly rational mind and a will of steel. On the few occasions I've seen her, I've been reminded of an Amazon without her quiver and bow.

The effect of her presence is enhanced by her being so rarely visible anywhere except on the bridge. No commander had ever come here in person. Then without a word of introduction, she interrupted with those five portentous sentences. It took about a nanosecond to see that everything, even the delicate balance of authority on the ship, had shifted and that our destiny had changed utterly.

One other aspect of this event was the well-known fact that Alison Rawls and her kind have nothing but contempt for our "band of dreamers" who lounge up here on our "talking deck" like the gods on Mount Olympus, indifferent to mortals below, glutting ourselves on the ambrosia of arcane speculation. The first impression I picked up as she entered the room was how distasteful to her it was to have to bother with us at all. But she's not a stupid woman and would never let resentment blind her.

So having delivered her message, she took the seat at the head of the conference table and in the continuing silence made a glancing survey of the Chamber, lined with books on one side and a large window on the other, framing a panorama of the cosmos.

As the consequences of her news sank in, our astonishment only increased. With a lightness out of sync with the occasion, member Claudio Rucai was heard to murmur, "This is first real event in our lifetime." He meant, I suppose, two hundred and forty years in space without anything happening that might transform the mission or alter our destiny.

By the way, my name is Ishmael Kahn, Recording Secretary of the Council of Elders on Starship Galatea, and my role is to introduce you to life on the generational starship.

Commander Rawls looked severely in the direction of Rucai's remark. Then, recognizing him for the first time, her authoritarian demeanor encountered his personal authority and she visibly wavered. Rucai is a tall man of exuberant Italian bearing, some sixty years of age, and the de facto spirit of the Council. He's a person who can electrify or silence a room just by entering. Rawls' single glance of recognition down the long conference table reduced her to life size and raised a question: What compelled her to consult with us in person, if you can call her announcement either consultation or personal? Why hadn't she sent a messenger? She's an intelligent executive woman as capable of charming as galling. And as the first female commander in the history of the mission, she is highly skilled in using her talents to intimidate or seduce as a situation requires, but in the crossing of glances with Rucai, her stern face softened visibly and she modulated her tone from aggression to geniality. She wanted—or needed—something. But what? Was she as far ahead of events as we were? Had she already seen that the news would shift the basis of authority on the ship to her advantage and to our disadvantage? If so, perhaps she needed to see how far our vision extended.

The important thing to understand here is the delicate balance between the technocrats in Starship Command and the Elders. Our Council consists of twenty of the best educated and most thoughtful people on the ship. We have met—the group has met—weekly since launch nearly three centuries ago. Because this Chronicle is largely about a self-perpetuating Council that was embedded in the ship by the first planners, I'll just say that our purpose has always been to consider the meaning and consequences of every act on board the ship, foreseeable and unforeseeable. We few have the leisure for such meditative thinking because we are rarely bound by time or immediate aims.

After the announcement, a spirit of gravity weighed heavy on the room. We sat for a time as in an old Quaker meeting, pondering the most fateful change since the ship was launched in Ulro Year 2075. Rawls squirmed almost invisibly as though we were wasting her valuable time until, gradually, the well-known differences between Council and crew seemed to subside, and she spoke again:

"I'll come directly to the point. My reason for being here is a problem of managing this information. Prevailing opinion on the bridge is that the news should not be circulated among the populace for fear of causing distress, even provoking disorder. But that leaves us open to later discovery. Conceal-ment might have consequences. At the very least it could erode confidence."

Wonderful, isn't it, that she regards truth as pragmatic, to be manipulated as utility dictates? Anyway, she went on to repeat other things we understood very well. I hope my colleagues didn't detect the condescension in her voice and eyes as she recounted how, during two and a half centuries of travel at near warp speeds, signals from Mission Control had often been intermittent.

It's true, of course. Messages received during the span of our generation had been chasing us for longer than we had been alive. Since she regarded "hard information" as the important thing, I wondered why, given the time lapse, she was taking the situation so seriously.

On the other hand, should the time difference matter since whatever information we got was new to us? Yet somehow it did. Occasionally when the ship paused to survey planets in one solar system or another, communications packets had time to catch up. Accustomed as we were to the expectation that eventually all signals might cease, there was still room to wonder why she had come. She was afraid. But of what? Dissension among the crew? That seemed unlikely in a quasi-military system. Or was this a concession to the fact that the Elders have the confidence of the populace and she needed our support with them? Whatever the truth was, once she had clarified the situation as much as it could be clarified, she put the question to us in an unaccountable tone of vexation:

"What is to be done now?"

Several Council members found the question incongruous and suppressed a chuckle. What's to be done when nothing can be done? And how much does a thing matter when it makes no difference? The relevance of the transmissions to the ship is mainly historical, and a public that lives in presence cares little about it. A reference point lost perhaps, but wouldn't that only be a psychological effect? The trouble is that no one knows what "only" means in that sentence.

When the members finally began responding audibly, the Commander was asked a few factual questions, and the tone of the room gradually modulated from astonishment to anxious deliberation. In our culture of debate, we considered the issue with the dispatch of an experienced team addressing an emergency.

Clive Dennet-Jones spoke first. But I want you to see him in the flesh as he speaks. Dennet-Jones is a tall, slender bachelor who stands as erect—some would say as stiff—as a broomstick. He's a linguist and your quintessentially tight-lipped Brit, the kind that, as a stranger, you would never speak to without first being introduced. It's an odd fact that although he does not have aristocratic roots, you find yourself acting as though he did.

Though he, like his great-great-grandparents, never set foot on the home planet, much less in a native region of the planet, yet he retains an amazing degree of cultural identity, as we all do. You begin to see from our names that our ancestors came from all over Planet Ulro, the Galatea having been a global project. It's curious that in the present homogeneity of language and ethnicity people take pride in their own traditions and preserve—sometimes passionately—the trappings of their ethnic uniqueness. What was once unconscious becomes something like an object of aesthetic desire, if the word is not too shallow. The more mysterious part is that so many ancestral physical features also survive, as though the traits of the past could be preserved by will.

But back to my story. In reply to the question "What now?" Dennet-Jones, addressing himself mainly to Commander Rawls, took the line that, beyond pure mysticism, the loss of signals from Ulro didn't matter. "I suggest that nothing should be done. The news changes nothing unless we intend to turn around and spend as many generations returning to Ulro to investigate. That being absurd, we should advise the Commander to carry on as usual with the systematic search for a hospitable planet. Even if we never find one, things will remain exactly as they are, so why make a stir? We have lived for nine generations in what once upon a time would have been called heaven. So here we are, in heaven if not in the heaven of the heavens! If we ever should find a destination, how many of us would care to trade the security of the mother ship for the inconveniences of a colony in a primitive terrestrial environment?"

What interested me most just then was Rawls' impatience as we began to wind our way slowly through the issue. She was clearly exasperated by our inefficient habit of holding a topic up to the light and turning it this way and that to catch every facet. She was like a fish on a hook and clearly wanted to be somewhere—anywhere—else. Which made her self-control exemplary.

The next to speak was our red-headed sociologist, Gwendolyn Burgess, who is a person of unrelenting "common sense," as it's called, however little sense she and Rawls may have in common.

"The Commander's news," she observed, "may have some temporarily unsettling effects when people realize that their feeling of destiny has been altered, but they'll get over it. After all, we've never known whether there was a human future outside the Galatea or not. I agree that our position should be: Nothing has changed. Do nothing. Say nothing. Get on with life as usual."

Claudio Rucai, a classicist, by the way, speaks rarely in these sessions and only on the most urgent topics, but this time he responded. "Mr. Dennet-Jones makes a good case, and in a literal sense he's right. Our voyage doesn't change. But I wonder whether, when the *meaning* of the voyage changes, everything changes? Isn't that why Commander Rawls is worried about public responses and why Dennet-Jones himself warns against 'making a stir'? Maybe we're on the way to becoming something different, something post-human—static human being after the struggles of history are left behind."

He chuckled. "That's when there's nothing more to be done, and we begin to fall asleep. Such questions are not exactly new to us. This change or mutation, however slow, will have consequences. Rather like the ancients adjusting to the knowledge that Planet Ulro wasn't the center of the universe. Or like surrendering the religious belief in life after death. Those changes also went unnoticed at first. But they altered the tone and texture of life so radically that, centuries later, people still struggle to define what difference their loss may have made."

At this point, Elena Bart, a small woman with piercing eyes and a laser-clear mind, retorted, "A better analogy is 'the death of God.' Gods, you may have heard, die very slowly. We're still trying to get disentangled from the last god we could recognize. We swept aside old Nobodaddy with the long white beard and have been trying one substitute after another ever since."

Elena Bart was trained in the ancient literatures of the Middle East and has spent about twenty years studying the history of religions. You may guess how out of place religion is in a totally secular, technological environment. So we smile condescendingly and call her our resident theologian. Maybe that's why I don't much like her. An austere, careworn face is matched by the eccentricity and sharpness of her remarks. In debate she can pin an adversary to the wall just with her eyes. It's enough to make her a scourge to the Council. But more of this when it's unavoidable.

Meanwhile, another member responded to her "death of God" remark. Oleksiy Hunenko grinned at her across the table and said, "I prefer not to join theological discussions, but"—now addressing the group at large—"there *may* be *something* in what Bart says." An unguarded chuckle took the measure of his coolness toward her mystery-mongering.

"The serious thing that has happened and may eventually be troublesome is the displacement of sovereignty."

At this emergence of Hunenko's well-known political passion, there was a muffled groan from several members. Oleksiy is a political historian who finds the issue of power in almost any topic that turns up. I'll tell you later about the deep tensions between Council and crew on this subject and why several people present have reason to regret Hunenko's bringing it up in the Commander's presence. He wasn't speaking to her at the time and is capable of having forgotten she was in the room. But she heard and took the full weight of his point. It was the worst possible thing to say in front of the enemy, unless he was trying to precipitate trouble. Hunenko is an astute thinker but can miss social realities out of pure innocence.

He continued unfazed. "No matter what the content or how out of date the message from Ground Control, it bears the authority of the origin. The *origin* of the mission is not a point in the distant past. It's a psychic anchor that secures the meaning of what we're doing here. The practical consequences of its disappearance may emerge slowly. Once sovereign authority dies, what takes its place? The king is dead. Now who rules? In this sense it may indeed be like the fugitive God of the universe."

Too late, Gwendolyn Burgess tried to soften his point. Without appearing to be speaking to Rawls, she shook her red hair in Bart's direction and responded to her instead. "I'm a humble social scientist so I'll leave aside the supernatural and cosmic dimensions of the question. I'll just remind you that the effects of this development may not be so different from others we've recently considered with some alarm. I mean the long-term effects of living in the artificial environment of a starship, knowing it's for life. The Council has been struggling with that problem for over a century."

What Burgess was referring to—I'll tell you more about all these people later, but I don't want to interrupt the conversation just now—she meant that in the past the Elders discussed several alienating factors: the lack of genetic and social diversity in a small, originally hand-picked population; the homogeneous intellectual and linguistic environment; the resulting diminution in the power of imagination; and much, much more.

"From the conceptual point of view," Burgess continued, "the disruption may have changed nothing. But with Ground Control permanently silenced, the future may appear in rather drab colors."

"Right, Gwen," Bart interrupted. "People live as much by hope as by bread."

To which Burgess replied, "And if we don't substitute a plan and a destination, even a hypothetical one, we'll live to see a contraction in all our spirits. In people whose rational grip on reality is less secure, the effects could be ruinous."

Elena Bart gave Burgess a gloating look and clapped her hands in mock applause. "Now look who's defending myth. I do hope you're not becoming disillusioned with the divine power of empirical measurement. Why not just survey public opinion: Ask everybody on board how they plan to feel about being adrift in space in, say, ten years."

During all this in-house banter among people who know one another's dispositions intimately and usually interact with goodwill, Commander Rawls was largely forgotten and clearly mystified. No one else seemed to notice, but I saw what a poor impression we were making on her. Through that admirable façade of self-control, her restlessness was visible, like having an itch you can't be seen scratching.

As a way of restoring the proper focus of the discussion, chief cosmologist Akira Kashimoto speculated on what conditions might currently be on Ulro. Kashimoto is the only member who enjoys the trust of the crew and the Council equally, the one because of his eminence as a scientist, the other because his head is still attached to his other parts. Usually he just sits quietly behind his Japanese smile, taking everything in, pondering implications, stated and unstated. Only when the issue is urgent does he intervene. When that happens, a hush typically falls over the room and everyone comes to mental attention.

At this juncture one could see Rawls following his remarks attentively. "Late in the twentieth century the Hubble Deep Probe could already read light across fourteen billion light-years. Theoretically, the signals from Ulro could not have been outrun and, however long the transmission took, they should not have ceased. That opens other possibilities that will multiply endlessly if we let this cat out of the bag. By some theories, the Galatea was launched in the first place because the planet was on the brink of destroying itself, and the gamble was to save humanity from extinction. Maybe that finally happened. Or there could have been a cosmic event like the one that killed the dinosaurs. Whatever it was, it happened many decades ago."

Anxious to bring the topic "back to earth," as Dennet-Jones put it, he filled the first pause in Kashimoto's speech. "Let's stick to what we know and not lose our way in pointless speculation. The question is, what's to be done?"

Bart glared at his insistence on practicality. "The fact that a question is unanswerable doesn't keep it from being urgent: He loves me, he loves me not? Real questions are the ones that refuse to be silenced by answers."

Hunenko added, "True. And facts aside, anxiety over the fate of the only known planet that evolved rational life will not die easily. It alters our responsibility. Absent Ulro, humanity is consigned to a sardine tin adrift in the void."

Apparently Dennet-Jones felt that, having spoken first, he had a certain prerogative. "On the strength of these very interesting speeches, I suggest the news be released along with an authoritative statement about the future of the mission—*as if* nothing had changed. Otherwise the very word 'mission' will come back to mock us."

And with that, the brief but momentous meeting ended. The Commander must have returned to the bridge counting how much time she had wasted letting us work our way around to the point of view she had brought with her. And that fact, if it is a fact, tells you much of what you need to know about the mind-set of Starship Command.

LIFE ON A STARSHIP

HERODOTUS SAYS he wrote his *History* to "preserve remembrance" of the Persian Wars "so that time will not abolish the deeds of men." All these centuries later I am writing this Chronicle for preservation *and* prevention: remembering without repeating. As it turns out, however, my project is more than a little absurd. It can preserve nothing and prevent nothing, since, once written, it must be suppressed.

The Chronicle was first conceived by the Elders, who charged me with preparing an account that would reveal day-to-day life in our space village, including samples of Council deliberations. The aim was to help our terrestrial heirs, if any, avoid repeating past mistakes during periods when there might be little leisure or little inclination to reflect on the life worth living.

I was an odd choice for the job because I am older and have a much simpler mind than most of my colleagues. As often as not the things they say confuse me. Especially when someone speaks as if we were all black boxes with egos, ideas, and neuroses, rattling around inside a largely unconscious inner space, or as if the simplest external object were only an empty field with electric charges dashing randomly across it. All this they call knowledge. I'm sure it's true in some way, but I have never been able to get it into my head that the causes of things are more important than things themselves. So how am I ever to give a fair account of these conversations?

The task of selecting a few representative exchanges—they've always been called "colloquies"—has proved especially demanding. I had three hundred-odd to choose from in the decade between the communications disruption and the time of writing. From this number I jettisoned many. Intellectual debates tend to run aground for various reasons: verbal ambiguities, repetitive quarrels, technicalities too abstruse to be useful, or topics too transient to be relevant. Others I dropped because no one at all intellectual needs examples of ordinary research projects or historical scholarship. Subsequently my choices were ratified by the members of the Council under two urgencies: practical issues of life on the starship and topics that might be useful to a colony should there ever be one.

Then recently, when the book was almost finished, I got a summons in the night that disrupted the whole plan and guaranteed no one would ever read it anyway. The problem was a dangerous political intrigue that I was required to include. The intrigue had been going on under my nose the whole time and was dangerous to us all. I'll tell you about that in due course, but for now I'm just reporting that including it retrospectively turned the randomness of the Chronicle into a plot and made my constraints much tighter. I had to make room by dropping half of the conversations already selected.

Eventually I resolved to focus on a kind of thinking you don't find by doing research in the memory banks of Alexandros. Instead I needed to catch the speculative impulse of the Council searching for new routes into the unknown.

One colleague has taught me to call these thought experiments exercises in "the higher pragmatism." That means practicality raised to a higher order and opened to a longer vision, always keeping an eye on what might wound where we're seeking to heal.

So, I have chosen to open my book with The Great Disruption, as it has come to be known, because it's the one fateful event since the launch of this one-way voyage of exploration deeper into the Milky Way. You've had a taste already of an inherent tension between Starship Command and the Elders. Operating the ship belongs to one, while questions of everyday life fall to the other. As for what the public should be told about the communications failure, Command sensibly decided to do what Dennet-Jones had recommended: *Tell the truth but tell it slant.*

From the beginning the object of the mission was to find another celestial body suitable for habitation. But the barest introduction to astronomy is enough to show what a gamble the plan was, given the distances involved and the rare conditions requisite for a human colony. Some of my colleagues see that as evidence of just how perilous things must have become on the home planet in the mid twenty-first century. Otherwise, they surmise, few would have ventured to plan and none to have joined such a mission. And there was the matter of the enormous global cost of building and deploying the starship. The Disruption hardly confirms this theory of doom, but it surely fits.

I did say, didn't I, that my name is Ishmael Kahn? Speaking of names, no one seems to know where the ship got *its* name. According to the memory banks there was a variety of possible sources, all descending from a Greek sea nymph named Galatea who was famous for her virtue. She's the woman whose statue was carved by Pygmalion and that Venus thought so beautiful that she sent Cupid to bring it to life with a kiss.

Another Galatea, the HMDS Galatea, was a survey ship in the royal Danish Navy, Denmark having been one of the nation-states in the period sometimes called "Late Modern." Also, Galatea is a moon orbiting Neptune in our native solar system, and 74 Galatea is a large main-belt asteroid between the planets Mars and Jupiter.

But my favored source for the name of the ship is a picture by the twentieth-century Spanish painter Salvador Dali called "Galatea of the Spheres." It is part Renaissance portrait of Gala, his wife and muse, and part Christian apologetics. It seems the artist had converted to Catholicism and was trying to reconcile his religious vision with the discontinuities of atomic matter. He painted the portrait as a matrix of spheres roaming in space, rather like this starship searching randomly for a home.

For the technological side of our odyssey—how we learned to travel at near warp speeds, fuel the starship in perpetuity, manufacture everything we need from basic elements, fabricate what foodstuffs we cannot grow—for all this information and much more about how the starship sustains itself, the curious reader may consult Alexandros. You'll have to excuse me, but I'm not a scientist and not much interested in machinery. My interest is in the human effects, and my charge is to shape a human story that makes sense of the isolated facts to help later generations grasp the non-technical meaning of their situation.

Our world is a long cigar-shaped cylinder, very sleek and aerodynamic-looking, I am told—since only a few living technicians have ever seen it from outside—rather like a cigar-shaped asteroid. It was designed as a self-sustaining habitat for several thousand explorers and colonists. For reasons that are both familiar and deeply obscure, the mission was planned under dire conditions on Planet Ulro.

The mystery is why our ancestors, accustomed to the open skies and seas, mountains and plains, found it desirable to transform their planet into a global machine in the first place, for that's essentially what happened over a span of centuries. Even less clear is why they would have volunteered to board a smaller machine knowing they would spend their entire lives in this womb or incubator or coffin without ever being outside again. It must have been some looming prospect of planetary disaster, but if so, the memory banks are unaccountably silent on the subject as on much else associated with the construction, selection of personnel, and launch.

Was the starship designed as a lifeboat or a luxury hotel? Either way it's many times the size and complexity of the ocean liners that once sailed the seven seas of Ulro—all needs supplied, security assured, and amusements sufficient to keep people distracted. Perhaps it did seem like utopia. We know from oral tradition rather than from those suppressed official records that these issues were much discussed among the elite group involved in the starship project, but the discussions went on under a cloak of taboo that was never lifted. We also know that the crew and colonists were selected with an eye to eventual intergalactic exploration far beyond our local cruise through the Milky Way. So, you see, the mission was never intended to return.

The starship, as designed and assembled in orbit around Ulro's moon, consists of many decks like the floors of a giant hotel, much longer than it is tall, all parts connected by elevators, staircases, and moving walkways. The lowest decks are devoted to manufacture, farming, water production, waste treatment, the transformation of energy, and dozens of other technical support functions that are off-limits to people who don't need to be there. An administration deck farther up is devoted to the managerial offices of a small city, like health care, housekeeping, and social services.

This and other public decks are organized like the long pedestrian streets, here corridors, of a terrestrial city, "buildings" on either side and side lanes or hallways that occasionally extend to the outer shell of the ship, and unpredictable smaller lanes off these lanes. All these are intended to make the environment as fresh and diverse as possible. Given the length of the "streets," the designers included segments of moving sidewalks alongside walking and running lanes. They, the planners, never forgot that residents here were here for life.

Ample room was provided for the expansion of the population and all the activities of any thriving, well-organized city, and near the top of the ship we come to the residential levels containing family suites organized into "neighborhoods" to accommodate basic functions of eating, sleeping, and nurturing children. Living quarters are interspersed with common areas that bustle "morning and night" with people going about their affairs. There are shops for the acquisition and exchange of essential goods and services, well-maintained parks for leisure activities, and performance spaces for the arts.

Above the residential levels is the Academic Deck, just below the top. It's for the schools of all levels and for diverse research facilities. At the very top—in restricted space again— are offices for Starship Command and the Chamber for the Council of Elders. Forward from these, at the very front, is the bridge. Only one level is higher, though if you grasp the cigar shape of the ship, it's only higher in being farther up the slant from the prow. That's the Observation Deck, reserved primarily for cosmological research.

The Observation Deck is extraordinary in design, like a dome open to the heavens. Since some of the clandestine activity in my suddenly expanded story occurs here, I must describe it. It's a large "swollen rectangle" capped by a dome that accommodates the telescopes and working space for a substantial number of people. One who is in the room when it's empty feels so exposed to the outside it can cause vertigo. The planners' solution is one of the wonders of the ship's design. To counter the effect of disorientation and exposure, the two ends of the rectangle extend beyond the circumference of the dome and provide enclosed space for research support. On the inner or dome side, these offices have sweeping concave walls, translucent rather than opaque, so that from the center of the great circle you experience contrary effects at the same time. Except for the office walls, the great transparent bubble would make you feel exposed and unprotected on top of the ship, in danger of floating away. But the enclosures at the office ends provide a sense of being contained and "grounded."

If you wonder why so much attention was lavished on this deck, consider that for creatures of sky rather than earth, cosmology has an importance similar to the geological sciences on a terrestrial planet. The heavens are our backyard, our park, our meadow, as well as our horizon, while the telescopes used by Akira Kashimoto and his students enable us to explore the distant corners of the vast playroom of the cosmos. Research was a secondary purpose of a mission that provided the unique opportunity to send the scientists and their telescopes where they had never gone before. For generations, the results of their work were exchanged with their colleagues on Ulro, though with the increasing time lapse, transmissions became a routine duty without the advantages of useful collaboration on either end.

Since the galaxy is our neighborhood, whenever this deck is not otherwise in use, it's open to the public, even at "night." People of all ages crowd into it like an Ulro city park on a holiday weekend. It's hardly too much to say that what the cathedral was for a medieval town, the Observation Deck is for us. One member of the present Council who is interested in the history of religions—but you've met Elena Bart already … Anyway, Bart likes to say that the Observation Deck and the cathedral serve the same purpose: one for worshiping the infinite and unnamable, the other for worshiping infinite scientific measurement.

Well, okay. I suppose cosmology and the cathedral do at least show a vague preoccupation with the heavens, but

Bart's manner is so annoying. Not just the connections she likes to force between unassociated ideas. It's her acerbic way. I see she's a perfectionist, and I can accept that shallow and sloppy thinking feels like a pea in her shoe. It irritates and she lashes out.

Perhaps I should turn the glass around and wonder why she annoys me so. Why am I sitting here right now compulsively disliking her when I should be getting on with my story? Besides, a writer must love his people if he's to get close enough to catch their outlines and weigh their characters. He doesn't have to *like* them; he has to *love* them. Claudio Rucai says that thinking *is* loving—its highest form. You see where that leads. Come to think of it, it also irks me that Claudio is so fond of Bart. But never mind that.

Back to the story. For clarity, I should note that we maintain Ulro units of measure. Time is artificially counted by the 24-hour clock, the seven-day week, and likewise for months and years. In a sense, there is no time to measure on a starship since nothing ever happens. Nothing, that is, that opens a new time and marks lived time as beginning *here* and *now*. We are told that "*there is a time for all things: a time to be born and a time to die; a time to plant, and a time to pluck up that which is planted.*" Well, planting and plucking up aside, if an event *is* a time and not a point on a scale, as some say, then isn't this sameness generation after generation a timeless existence? Maybe all that depends on how you conceive of history.

However artificial these units of measure may be, for us to function in the shifting cosmic environment, the parameters that give shape to life must be maintained. Thus, early morning, noon, evening, and night are marked by changes in the artificial lighting that is never allowed to go entirely dark. Likewise, the rhythms of weeks, months, and years—all are maintained much as they ever were. So you see that though no one now alive has ever set foot on Ulro or any other planet, the ship is an "Ulro bubble," and we remain the disinherited children of another world.

You may wonder why I'm always making comparisons with Ulro. I suppose it results from a preoccupation with the past that developed very early. My father was a historian, and he was always puzzled by time. Among my most treasured memories are the weekends when I was home from school and he read me stories from history. Sometimes he would stop in the middle of a story and begin musing on time.

In those days I didn't understand what it meant and, to tell the truth, I don't understand much better now, but with real sorrow in his voice—with perhaps a dash of good old Jewish guilt—he would complain about "getting time wrong." One night stands out in memory. He said that time was a snowball and things to come were accretions covering over a past that must never be lost. Then he stopped to think and admitted there was something wrong with that image. "It doesn't fit experience," he said. "Especially the experience of forgiveness."

He went on musing about other spatial metaphors for history—a circle, a wandering dotted line, a series of isolated dots popping up erratically like an archipelago in the sea. Those at least are the ones I remember. But he always bounced back to the path of that snowball rolling down a hill. Many years later I learned to wonder if his problem might lie in accepting the idea of chronology as the whole story. If so, that's Alexandros in a nutshell and a warning to me not to lean too heavily on the word "chronicle."

By the way, Alexandros' memory banks provide us with "total recall" of planetary history. It's a complete media record—every book, journal, recording, and film ever made on the mother planet, except for the pre-launch blackout! Otherwise, everything not lost before the technological revolution. All of it was loaded into Alexandros before launch, and that record was perpetually supplemented by the communication packets for almost two and a half centuries.

Oddly, no one at the last Council meeting thought to mention it, but our further insulation after The Disruption may prove a still more severe loss to our island culture. Except for what's produced by our tiny populace, there will be no new books or films, no new music or science. However "out of date" the ones transmitted were by the time they arrived, they were new to us. It would appear for this and other reasons that chronology is a concept with a limited provenance. Perhaps the time of measurement depends on a more fundamental experience of time. To us a new book a century old is—or was and may be again—contemporary and no less inseminated with the creative spirit. What's the difference between reading Homer or Shakespeare or Kafka after all? The singular work is "eternal." But since I've never been sure what that word means, I'll get back to the ship.

Our social structure is simple. It consists of four classes. The classes don't correspond to the ancient hereditary divisions of Ulro history or to the distinctions by wealth that came later. Differences on the starship are not based on material inequalities but on a rational division of labor that acknowledges only tasks and talents and skills. Material conditions, being uniform and sufficient, largely go unnoticed. What class distinctions there are consist of different jobs: Providers of goods and services, Technicians, Elites, and Children—all conceived as functions rather than individual persons. It may seem odd to count the children separately, but I'll come to that.

First, the Providers. Most of the adult population is engaged in services necessary to the space village. There can be little significant material growth where resources and space are limited and the birth rate is ultimately static. Such industrial production as we have is performed mainly by robotics, so there's little labor. Where there is no scarcity or need, there is no poverty, and the notion of private property is largely obsolete. Not that it's forbidden or that we are more virtuous. It's just that without the impulse to ownership or to economic competition, the concepts and the notions of economic equality and inequality have largely worn away.

The utopian dreamers of Ulro history were occupied with class struggle and quantitative equality, but here those simply don't apply. The very word economics, *oiconomia*, has largely returned to its ancient sense of ordering the house. There is still dissension, of course, but it grows in different soil. Where there is little to fear and less to hope, temptation lies in the direction of such enervating vices as complacency, boredom, and sloth. About these there will, unfortunately, be much more to say.

The Technicians. I think I mentioned that the crew who operate the ship are organized in a quasi-military structure under the Commander and her mates. Well, the crew is at the top of the ladder of Technicians. This structure derives from the long history of ships on the high seas of Planet Ulro and the subsequent history of airplanes and spacecraft. But the Technicians also include those responsible for modes of production, all manufacture being from materials of microscopic or molecular scale and requiring complex technology and skill. Even general security, once called law enforcement, is a technical operation under the ultimate authority of the Commander. So this class is almost as numerous as the Providers.

However, the broad operational decisions about the purposes and conditions of the mission are not the prerogative of this class alone. On these points, authority is divided, and the result is the major point of stress. But since that's what this Chronicle is largely about, I'll leave that for now and pass on.

The Elites. These are much less numerous but far more diverse than either of the preceding classes. Some people are offended by the term itself so it gets understated, but euphemisms may only distort language and loosen our grasp of reality. The term is necessary for understanding possibilities inherent to our circumstances. The naval command structure aside, the fact that the Elites are a disparate group with permeable boundaries weakens any threat of oligarchy. The class system, based on merit, is less rigid than it may sound. It is largely invisible and quite flexible. Intellectuals, artists, teachers, researchers of various kinds, but also people whose pursuits later in life ally them in spirit to such company—these do not form a parallel ruling class but *a way of living*. It is possible if a bit unusual for a person to begin life as a Producer and become a member of the Council of Elders.

Then the Children, the fourth class—and always the first because the future of humanity! The best way to take you deeper into the mind and sensibility of our people is to speak of the education of children. Not just the facts. The facts are the very things that need explaining, and this will be done best by letting you look more closely at how the schools are ordered.

On a generational starship where all but the first generation are born, live, and will likely die, life is oriented toward an indefinite future that rests in the hands of the unborn. No mystery, then, that education should be a primary concern and be supervised by Elders committed to nurturing all human talents. The last thing we want is shortsighted and arbitrary "conditioning" of unique children to easy conformity, like animals, to their environment. To instill stultifying norms and popular values would only lead to repetition and thoughtlessness that might be called de-volution. The Council's aim is to initiate the young into the non-conformity of living and thinking inventively. The aim is to develop courageous openness of each person to all that offers itself for appreciation and understanding.

To that end our children begin school at about age three. A bit later but still at a tender age they leave their parents and live in "houses" on the Academic Deck, designed and staffed for the purpose. They return home on weekends and holidays, but the point is to wean them from the family unit as in the olden-time boarding school and shape them to life with their peers in the public space. The nuclear family is regarded as the best incubator but fundamentally inadequate for nurturing citizens. Often this means that the family itself is a temporary social arrangement as, for better or worse, it had largely become on Ulro before the mission, though *there* it often abandoned the welfare of the children and responsibility for the future. No doubt our system would have scandalized the individualists of that day, but the mission planners had become all too aware of the disintegrative effects of individualism as encouraged by the family structure of the time.

In their early years, our pupils study a universal curriculum in the liberal arts, sciences, and fine arts. In addition, all are required to practice some aspect of gymnastics or physically vigorous sport. Each child continues in each field of the common curriculum as far as talent allows. When differences of aptitude become evident, they are directed into branches of study best suited to their intellectual, affective, and manual gifts. In the teen years, individual inclinations are also considered, but it is never left exclusively to the students to choose their own direction. Where, after all, is individual welfare less separable from long-term public welfare than on a generational starship? And yet, understanding that pedagogy is also seduction, the Council strives to put a charismatic teacher in every classroom and every lab.

Here's what I mean. I was a fair example of the mediocre Level I student—the highest of three levels—who needed to be pushed beyond my own interests. When I was taking the year-long survey course in astronomy and cosmology, I spent a lot of time in the observatory. But, having always found human beings a greater mystery than the stars, I mainly gazed at the people gazing at the stars. Younger students would arrive under the great dome, look up, and lapse into silence as they stared dumbly into the dark, as indifferent toward innumerable points of distant light at first as I. But when the guide, an assistant to the cosmologist, drew their attention to one dot that looked much like all the others and began weaving a story about how an exploding supernova scatters the elements of nucleosynthesis and all that follows, the dead faces sprang to life.

Just here, in native capacity and disposition, nurtured by masters of seduction in the classroom or lab, lie the roots of our class structure. It's not about rules; it's about love that inspires understanding. Thus every precaution is taken to prevent life's being reduced to useful purposes. What is easy and quick is discouraged. Anyone can see that the inclination toward instant gratification ends in a life of diminishing returns and that on a starship, when any person lives idly, everyone loses. The class system results from the necessity for excellence. Sometimes it's referred to as a "natural aristocracy," where excellence is not eroded by shallow notions of equality among unique beings. It's also called "democratic aristocracy," shifting the emphasis to participation without compromising the ideal.

No one is limited to one place for life except by capacity, achievement, or choice. The lowest manual job may be performed by a person who spends his leisure time on the Observation Deck studying the heavens or on Alexandros reading the classics. I know of at least one instance when a person of the most ordinary talents and achievements rose to become a member of the Elders, and there are members of the Council who spend their leisure hours watching old Ulro movies or playing racquetball.

Because our circumstances require excellence of many kinds, we encourage diversity beyond what can be foreseen by social engineering. And yet mediocrity in any line of development is discouraged in favor of achievement in another. Collective well-being forbids the kind of dilettantism that dabbles life away, shifting from one shallow interest to another. Even as specialization and division of labor are essential, ample opportunities are provided for hobbies and avocations of all sorts. One person can't be a research botanist, a ballerina, a learned elder, and a good violinist, and yet living well requires broad interests and lifelong growth.

From this cursory glance at the social order, you may already see that our way of organizing life serves more than utility or convenience. It responds to needs acknowledged for centuries, but it certainly does not result in a perfect existence. The mission planners may have thought they were offering volunteers for the Galatea odyssey a kind of paradise rather like a return to a virtual womb. Perhaps people who regarded nature as a machine could not foresee that life limited to an actual machine, however comfortable, might lead to the death of desire, or that life in space might lead to an epidemic of anxiety. More on this too—later.

IN PRAISE OF ANXIETY

AFTER ALISON RAWLS MET with the Council, the urgent question quickly divided: For the crew it morphed into "Where do we go next?" while for us it became "Why go anywhere at all?" Between that "where" and that "why" lies the vexed history of the starship.

The chief danger of the moment is the embryonic conflict between two cultures: Command and Council. It duplicates one of the many fault lines that ran through Planet Ulro itself. More or less the eternal rivalry between theory and practice, utilitarian aims and "aimless" understanding. Not a rivalry in the nature of things. More like an illusion indulged when we are unprepared or unwilling to take the long view of what practical conditions mean and where they might lead. The distinction is forced on us because trouble can arise between us and the Technicians by a thoughtless remark on either side. The new political danger is that, as the nominal authority of Ulro vanishes, the balancing influence of the Council will diminish, and real authority may shrink to managerial power. The sticking point du jour.

The Elders are sometimes laughed at or, even worse, regarded as a club of talkers who do nothing useful. It's true in a way. At least where there is leisure to consider life as a whole and to follow complex issues through to the end, talk is endless. Why not, since to con-verse is to live by keeping company with others in language? Our colloquies have occurred weekly for two and a half centuries. The result is that every aspect of life on the Galatea past, present, future is regularly examined and re-examined. Literally thousands of meetings have been devoted to the widest imaginable range of questions, from the ridiculous to the sublime.

In this Chronicle I have preserved a handful of these discussions but not just as historical information. As one member, philosopher Hannah Jaeger, said a century ago, "Preservation for its own sake is an effort to stop time and change. And that's doomed in advance." Her remark suggests that memory may be a stranger thing than people think. Those who want history unadorned may consult "the memory of man" in the archives of Alexandros, but if they read the colloquies as collections of historical facts, they will understand nothing. We entertain instrumental, practical questions only as they bear on the quality of public life. Otherwise, they're left to the various officials. The polestar of each conversation is the single question, "What does it mean to live well?" There may be no final answer, and yet every human act assumes guiding ideals.

In the commotion surrounding the communications failure you have already glimpsed that our existence is not exactly idyllic. To call the Galatea an incubator may be unfair, but The Disruption brings to a critical point something that surfaced slowly in the early decades of the mission. As the hope of our ever finding a home faded, people began to feel a nameless anxiety associated with the deadness of time and with a sense of groundlessness. It was, and remains, a background uneasiness, invisible but pervasive like the cosmic microwave background. Not suffering from anything in particular but unsettled, haunted, anxious.

You might think that the memory of the terrestrial platform and our kinship with earth would eventually have died out like an old habit. Instead, after generations of absence, the loss returns like a repressed trauma. Losing touch with Ground Control is like losing the long-sustained voice of the deceased mother. Or like the cartoon character who doesn't realize he has overrun the cliff until he looks down. That's where you end up if you try to live by the facts as though imaginative contexts were unreal.

The symptoms of anxiety were first recognized around Ulro Year 2170 in what the medical staff called "Starship Syndrome." In other words, speaking of imagination, they knew something was wrong but had no idea what. No less real for that! The usual result was, having given it a name, there had to be a cure. Call it what you will, it has been our primary mental health issue ever since and appears related to the artificial and confined environment. In truth, life for us is static. We might be moving ever so fast through the cosmic void, but speed is just an abstract quantity. From where is a ship blazing a trail across the galaxy distinguishable from stasis? Not from inside! To us it's like going somewhere without moving, except that where there is no motion there is no space and nowhere to go.

No shortage of inside space, of course. Plenty of room to move around in a ship as large as a small city with windows and portholes and an observation deck. In a sense, enclosed as we are, we live more exposed than terrestrial beings ever did. The sphere of the heavens extends before us in every direction, and there are innumerable things to see that no one has seen before. Yet it's possible to feel like an animal in a luxurious cage, homeless, groundless, adrift, waiting only to die.

Even though we have never had a positive destination, knowing that we are no longer connected to a beginning or an end intensifies the symptoms. Once we were drawn forward toward the possibility that somewhere down the corridors of "time" we would find a new earth. That gave hope. Each time we altered our course or sent probes to make closer surveys of a planet, it felt like progress. Even after it became clear that suitable planets for human habitation, if any exist at all, are far less numerous than twenty-first-century science had predicted, we remained beings attuned to the future.

Repeated disappointments have fostered complaisance. From afar a comfortable life is more attractive than the hardships of colonizing a hostile planet, but "more . . . than" still holds a vague promise of something other than repetition. So the search goes on more or less as it always has because it's indispensable. The difference is that where once we kept ourselves ready for the unexpected, we have become disheartened and a bit lax. You can see why the decision on how to manage the news about The Disruption was critical, even a turning point in the mission.

In Ulro Year 2314 we had made an unusually thorough survey of one planet therefore called P2314. During the survey, hope was on the rise, not so much because anyone wanted to live on that desolate space rock, but because it gave shape to the mission and to our lives. Eventually the judgment was that while the planet might be adapted, it was not ideal. So we moved on, and public spirit plummeted. Which proved that the communications issue was critical and Commander Rawls' concern was sensible.

The decision when it came took the form Gwendolyn Burgess had advocated when it was first announced: Supply a substitute destination, even a hypothetical substitute, to sustain hope. Hence the announcement—without further consultation with the Council! —that, having lost touch with Ground Control, we were returning to Planet 2314. We were then ten years beyond that planet, but since our flight path had not been in a "straight line," we could return in roughly six years. As a result the shock of finding ourselves isolated in space was softened by the plan to return to the scene that had raised, then dashed, our hopes a decade earlier.

And yet the decision, benignly practical as it appeared, would prove to be one of those moments when a contingency comes along and changes nothing . . . but destiny! At that moment, the poles of our little world invisibly shifted, though realization of the fact would come only in the future perfect.

A surge of excitement followed the announcement, but soon afterward we were blindsided by a virile return of the starship malaise. Faces that had been restored to the glow of health lost their luster as unexpectedly as a punctured balloon loses air. It was as though they suddenly awoke from a happy dream and faced the same drab world. At that point I took it on myself, as designated historian, to research

Council records of the year 2170 when it had occupied so much of the Council's attention and resulted in an overhaul of public welfare.

One evening a few months after Commander Rawls' meeting with us, we gathered and, having no particular agenda for the session, sat around the table chatting informally about the morale issue. Remember, the twenty Elders live much of our lives in the Council Chamber. Not always sitting, of course. We frequently get up during a discussion to stretch our legs while keeping tabs on the progress of the topic. That night as I happened to be passing behind the chair of Gwendolyn Burgess, our sociologist, I mentioned a colloquy on the subject, discovered during my research. She turned around in her chair and began interrogating me about it.

Leaning against the back of the empty chair next to her, I replied, "The colloquy was conducted by a colorful group of people in Ulro Year 2170. It grew out of still older conversations on the psychosocial effects of living for extended periods in this closed, no-growth environment. Nothing surprising. Except that the symptoms were the same as we're seeing now."

She continued, "Anything useful to us?"

"In part it was historical, but something new to me was a summary of problems the mission planners had always anticipated. Relating to increasing homogeneity on the ship."

"What symptoms?"

"Well," I answered, "that caused some debate. The member who led the discussion was a social scientist who had done extensive research on it. Her name was—is—Parvaneh Sarosh, of Iranian descent. I've just learned that she is the

36

great-grandmother of our Ava Sarosh, whose interests lie somewhere in the field of social anthropology."

I gestured toward the young Sarosh down the table and, as our gazes happened to cross, she nodded and smiled from the warmest, hazel-colored Persian eyes you can imagine. I continued to Burgess, "The conversation is very interesting. Probably worth consulting in relation to our circumstances."

"Then summarize it," Burgess replied, turning to include others in her request. "Or tell it all. We seem to be out of ideas. Some historical perspective might be useful. All I remember about that period—twenty-second century, did you say? —I remember that social life was reorganized at about that time. Were the two things related?"

As I walked back around the end of the table to my place, I answered, "It is worth reviewing. I've even made an abridged version of the video recording. I can play it if you like."

This was a novel idea and it met with general interest, as much out of curiosity to see the Elders from a past era in person as to observe together a dialogue from the past. Anyone might consult these records at any time, of course, but it's a well-known fact that where resources are unlimited, the sheer quantity discourages access. The old adage, I suppose, "Proportion is all."

So we cleared the far end of the room and I turned the video on. It flickered a moment then virtually doubled the length of the table and the Chamber. There, just beyond us, sat our predecessors in the same room, at the same table, discussing the same topic that occupies us now, except that what happened at one end of the table was separated by a century and a half from what happened at the other end. It felt like a joint conference between the real and the virtual in which the boundary was blurred. By way of introduction I said only, "The year is 2170, nearly two centuries ago."

(As an aside, I should say that, for the convenience of future researchers, I record an inconvenient number of names here, but there is no more reason to worry about remembering all these characters than keeping the details of chronology clear. We follow the tale, not the people.)

First the virtual figure named Parvaneh Sarosh reported on her recent research. A lovely woman of great dignity: light olive skin, dark brown hair, even features accented by high cheekbones. Her exotic appearance with the most expressive eyes you can imagine would get a hearing whatever the merit of her words. She began with characteristic dignity by describing symptoms, in her most clinical voice:

"The medics first noticed this phenomenon. They call it Starship Syndrome. They report that the health-care system is increasingly burdened with nervous disorders without detectable organic causes. It's a general feeling of agitation and disorientation. When they are questioned, most people fumble for a description and when they find none, they become more anxious. Those who have an answer give strange ones."

Manuel Didière, a historian of technology, was a small Frenchman full of petit-bourgeois intensity. He wore inner turmoil on a pinched forehead that occasionally glowed like a flag of distress. With the impatience of a man who thinks every problem has a corresponding solution, he asked, *"What are they afraid of? They must know they're probably safer than anyone else has ever been."*

"What they know has little to do with it, Didière. It's not fear. They don't feel threatened by any present or future thing. Anxiety is different from fear. It's insecurity without an object, and the patients are the first to call it irrational. Some are clever enough to invent explanations. They mention things like agoraphobia and claustrophobia and acrophobia, knowing it's not fear. And they know it's not about space. They were born in space. Some of them feel anxious when they look out a window at what most of us think is beautiful. In one case a patient whose job was to make outside repairs to the shell of the ship said he had to change jobs because he constantly felt that he was flying away without a tether. That may sound like fear, but he added that he had also stopped going to the Observation Deck because it made him feel disoriented.

"Another patient says the opposite: She feels trapped inside a container she can never escape. To counteract the sense of being enclosed she takes long walks the length of the ship, trying to convince herself that the sensation is false. Yet it always returns. By the time these people seek help they have come to feel that life is at a standstill. Another, who avoids the Observation Deck, also avoids the long escalators going down—not up—because he feels he's falling.

"The cases associated with space are odd and interesting but not typical. The majority just complain of insomnia, nightmares, and being irritated by everything and everyone around them. One situation is even more alarming for the long term. Teachers report an increase in restlessness among bright students who seem to be losing the capacity to concentrate on their studies. Not the slow ones. The quick ones. All these cases seem to have in common is a nameless distress that makes life a torment."

One member of the virtual Council, Robert Forsythe, also interested in the history of science, was a pleasant, lighthearted man of American heritage with a bushy mustache and side whiskers. He asked, *"So what's been done? Does anything help? What's your best guess about the causes?"*

"I can only guess," Sarosh replied. *"But I'm not alone in suspecting that the phobias are imaginary, which isn't to say unreal. We doubt that space or time or anything environmental lies at the source. It's possible that the anxiety is an extension of dissatisfaction with themselves. They all seem ill at ease, like not being at home with themselves. The councilors who have most experience with the problem tend to agree that it is a reactive response—a more and more common one—to conditions of life that we all share. That doesn't explain much but it raises the question, why not everyone?"*

"What's been done?" Forsythe repeated impatiently in a tone that made it sound as though the doctors, all things being possible, weren't doing their jobs.

Sarosh controlled her evident displeasure with his peremptory tone. *"Since no one pretends to understand the disease, much less to have a cure, the pharmacy goes on dispensing ever more antidepressants, sleeping pills, tranquilizers, and the placebos that often work as well. It's understandable. The symptoms are real and the causes are hypothetical. So you treat the symptoms. But long-term, the mission itself could be threatened."*

"Threatened how?" Didière asked, this time genuinely puzzled.

"There's a fear that social life may be mutating in ways that could be undesirable and irreversible. I suppose that's a

sociological question stacked on top of a biological question on top of a philosophic question, but we do know that the problem has been steadily increasing for at least two decades. I don't know what 'normal' means, but this is clearly abnormal. It's urgent that we understand such debilitating phenomena."

That ended Sarosh's summary. In the interval as Council members at both ends of the table sat weighing the situation she had described, I studied her. At my first viewing I hadn't seen how much our Ava Sarosh is like her ancestor. The physical features, the modest dignity, even the grace of gesture and warm vocal intonations have passed intact down to the fourth generation. It made me wonder again how so many of us bear inherited traits from even farther back. If you look from the right angle, you sometimes see ancient experience stamped in the organism just in the way a person walks across a room or exposes herself to a glance. It's as though we had chosen to skip over centuries of history and replicate ancient ethnic traits. I must remember to ask our biologist Ang Yimou if such things are genetically transmissible even if they begin in social experience.

A voice from the past that I didn't recognize eventually broke the silence in the room and jerked me back to virtual reality: *"Good work, Parvaneh. Clearly the issue is urgent but I for one am at a loss. I'd hate for us to panic and turn in desperation toward social engineering."*

She replied with light irony, the almond-shaped eyes glowing with amusement. *"You think our record at engineering human responses is less than encouraging?"*

Then she continued, more seriously. *"True, it leads nowhere anyone consciously wants to go. And there is a danger that we might institute repressive social policies. Totalitarian systems are very imaginative in discovering solutions that make things worse."*

As people in both eras sat figuratively wringing their hands, I remained a spectator observing in wonder the intensity of engagement at our end of the table with what was going on twenty feet and a century and a half away. Proof that as the Council has grown over many decades, it has become a unique bond of past, present, and—because what is said is said no less for them—even future members.

Quite suddenly a voice from the past that we hadn't heard before pushed the topic in a curious direction. A woman named Chetana Dubashi.

You may have heard of Dubashi. Her primary interests were literary, especially the ancient books of the Indian subcontinent, though that wouldn't appear to have much to do with the subject under discussion. Chetana is a short, sculpted woman with dark, dramatic features who would seem more at home in a sari than in a starship uniform or a Council robe. As the camera suddenly confronted me with the *bindi*, the bright-red "third eye" on her forehead, I was reminded of the inner gaze or center of consciousness descending from the Hindu hymn of creation.

Dubashi began by throwing a gleeful barb at Parvaneh Sarosh. *"It's good to hear a social scientist admit that there are realities beyond social and statistical norms. We may even have stumbled on the possibility that the human horizon might be wider than the facts!"*

This sounded important in a way I couldn't make out. Did she, do you suppose, mean we aren't creatures of chronology, that we belong to a different time? Anyway, at our end of the table Elena Bart audibly snickered at the criticism of behavioral science and cast a significant glance at our own sociologist Gwendolyn Burgess as though to deposit the remark at her door.

Meanwhile, back among the virtuals, Parvaneh Sarosh smiled at the salvo from Dubashi and answered coolly with a remark that was more than slightly dismissive. *"My attention has been confined to trying to discover the facts of experience. Naturally I've thought about what the facts might mean—not very successfully, I admit—but I don't care to confuse the two."*

Dubashi had a way of startling others by coming at an issue from the ozone and did so again for the company at large. *"We might reformulate the question and ask where on a starship there is space for desire. It's a nest, and when we've nested down, secure and well-provided, what's left to hope? Maybe these patients are canaries in our mine shaft. Our prophets. If Sarosh is right, they can't even translate their anxiety into something to fear. Their surroundings don't have that much significance, and they're left facing something about themselves they can't face."*

Forsythe turned red with frustration and slapped the virtual table violently with an open hand. As though it was Sarosh who had precipitated this extravagant speech, he shouted, *"Why do you weave such a tangled and pessimistic tale? It's purely fanciful. It just gives Dubashi a chance to extol her Eastern mystics."*

You need to know only that Forsythe was the most prominent historian of that generation and formidable in debate. He continued, *"There's nothing here that isn't perfectly normal. In the beginning nobody thought the search for a habitable planet would be easy and nobody has thought so since. So, it's been ninety years, and people have gotten discouraged. It's natural. Of course we all need something to work for. Your point—aside from its gothic embellishments—is so obvious it's trivial. We need goals at shorter range. Rewards for smaller tasks. Let's try to stick to the point."*

Dubashi shot back, *"A Band-Aid over an abscess!"*

Forsythe: *"Life consists of Band-Aids. Preferably real ones!"*

Dubashi: *"Here's the point, Robert. How we occupy the situation we're given. We're born on a starship where we look out into the void every day with few ideals that give meaning to our situation. And yet I have a say in my disposition toward my circumstances. I can be grateful for having a life to grouse about. Grateful or discontented, terrestrial nature aside, we have the greatest things ever created by the human spirit at our fingertips. We can develop in infinite directions or we can fixate on what we lack and plunge into despair. What's wrong with people who live free of need, free to live like the gods, and yet turn life into a disease to be endured? Taking pleasure, I might add, in their discontent. I say that's a disease of the spirit!"*

Sarosh answered in all her imperturbable Persian dignity with a verbal shrug. *"Yes? So what? Where does all that get us? To the salvation of the soul of every lazy child on the Galatea? Psychoanalysis interminable? To what?"*

"*Careful, Parvaneh,*" Dubashi replied. *"Don't alarm Forsythe by confusing the pathology with the cure. If there is disease and we get the description right, we might find that it foreshadows a new kind of health. Even the metaphor of illness*

*and cure may lead us astray. Anxiety shows care where indiffer-
ence would be the death of the spirit."*

Sarosh: *"Let's say we all agree with you, Chetana. Then
what are we to do?"*

*"If that's a real question, it's a good one. While social engi-
neering tries to adjust collective dynamics and biologism looks
for a pill and skepticism wrings its hands—we might look more
closely at ourselves and our predecessors. How is it that twenty
people come to this room week after week, generation after generation to face the mystery of things, always starting the adventure
over, devoting our lives to the pursuit of wisdom, while some of
our neighbors one deck down neglect their talents? One group lives
a rich life while the other spins its wheels, bored out of its mind.
Where does the difference lie? The question is this: What can we
do for them to make them stronger people?"*

The short, square figure of Viktor Pastukh, who looks more
like an Eastern European peasant than an intellectual, shook
the bald head with the cotton fringe in vigorous approval. As
he tried to ask how education could cause a person actually to
do what he already knows is good, Didière cut him off sharply.
"Don't fret, Viktor. She's really preaching a new religion."

Manuel Didière was trained as an engineer in his youth,
then got fascinated by the history of technology and eventually
became a kind of social planner and member of the Council.
For him, even in the depths of cosmic space, reality consisted
exclusively of an object-world and its processes. His protest
continued, *"This is all arrogant elitism. Of no use whatever."*

And that provoked Dubashi. *"Okay, if it makes you feel
good to say so, Didière. But your imitation of the passion for*

ignorance isn't very convincing. Leave that to people who resent hearing their complacencies named. It's redundant to call excellence elitist. And the addition of 'arrogant' is just defensiveness in hedonists whose sloth prevents their doing the work it takes to be good at something. You are better than that, Manuel."

Before this exchange descended into a quarrel, as I knew it would, I turned off the recording, and we sat quietly until Gwendolyn Burgess took up the case in time present.

"Some things appear to have changed since 2170 and some "haven't!" she said in a tone of amusement. "Our people aren't so much anxious as indifferent. Bored. Instead of avoiding escalators, they wander around with blank faces or retreat into work. They don't just suffer from being idle; they enjoy it."

"I hope you're wrong!" our colleague Joseph Kern wailed in what sounded like a cry of sorrow. "We might as well put brains in jars and feed them stimuli. If there's any truth in what I'm hearing tonight, then the mission has been at risk for a long time. Life in space certainly gives the lie to the notion that what I do with my time is my own business. My time, my talents, and my habits pass into collective experience and bear on all of you and on the unborn."

That outburst confounded all Burgess' psychological convictions, but she only withdrew her use of the term "indifference." "People who take so much trouble finding diversions don't seem indifferent. And most people certainly aren't idle. So why take boredom as a general threat?"

"Oh, they may be in perpetual motion. Even in a frenzy of activity," Bart replied. "But the aim is to hide from the emptiness. It—the emptiness—isn't theirs, you know. They experience everything around them as being indifferent *to them*. Unrelated. When we refuse to engage with it, the world becomes indifferent. This breakdown of the relation *between* people and their world means the death of desire. Boredom."

"That's not bad." Burgess replied. "Why didn't Dubashi say that?"

"Because they"—pointing to the now blank screen at the end of the table—"didn't want to hear it!"

"Still, it's a little hard to look out the window and feel at home."

Bart pressed the point. "Then look somewhere else! We have intelligent and creative people to converse with. All the arts to give us joy. Infinite variety. All learning at our fingertips. Why should anyone turn her back on what's in *our* world here and fixate on the void outside the window? Why not bless it? I think it's because we must feel something, and it's easier to feel deprived!"

"Still most people are functional. Even busy."

"There you're missing something, Gwendolyn. People who are just going through the motions of living cling to the very things that bore them. When they're off balance, they escape into busyness. Diversion conceals how much they love their little disease. Provide more diversions! Keep the empty people running!"

Burgess didn't even try to hear that. "I want to get back to what the historian said. What was his name, Kahn?"

"Forsythe. Robert Forsythe."

"Thank you. Forsythe made a suggestion that the metaphysicians didn't want to hear."

" . . . As you're not hearing me!" Bart said aside.

Again Burgess ignored her. "Forsythe recommended inventing temporary goals. Distractions, if you like. I don't see that distractions are so bad. Many of our leisure activities date from the time of this timely old colloquy. In that era they developed the crafts and expanded participation in sports. I believe art education even got a boost. These may not have been permanent solutions, but they seem to have improved the quality of life without resorting to ancient spooks or modern superstitions."

You can see that Burgess and Bart are destined to continue the same debate Dubashi and Forsythe had begun, so here I'm cutting off my account of this unusual session with only one auspicious detail: Somewhere along the way—in our time—Burgess happened to remark on how frequently one or another of us referred to what she called "the time thing."

Then she added, "It reminds me that the person on board who has the most experience with the boredom problem is the psychiatrist Nacho Rojas. He's always saying that the most ordinary things involve how we experience time. I've no idea what that means, but maybe we should invite him to tell us about it sometime."

And so it was decided to consult a person who, as a result, was destined to become a new and important member of the Council.

REINVENTING EDUCATION

WHEN THE SHIP REVERSED course, the idea of a colony shifted from an indefinite possibility to an imminent event a scant six years ahead. This initiated re-examinations of technical surveys of P2314 made a decade earlier and raised an alarm in the Council. The new environment certainly changed my life, since I was commissioned to begin assembling this Chronicle of life in space. The original plan, suggested by Claudio Rucai, was to focus on the crucial period we were entering between the turning back and establishing a colony.

I should repeat: Don't bother trying to remember all the names I've been throwing at you. What matters is not the individuals but the unique condition of life on the ship. Don't get me wrong. Each person is important, but our concern is collective life and how it is and might be structured. In the schools, for example. The last time the Elders revamped the school system was over a century ago, but just now an order has come from Command for a comprehensive evaluation at all levels. In their view the prospect of "planting" a people on a terrestrial body seems to raise a pressing need for changes in the curriculum. I can tell you that the news got a cool reception in the Council.

Here's how it happened. Akira Kashimoto had not turned up for one of our regular meetings and Claudio, who might have known where he was, didn't know. Thus began what promised to be a lackluster discussion of another topic related to the social malaise, since that was still on everyone's mind. Suddenly the door opened and the dignified Kashimoto, who was never in a hurry, burst into the Chamber.

Without the customary Japanese bow, he made a perfunctory apology and announced in a breathless voice. "Forgive the interruption, but I've been delayed on the Flight Deck. I come with a message." Then, realizing he had disrupted our conversation, he added, "When you're ready, of course." Kashimoto took his seat at the large conference table and regained his usual poise. No such urgency had ever disturbed our quiet proceedings except when Commander Rawls came with her news about communication with Ground Control.

I hardly need say that we wanted to hear Kashimoto immediately. You may remember, he is the only Council member who maintains close relations with the technocrats. It's because he's the most distinguished physicist of the present generation and the best cosmologist since the voyage began. Command often consults with him about celestial phenomena or problems of navigation or simply where we should go next. Hence the messenger.

He unfolded a formal-looking document and began reading:

> Starship Command respectfully requests the Council of Elders, per their responsibility for education on the Galatea, to promptly begin a review of the order of studies in the schools. The aim is to speed

development of all skills critical to life on Planet 2314. This request requires deliberate haste for two reasons.

(1) During the 240 years of the mission to date, the school curriculum has been allowed to drift away from the rigorous technological focus appropriate for a project of this kind. So long as there was no destination in view, that fact caused little concern. Now the situation has changed. We can no longer afford to spend valuable time on the niceties of studies that serve only as leisure activities and arcane intellectual hobbies. We must renew the commitment to serious technical training.

(2) By present calculations, the time required for reaching orbit around P2314 is six years and five months. That provides ample time to bring future colonists up to speed on the survival and technical skills required to support colonization.

Thus Starship Command formally requests that the Council begin posthaste and send regular progress reports and concrete proposals to First Mate Talib Nasser, who has been appointed project liaison between Starship Command and the Council.

When he finished reading, Kashimoto added nothing. Just folded the document without lifting his head, passed it to me as Council Secretary, and resumed his seat. There was silence for a minute or more as questions rushed in on us.

I passed those moments watching the venerable Claudio Rucai. I have examined no face so closely over the years as his. It's an open book of changes. The dark eyes and mouth are like lakes set in a landscape of wrinkles with a ridge of Roman nose rising between. Each crease is a memoir of experience. Taken all together, it sums up a life well-lived and reveals a character like no other I've known. Do all our faces reveal so much truth? I wonder. Anyway, after Kashimoto had read the extraordinary document, Rucai, who rarely speaks, spoke first:

"I don't want to speculate on why this document has been sent except to say that the members of the crew are all graduates of our school system, especially of the sciences. A number of them are teachers themselves, as some crew members have been from the beginning. Yet the document mentions no part of the science curriculum that needs strengthening. I have the honor to have been a member of this distinguished group for nearly forty years and I recall no official complaint until tonight. When there were new developments in the disciplines, we were responsible for them and always acted accordingly. We regularly offer training for our teachers to help them stay abreast with their fields. Responsible criticism when it has come has always started here." Then, turning to face his friend Kashimoto, whose almond-shaped eyes were fixed on the table in front of him, he continued, "What can you tell us about this, Akira? The formality of it—is that poor judgment or a very bad omen?"

Akira raised first his eyes then his arms from the table and extended his hands, palms open. In a subdued voice he answered, "You know everything I know, and I've only known it ten minutes longer than you. All I can say is, whatever we think of this document or the motives behind it, we dare not ignore it."

The somber tone of that question and that answer were enough to underscore the seriousness of the situation. If any present could have read the tea leaves and foresaw what the message meant, it would have been Claudio and Akira, though in this instance, none of us were far behind. Most saw instantly that Oleksiy Hunenko's prediction was already fulfilled: With the authority of Ulro silenced, Starship Command was taking aim at all the prerogatives of the Council by striking a quick blow at the schools.

This was to be a night for unpredictable responses: from the reckless, caution; from the cautious, passion. In response to Kashimoto's remark, "We can't ignore it," the usually quiet young biologist Ang Yimou pounded the table with a fist and almost cried, "Why not?" Minds were darting to and fro so fast that faces went blank searching for his reference. He meant, why not ignore the command?

Presently Clive Dennet-Jones provided a full answer. "Power. We can't ignore it because of power."

Claudio added, "And we must be compliant. Otherwise, Command will begin taking over the schools themselves. They want the schools redirected? Then redirect them. Only do it by our own lights."

Ang answered, "But they've no right. Education has always been the province of the Council and was intended to be. As well make one of us commander of the ship."

Hunenko, who may in all innocence have handed Commander Rawls this trump card by mentioning sovereignty in her presence, now responded more sensitively. "The way to reduce the chances that a disagreement will turn into a power struggle is not to inflame the issue. No court or constitution stands between us and them as judge. We balk, we lose. And the mission loses. In this instance it's not histrionic to say, humanity loses."

Silence again. And in that ponderous silence I want to say how wonderful it is to be part of a group where, when there is nothing to be said, no one speaks!

Eventually, Claudio cleared his throat and continued quietly as though to prevent being overheard by eavesdroppers. "Hunenko is right: This is our moment of greatest danger. Ulro is rising from its own rubble! I propose that we send an immediate response to Command, equally formal as the request, blanketly acceding to their wishes."

For a moment everyone waited respectfully as he pondered what compliance might entail. "Then, we should begin a highly visible review of the schools. Where we don't find problems in the sciences and technological disciplines, we can repackage courses in ways that signal their relevance to colonization without diluting or reorganizing the science. Whatever the phrase 'leisure activities and arcane intellectual hobbies' intends to say, we may accept the pretense that it's the sciences they're interested in. So we make them our priority while keeping a benign silence on the arts. We must provide no excuse for intrusions into the rest of the curriculum."

He pointed at the piece of paper lying oh-so innocently on the table in front of me. "That is a command, intended as provocation."

Rucai bowed his head a moment before adding, "I'm sorry to be talking like one of those old Fifth Avenue advertisers who did their best—and enjoyed their success—in ruining language, but occasionally, when the danger is great, political realism is the only expedient."

That was the longest speech anyone could remember from Rucai, and his proposal was accepted without comment. Then someone, I forget who, asked, "So how do we proceed?"

Gwendolyn Burgess took that one. "Since Command trusts Akira and he can speak for the sciences, why not ask him to organize the review? If difficult questions pop up outside the sciences, his being a scientist would give him license to temporize and consult. We all know that, for whatever reason, this document is ultimately taking aim at the arts and historical disciplines, perhaps because competition in the colony is expected from that direction."

From that point the discussion descended into administrative arrangements of only temporary interest until Akira spoke again.

"Even as we respond by welcoming this opportunity to review the schools, I suggest that we keep a thing or two in mind. The crew is driven by the practical affairs of the busy day. They don't have time to spend looking over our shoulders. If we find they are, it will help us see where exactly we stand. Meanwhile, we should do what thinkers always do: Start over.

"If we must do what is asked, then we needn't waste time playing at the margins and tinkering with details. Let's reinvent the wheel as a way of reminding ourselves what wheels are for. That hasn't been done in living memory. I suggest we begin with what human beings require to realize their potential and why. While you're busy with that, I'll get a review of the sciences underway without wasting the time of our teachers. If you accept this suggestion, the only other thing we have to decide now is where to begin."

When that suggestion met with tacit agreement, Clive Dennet-Jones said, "Then let's begin at the beginning, with the Seven Liberal Arts, later called the Arts and Sciences. That's the historical foundation."

That remark roused Aurélie Lefèvre, who speaks for the Fine Arts on the Council. She's an unprepossessing person, French of course, in appearance stylish even in an ordinary uniform or a Council robe. But she also has depths that one would not expect, along with a surface manner that can be prickly on occasion. I've always suspected that between her and Dennet-Jones there are relics of the age-old suspicion between the Gauls and the barbarous islanders to the north. She had no charity to spare for Clive's historicist pedantry. Giving him one of her withering ironic glances, she declared, to the delight of everyone present: "No doubt you are prepared with an order of procedure, Clive. But do please start somewhere since the fall of Rome."

And so he did, but not by much. While the rest of us threw paranoid glances toward the door as though Commander Rawls might burst in at any moment, Dennet-Jones assumed his formal dignity and began:

"Since I'm denied Rome, presumably therefore Greece, I'll begin with the medieval curriculum. The chief bone of contention between Command and the Elders has been recognized since medieval Europe. Our last revision came in Ulro Year 2170, sometime after the colloquy Ishmael Kahn replayed for us at a recent meeting. At that time the Council reaffirmed the ancient hierarchy of the liberal arts. And 'hierarchy' is the important word. Not important because it's ancient. Important because it gets something profoundly right."

It was not that Dennet-Jones was insensitive to the crisis at hand. Not at all. There was more handwringing in his speech than history, but no one was listening because we were all preoccupied with the idea of a cold war we were sure to lose. Oblivious, Dennet-Jones rehashed Command's misunderstanding of education as training in skills rather than nurture of persons.

"They just don't see that specialization ghettoizes knowledge to everyone's detriment. Unlike practical affairs, our deliberations lure us beyond our special interests in physics or history, psychology or literature."

Then he went on to review the hierarchy of disciplines "by threes and fours," what once was known in the West as the *trivium* and *quadrivium*. There was wisdom in all he said and people who had never thought about the subject might have gotten an education from it, but here he was preaching to the choir, and the choir was otherwise engaged with that piece of paper lying still on the table.

While most provided the occasional obligatory nod, the four youngest members of the Council—Joseph Kern, Ang Yimou, Ava Sarosh, and Hans Rückert—were abuzz with interest. They hadn't been soaking in this topic for years and, huddled together at the far end of the table, they may not have appreciated fully how desperate the situation was.

As a specialist in European literatures, Kern must have found the topic down his alley. With a touch of impatience he asked, "So where do we actually begin?"

Dennet-Jones replied, "Start over, as Kashimoto suggests, with grammar, logic, and rhetoric, treating all three as performance rather than structure."

To us slightly jaded older heads there was more in the remark about performance over structure than the younger members heard, but their readiness to take up the cause was reassuring. Their eagerness was to think the tradition through for themselves. To the young, starting over is not arch conservatism. It's next of kin to revolution.

Kern was teeming with enthusiasm. "Good. We start with language because we are speaking beings. If we get language right, the other disciplines will follow in course. Since grammar comes first and since there's destiny in names, why not reaffirm the point by resurrecting the old term 'grammar school' as our guiding idea? Isn't it wonderful that when we begin by inducting the young into the conversation of humanity, we share the love of 'letters' with them and 'liberate' them into being human?"

Burgess wanted to know why start with grammar instead of logic or rhetoric or why not do all at once. The irrepressible Kern replied, "Because to get language right is to get from no psychic space at all into the opening on infinite worlds. That's not grammar as in nouns and verbs and complete sentences.

Think of childhood: We don't start with abstract categories. We start with babbling. Then names. Then stories."

Lefèvre suddenly interrupted with considerable force: "Right! Except that, we actually start—language starts—with music. With music and the muses!"

That remark momentarily startled everyone. To me it made no sense at all. After taking a moment to recollect his point, Kern continued. "Well, at least we don't start with meanings. Not even *the same* ideas, as though a meaning were stuffed inside a word like a letter in a box. It's all about accessing a world by participating in words. Do this, and logic, rhetoric, and all the rest will have a place and an address."

Well, there were two conversation stoppers at once! I don't suggest that they both didn't make sense. Only that I wouldn't know what sense to make of either until much later.

At that point Hans Rückert, the young philosopher who had been a student of both Oleksiy Hunenko and Claudio Rucai, did what philosophers do best: He made a distinction. "Kern is right. Starting with the practice of a rich language is the right thing to do, and when we do, there are two ways to go about it. We can start with the building blocks and proceed in rational sequence until we reach some ideal goal, or we can take the all-at-once approach and start where we all started, with complete worlds that are already embedded in language."

Ava Sarosh, whose virtual great-grandmother you met earlier, asked, "Then isn't it more realistic for us to take the all-at-once approach and start with the stories we tell the children? That's Kern's world in one gulp."

For the moment Hunenko skipped over that suggestion and raised an astonishing idea. "Since we're proposing to *conserve* a tradition by *starting over*"—he smiled at the oxymoron—"I'd like answers to two questions about the liberal arts. But first some context: Before the mission, knowledge on Ulro had dwindled to information, language to communication, art to culture, people to producer-consumers, and history had reached its apex in the global free-market economy. Perhaps by a kind of subversion, the Council was put in charge of running the starship schools on the age-old model of the liberal arts. So, if we genuinely intend to reinvent that wheel, I suggest we explore two things."

He stopped and closed his eyes.

After a moment Dennet-Jones, afraid, I suppose, that Hunenko might have fallen asleep, said, "Yes?"

He opened his eyes and raised a thumb. "First, do the liberal arts really offer an alternative to the Ulro ideal? More to the point—leaving the sciences aside—isn't education in the humanities a kind of anachronistic finishing school for the leisure classes? Historically it was rooted in the aristocratic life of feudalism. I'm not saying that's all it was, but I am asking if we're blindly instilling the cultural pastimes of a class of leisured dilettantes. Are we continuing a reactionary, aesthetic hedonism? One might answer that leisure is exactly what people in our situation most need to learn to use but, on the other hand, hedonists make poor citizens."

Dennet-Jones, staring at Oleksiy's thumb still hoisted in the air and wishing no doubt to get these questions out of the way as soon as possible, called for his second point.

"The second question is this: Aren't the liberal arts anthropocentric? As though we were supplying an operating manual for a well-defined object that we call human? If so, wouldn't that path result in narrow little egos adapted not to a boundless cosmos but to a conventional picture of a world? An alternative preparation might make students responsive to the lure of all things and open to continuous invention. I won't take the time just now to show the radically different consequences these alternatives lead to."

Young Rückert responded to this blitz with a passion we hadn't witnessed before. "Oleksiy, this battle has been won and lost and won again many times. As the humanities became sophisticated amusements, science became the handmaiden of economics: biology as health care, physics as machines, and chemistry as toothpaste. Do we need to rehash these arguments as though we'd learned nothing?"

"You're right, dear boy," Hunenko replied. "I am playing the skeptic. But these misunderstandings never go away. They are congenital diseases that rise again in every generation. I'm only underscoring Kashimoto's suggestion that we remind ourselves of what we know and how we come to know it. And, in the process, one more generation may understand what it means to exist as the political animal."

This was a night for drama, Akira's message from the bridge followed by Hunenko's casting a pall over everything. Only Claudio had the presence of mind to respond coherently.

It was the mood he put into words. "Commander Rawls' message may have been intended to open a jar full of evils on us, but whatever they are, evils or goods, they're beginning to swarm. I wager that Hunenko's excellent questions will get answered piecemeal and concretely as our discussions proceed. Meanwhile, as this introduction has gotten our attention, let's adjourn until next week. By then each of us will have been stung by one or another of the gadflies in the Commander's jar and we'll be ready to take on the swarm."

THE TIME THING

THE NEXT WEEK we did not get underway with our reinvention of all knowledge as planned. Clive Dennet-Jones postponed that topic and followed up on Gwendolyn Burgess' suggestion by inviting Nacho Rojas instead. I won't turn aside just now to muse over why Clive might have done that when it was he who suggested where we should begin the curriculum review, but I daresay it had something to do with his being as flummoxed as I was by Hunenko's impious criticism of the liberal arts.

In any event, the invitation offered a new surprise: Rojas accepted—with conditions. Another first! Little would be accomplished, he said, by cataloguing examples of the boredom epidemic or rehashing interventions that were largely guess-work. It would be more useful, he said, to describe a single case that seemed to expose symptoms of the starship malaise.

But first, I must tell you about Rojas. He is something like a psychiatrist. At least that's the work he's best known for. And yet a medical officer in a populace as small as ours must play many roles, rather like a tribal medicine man. Alexandros may put all information at our fingertips, but there's no way we can duplicate the diversity of understanding and depth of research that occurs in a mass culture. In Rojas' case a firm grounding in biology and chemistry, followed by preparation for general medical practice, was only a starting point. By now, in seasoned middle age, his studies have carried him far beyond the ordinary physician. He has read and practiced widely in psychiatry, in the kindred fields of neurology, and in various styles of psychoanalysis.

Being well-known to several Council members for practical wisdom as well as scientific learning, he had been invited to join our circle several years ago, but he declined. To my knowledge it's the only time that has ever happened, so I have looked up his written reply, which is worth recording here:

> I am touched by the honor the Elders do me; however, I must respectfully decline the appointment. It's a time thing. One might think that anyone could squeeze out a few hours a week for a Council meeting. But my practice is very demanding and the changing health needs on the ship require constant research. This leaves time for little else.
>
> My work is research. Yours is thinking, and that's a different state of mind. You must ponder imponderable subjects for as long as it takes to reach clarity. One can't rush breathlessly in and analyze such issues while counting the minutes until the meeting ends. Again, I thank you for the honor of your offer.

Rereading Rojas' reply, I'm struck by how much people with his clarity are needed on the Council. When he turned up in the Chamber, I hadn't seen him for some time, and I was surprised by a bearing that I struggle to describe. "Centered and still" is the best I can do. He's a slightly rough figure, a bit careless of his appearance, as busy people can be. Of average height, tending toward stout, with a quiet and kindly, slightly gruff manner. All the older heads know him, and the younger know him at least by sight and reputation.

He opened with a word of caution typical of him. "I'm going to tell you about a case history, so I begin with a serious caveat: The psychic experience of every person is unique. That means that the story I tell is not typical of anything, yet it may shed oblique light on the wider context of your interests."

Then, like a man accustomed to efficiency, he plunged directly into an account that held us spellbound for the better part of an hour.

"The person I come to tell you about—we'll call him by the fictional name Fyodor—was a middle-aged man, a successful engineer when we first encountered him. Fyodor's job had something to do with the conversion of nuclear energy that runs the ship. From youth, he had been an exceptionally intelligent science student who neglected all his other studies as unimportant. 'Nonsense' was his term for whatever related to imagination. He was all for 'the facts!' This resulted in his taking a Level Two degree and making a career as a technician.

"Though Fyodor was driven by a powerful will to succeed, he expressed no regrets about his school years. His mother had died while he was quite young, and his father chan-neled all his care into the boy's development. He was already in school, of course, but his father now began fanatically following his work, perhaps filling the vacancy in his own life by demanding perfection in the child. In retrospect, the result seems almost predictable.

"Once he had finished school, Fyodor's ideals took the shape of self-denial and sacrifice to duty. The demands he made on himself included relentless discipline to become the best in his field, and that served him well for several years as he rose to a position of responsibility. So much so that when he became ill, it was a considerable problem to find even a temporary replacement for him in his shop.

"Now we come to the symptoms. When he wasn't working, he would sit for long periods of time staring at the walls of his room or go to lonely places where he could look at the stars. Not thinking about anything, not curious, just vacant. It became a daily struggle for him to fulfill his duties. He could control his anxiety and sleep only with the help of drugs, and yet repeatedly he referred to his symptoms in terms of 'weakness' or 'self-indulgence.' Aside from the drugs, he sought no help until he could no longer perform his job safely. Then he was seized by an overwhelming sense of failure. He expressed the vanity of life as an obligation to do away with himself.

"When Fyodor first sought help, I didn't meet him. The colleague who did later reported that Fyodor described himself as dead inside, like a stone, without feeling or interest or initiative. He had always been a reader but the ability to concentrate was gone. After he entered analysis, he began to remember repetitive dreams, mostly about school. The dreams were habitually repressed as 'nonsense' and 'sentimental self-pity.' In them he was typically unable to focus on his studies and eventually had to face an examination written in a language he didn't know. When inevitably he failed the exam, his teachers appeared as scowling schoolmasters—just their faces looming over him, excoriating him, again in unintelligible languages.

"Eventually the school dreams subsided and were replaced by a series about the ship. Now he was in a position where the Galatea depended on him alone. The sense of power was torturous, because he had to hold the ship in place moment by moment. Any lapse in his attention, like going to the toilet or falling asleep, would spell general disaster. The danger was so great that even when he wasn't at work he could risk no interruption of consciousness.

"The first efforts by our team to treat Fyodor consisted of trying to show him that these monomaniacal fantasies were illusions. Hallucinations. That rationalistic approach only made things worse. It caused him to retreat from the therapist into moody silence. When my therapist colleague insisted on 'realism,' the whole analysis came to a head and he shouted, 'What are you? Stupid? You think I don't know this is all nonsense?' Then he stormed out of the office and didn't return.

"That seemed like the end of the story until Fyodor was brought into sick bay unconscious after having slit his wrist in the shower. That's when I inherited the case and began building a relationship with him. Lying in his hospital bed he bore little resemblance to his Russian heritage. He had delicate, sensitive features; blond hair; a slender build; and the dull, sad face of a victim of sensitivity inconsistent with his life so far.

"After a few days, he was released but scheduled for follow-up visits that he knew were not necessary for any physical reasons. But he kept all the appointments. Showed up exactly on time in as clear a call for help as we get. By tacit consent, the sessions continued along the lines of psychoanalysis.

"Soon enough he confided his symptoms and the history of the prior medical intervention. The only thing out of the ordinary was a change in his dreams. Now he was plagued by faces and voices of creatures on the ship who, he was quite sure, were 'alien species.' 'They only appear to me visually, at night,' he said. 'They don't look at me the way people do. They look all the way through me as though I were a kind of screen. They see all I do and hear all I say like the white coats who know my insides better than I do. Like being inescapably known but only in the mode of an object.'

"This time no hint passed on either side about his specters' being unreal or irrational, nor did we make any effort to ameliorate his alternative reality with drugs. All were treated as worldly realities. It's remarkable that for long periods he seemed to find nothing unusual in that.

"Once, when he referred to events in a dream as being impossible, I asked, 'Do we really know all that's possible? Don't we hear what we hear? And see what we see? Maybe dreams are one more way of accessing the world around us.' At that he raised his eyes in the first expression of vitality and interest I had seen so far. The dullness and vacancy vanished, replaced by bright intelligence. In that moment he simply skipped over the rigid childhood and the stifling life of the technician. It was as though he had been allowed to respond to what he confronted in his dream without the intervention of theories and norms.

"This was no cure, of course. A hiatus at best. Thereafter he was afflicted with a different kind of dream that might seem even worse. The ship was still under invasion by the aliens, and this time they intended to take it over and prevent a colony. His aliens came at night and made it clear that only he stood between the ship and disaster. Now instead of having to keep the machinery running, he had to watch *them* constantly. They only appeared at night, but he could always hear their voices planning the seizure of the ship. By this time he had returned to work, but he heard the aliens in the human voices of the public corridors discussing plans for taking over the ship. He heard them in the mechanical sounds of his workplace and in the background hum of the ship. It was like a language that translated the meaning of generic noise. Only his perpetual readiness prevented catastrophe and the ship's passing into oblivion."

Rojas stopped for a moment as though considering some tangential idea. Then he added parenthetically, "Until this moment I had never seen that these dreams might be read as an allegory of what's actually happening before our eyes as we prepare for the colony."

I, Kahn, still don't know what Rojas meant by the "allegory," but he brushed it aside without explanation and resumed the case history.

"Fyodor's account had all the drama of a diseased, megalomaniacal imagination, but instead of treating his voices and apparitions as symptoms of psychic wounds, like the residue of an early trauma, we dealt with them once more as real creatures approaching him and demanding acceptance as part of his world. We might call it fiction, but that would explain little. Remarkably, when he became confident that his analyst accepted his apparitions as real, he entirely stopped discrediting them as unworthy of a rational person. The code of the detached, objective technocrat simply vanished."

Rojas paused again as though to give us breathing room but— remarkably, I thought—no one seemed disposed to speak. So he continued. "At this stage the effective treatment proved to be the following: 'What if you were to let the aliens have their way? Let them be right? Make room for them? If they *are* spying, then they must regard the ship as a threat. But if they can infiltrate it and choose who they should appear to without the others knowing, then it's less likely that they can be threatened by us. So why not treat them hospitably? They must want something. Find out what. Answer their questions. Make a game of it. Give up and see what happens.'

"Once he was given permission to respond to his aliens in an adult way, without dividing the universe between the evil and the good, the most extraordinary thing happened. At his next session, he turned up with clay models of his creatures, several of them rendered in exquisite, loving detail. We sat on the floor like two boys playing toy soldiers and he told the story of each, repeating what demand or threat each had made. All this passed without the least self-consciousness in either of us. This extraordinary event—what we might call age-regression—happened not once but a number of times. Fyodor appeared to be enacting an early relation to his world before he had become enslaved to the goal-oriented work ethic that had distorted his development and destroyed his joy in living.

"On one of these occasions he erupted gleefully, 'This is the first time I have ever done something without a purpose. Before, I have only done what was required of me. Now the aliens who were my enemies are my friends. I would like to run through the corridors of the ship singing.'

"'That's play!' I answered. "Maybe all your discipline made an enemy of imagination, and yet to live a coherent life, don't we need the imaginary too?'"

Rojas added a cautionary note. "You mustn't think that this was a magical solution and that the sun shone for him forever after. Anything but Nirvana. Even after one is reminded of what it feels like to live in a free relation with the world at an early age, there's a lot of ground still to cover.

"Shortly thereafter Fyodor's dreams opened on a new scene of horror. It was like an entirely different case, rooted much deeper in his early history. As early as toilet training. I won't take the time to develop this stage of the analysis in detail because it's not that unusual, but his dreams came to be dominated by defecation. His new friends, the aliens, didn't come with human plumbing. They had no alimentary canal. This made Fyodor ashamed of his own bodily functions. When he visited their spaceship, he passed the time in dread of needing to use the toilet where there was none. He endured physical and emotional torture until he could control himself no longer. Then he began defecating and couldn't stop. The aliens were repulsed by the smell and the growing human ordure that became knee-deep, then waist-deep, then neck-deep."

Hunenko suddenly interrupted, "It's allegory again! The body excluded from pure reason!"

Rojas stared in astonishment for a moment before his eyes lit up with recognition, though I have no idea what those two saw in all this. Maybe because I, like Fyodor, think the alimentary canal is rather a flaw in the human design.

"It's sufficient to report," Rojas concluded, "that he eventually came to see—or rather to experience—that his bodily, earthy existence had been closed off just as the realm of imagination had been closed, that to live on a starship where everything was fabricated and clean was to be confined to a dull middle state of existence without flesh or spirit. Like one of the neutrals who float aimlessly on Dante's lake Limbo. In fact, trying to live like an android, he had been brought to face despair. And the result was a tortured life."

Rojas' report generated an extraordinarily lively discussion that I omit here, except for two points. Several members showed great interest in his way of treating dreams as oriented toward the world—dreams speaking for themselves rather than being ciphers with hidden meanings or symptoms of forgotten traumas. That was new to most of us. But it was the second point that generated the greatest interest and perplexity.

Yu Wang, the chemist and quintessential scientist, who is often skeptical and usually silent in these conversations, asked about the pretense that Fyodor's dreams were realities. "Isn't that disingenuous? Aren't you reinforcing his confusion of illusion and reality? How could such an intelligent person accept that?"

Rojas didn't bristle at the implied contradiction but pondered the question carefully before speaking. In that moment I recognized something extraordinary about the culture of the analyst: He has to love the other enough to allow, even to credit, every mode of behavior as a step in the direction of a healthier life.

Eventually he smiled benignly. "It's a matter of how we order things, Yu. A while back Aristotle warned us against confusing what requires proof with what doesn't. There is no way to prove that a particular event has or hasn't happened. After the fact, we can argue about what it means but not before. Another way of putting the point is that we must get our ideas in proper order so we don't end up with a hodgepodge. I can regard an event in either of two ways. I can presume to be the legislator and approach it with the theories, codes, or norms of what is and is not acceptable. Rather like a literary censor. Or I can respond to the event by letting it unfold in its own time and its own way as Fyodor finally does for his aliens. In the first instance, I decide on the event before I let it happen. That's simply confused. In the second I give it time to have its way with me. That may sound like I have a real choice, but it's simply a productive way of ordering things."

Oleksiy Hunenko was mumbling something obscure about mental illness and moralism as Yu answered, "I don't see what you mean." Not that Yu is stubborn. He's just starting where a chemist starts and trying to make sense of something that isn't on his map.

"You think Fyodor actually saw aliens, talked to them, buried them in shit?"

"I think we really were dealing with alien realities of some sort. Perhaps, for our own sanity, freedom of speech should apply to chemical elements, black holes, aardvarks, and Greek gods as well as to other people. How do we learn if we don't start by giving credence to the incredible? In Fyodor's first analysis, the aliens were filtered through a mesh intended to remove impurities like hallucinations. That procedure demands credentials first. But how can we judge an experience until we let it show itself in its own way?"

"We can say 'No' to illusions."

"Yes. Soon enough we must deal with those issues, but not too hastily. The real difference is—and this is all-important in analysis—it's between loving what's given and recoiling from it as though some evil genius were out to trick us. That just lands us in a moralistic muddle. The confusion is much worse than I've described. Theory is for making sense of experience. To make it a litmus test in advance dooms understanding, *and* it's a detriment to psychic health. This includes our learned disciplines of science, history, philosophy, and so on."

After all that, it only remained for Dennet-Jones to ask his usual question: "And this is related to the boredom epidemic how?"

Rojas smiled and answered, "We are dealing with despair over a present mode of being. We want what's given to be different. To put it in archaic terms that may still be the most accurate, at root it's wanting to be God: 'I'm not willing to play the crappy hand I've been dealt, so I quit the game.'"

At the end of this discussion Rojas was offered, by tacit consent of the members, a permanent seat on the Council, and this time he accepted.

BIRTH OF A CONSPIRACY

I HAVE MENTIONED that from the beginning contradictions in this space odyssey have lain hidden like sleeping giants in the dark corners of the starship. The Elders have always realized that if the mission were to succeed in establishing a colony, the giants would stir, perhaps with deadly consequences. The rift between Elders and Command reaches back into the deep history of the mother planet. Whatever happened at the beginning of the mission must have happened by stealth, as all things happened in those last days on Ulro, when decisions were subject to the tugs and pulls of opinion. Hence our ignorance of those events.

I have also described how this work began as a kind of bequest to colonists who might eventually profit from an account of life on the starship. As projected, such a sequence of episodes would have fit the form of the Chronicle. Who could have known it would morph into a narrative of the cloak-and-dagger variety? My episodic account got sabotaged by unexpected events when strife between Council and crew turned into an epic struggle. Thus the form of *Starship Galatea* is neither fish nor fowl, as people used to say.

What happened, happened like this. Once the plan for establishing a colony was settled, Akira Kashimoto and Claudio Rucai devised a secret scheme for subverting the intentions of Starship Command. For several years what those two set in motion was known only to them, but their foresight was to prove exceptional. If they had disclosed their thinking to the rest of us, they would have been regarded as alarmists, and we would have failed in the very thing the Council existed for. After the fact, it was clear for anyone to see that the struggle always had been over the issue of sovereignty. Who—or better, what ideals—were to be supreme? Who or what was to rule?

Only when the plot was eventually revealed did this Chronicle acquire its narrative arc. As surreptitiously as those two worthies tried to subvert the colony, their conspiracy turned my innocent document into one so dangerous that it now seems only one copy is to survive and perhaps never be read at all. The single copy is to be deposited for safekeeping with Claudio Rucai himself.

Given the homogeneity of life on a starship the very idea of rival cultures may seem baffling to the practical mind. For generations the nascent rivalry between Council and crew mattered little. Each turned a polite cold shoulder toward the other while sharing the same language, the same teachers, the same curriculum, the same social structures, and the same habitat. How could so much harmony conceal a mortal fissure, especially as the fissure didn't explicitly run along the lines of power?

We all depend on the technicians to care for the physical operation of the ship, and on the Elders to care for the quality of life on board. And yet, I say again, two scales of value masquerading as one were destined to collide when the time

was ripe. To understand that collision and the plot to avoid
it or, failing to avoid it, to win the battle when it came—to
understand that much is to understand all. Thus it happened
that Rucai and Kashimoto were at the center of all that
occurred between the communications failure in Ulro Year
2324 and the disastrous event that would bring my book to
a swift conclusion.

The plot began with a secret meeting just after the
Council received and replied to Commander Rawls' demands
regarding the schools. Claudio and Akira met on the Observation Deck one morning when it was closed to the public. You
already know that it was Akira's observatory and that as chief
research cosmologist he always had access to the telescopes.
On this morning he had given his graduate assistants time off
so the two could meet without rousing suspicion.

Akira, younger than Claudio by a generation, was inspired
by the wisdom of the older man, but he also enjoyed the
confidence of the crew. He and his telescopes are essential
to the exploratory voyage of the ship, and his research does
credit to the Galatea. For several generations, collaboration
between the ship and the home planet had been fruitful, but
by Akira's day distance rendered the sharing negligible. Now
it has ceased entirely, and the glory is in discovery itself. But
since the cosmos is our backyard, his celebrity among crew
and populace alike is unrivaled. When a new discovery is
sufficiently promising, the Commander may even order
an adjustment in the flight path to allow for more refined
observations. Occasionally Akira gives public lectures, and
people flock to the Observation Deck to hear him. The very

status that makes him de facto mediator between Council and crew also gives him latitude to serve quite different purposes with impunity under the noses of Command.

When Claudio arrived on that fateful morning, Akira was sitting in one of the observation chairs from which one can survey half the visible universe. Claudio took the seat next to him without so much as noticing that, given the orientation of the ship relative to the Milky Way, he had a spectacular view of Andromeda.

Akira spoke first. "You look distressed this morning, my friend. Not much sleep I would imagine."

He shrugged the suggestion off with a casual "True." I have told you what an imposing figure Claudio makes: distinguished in a rough kind of way, virile and magnetic. His Italian sensibility is set off by the olive hues of an Etruscan complexion. Despite their difference in age, these two are close. Trusted friends for decades. They and their wives used to have dinner together once each week until Claudio's wife suddenly left him for reasons unknown but presumed to involve a third person. However, the women don't figure much in this narrative though they might, both having taken Level One degrees and devoted their lives to the arts, one to writing and the other to painting.

Without knowing what he had come to hear, Claudio opened the conversation. "In Council you handled the shock of the message from Rawls very well. Your expedient of the reply to her demands, then the quick move to consult with the teachers, set some distance between us and the disquieting moment. Gave breathing space and thinking time. It feels like we have the initiative again, even if you and I know better. Now tell me what you know that you didn't say in Council."

"Not much, "Akira answered, "and that worries me. When the Commander gave me the message, she betrayed no sign of ill will or even of having to exert herself to keep it low-key. All routine and efficient, though it was anything but. For me the room was filled with the surplus consciousness of a well-rehearsed scene. Later, when I delivered the response to her and Nasser, once again the only warning signals were atmospheric."

Claudio's deep sigh was the only sound in the silent universe or the observatory. "What after all can be done? Something must be done." Then, more pensively, "I know nothing can be done."

Akira nodded. "We have our first indication of how far Rawls sees. She knows as well as we do that the Council and crew are destined to collide over any possible colony. Either she's getting in front of the problem and warning us off, or she sees that the mission itself is at stake and is giving us time to count the cost. I'd say that from her point of view if one ideal succeeds—the technological or the historical—the other must fail whatever the cost . . . *from her point of view.*"

"And yet if either fails, all fail. They don't have to be at enmity. The differences might be neutralized."

Akira, ironically, "She's smart enough to know that too."

"If you could rely on people to act from what they know, life would be simpler. There's a great gulf between knowing and choosing. People swim in that gulf."

"Yes," Akira answered. "It's the people who are at enmity. From the point of view of the technocrats, *they* are on the cutting edge of 'progress' while *we* pass the time blowing soap bubbles and smoke rings. If *we* fail and the colony becomes an outpost for technological experimentation like the old space platforms, *they* won't know the difference until there's another planet like Ulro pulling its own lynch rope. The anxiety epidemic on a starship is only a hint at what the human condition might become. It's an odd thing to say, but in a way, anxiety is our hope."

The idea deepened the premature lines in Claudio's weathered face, which might at that moment have been a relief map of human history. He pondered their situation for a while.

"I underrated them. I thought they would not look so far ahead. It's Rawls of course. None of our male commanders, being consummate rationalists, would have listened to their intelligent instincts. She knows we're on a collision course, that once survival is secured in the colony, either their kind must relinquish governance to our kind or face trouble. Meanwhile, we shouldn't expect her to be shortsighted or asleep at the wheel."

Akira adjusted the back of his chair until he was gazing upward through the dome as though searching for a different flight path. "Then we must find another way."

"But what other way?"

Akira studied the problem before replying. "Where nothing can be done, you add energy to your opponent's motion until the momentum exceeds his control. We must cooperate and go underground. Become snoops and spies." He chuckled dryly. "If 'underground' can mean anything to people who've never stood on a ground.

"An idea has been growing on me that's only for the desperate. It's why I've asked you here. No one goes casually down the path I'm imagining. Only if the life or death of the human spirit is at stake. It would mean subterfuge on the scale of the *Résistance* in the second great twentieth-century war, with even higher stakes. If we are to act with greatest security, only you and I can be parties to the subterfuge"—he turned to look Claudio full in the face—"from this moment on."

The old philologist replied as lightly as possible, "You're speaking in the indicative, not the subjunctive. You have a plan!"

"There's no time to *sub-join* possibilities. Those who can read the *indications* must prepare to win the conflict to come . . . or die in the effort." Again Akira chuckled, time still more gravely, even as he took satisfaction in showing that a physicist could also know his way around language.

Claudio, "Am I hearing that your resolve is fixed?"

Akira returned his chair to upright position and swiveled around to put them face to face. Leaning forward, he spoke *sotto voce* but fiercely. "There is no choice. Others will see, but not until it is too late. Even our friends on the Council who might be prepared to help. There's no need to draw people into danger who are extraneous to the purpose. And yet no one can rely solely on his own judgment. This must be debated vigorously every step of the way, and for that I must rely entirely on you. Open debate would leak, and while others dithered, the mission would be lost. So without missing anything, we must appear to see nothing and do nothing."

"I would like to disagree with your view of the situation, but I cannot. It has always been foreseen. Now we must position ourselves for the worst, while, as you say, doing nothing we can avoid doing. I see no alternative but to wait and watch. If, beyond that, you have a plan, I'm happy to listen."

"For starts, here's what will happen when we get back to P2314. Since we mapped the planet a decade ago, a few additional orbits will be sufficient to confirm our readings and select a landing site. We know what we need to know about the physical environment: the chemistry of the atmosphere, surface temperatures, underground aquifers, minable deposits, and so on. So the first landing will quickly follow our arrival. It will include enough people to establish a base of operations, and they will be the likely nucleus of a settlement."

"Yes. The settlement is the crux. What can be done?"

"We must infiltrate that landing party with people who are the best technicians, but much more. Otherwise the momentum toward technocracy will be irresistible. If the colony becomes a machine, the Galatea mission will have failed."

Claudio met this with a sober smile. "Plato wanted philosopher-rulers. After that it took two millennia to get the scientists out of philosophy or vice versa. Now Akira wants philosopher-scientists. Extraordinary!"

He paused for a few moments without relinquishing the floor so to speak. "Getting a bunch of intellectuals to agree on such a scheme and to implement it clandestinely would be a social engineering feat on the scale of herding cats. In any event, they would make a terrible racket. How do you propose to manage it?"

"Not that way! Fortunately, we have several years to prepare. The time it takes to return and explore the surface of the planet."

He went on to outline how they might select the most promising young students in the technical disciplines, speed up their training in line with the current instructions from Command, then create an extra-curricular social environment to nurture the political imagination and prepare them for citizenship.

Having said so much he acknowledged the broad grin on Claudio's face. "Yes! We make them philosophers. We get them to see that living wisely requires more than know-how. That it's beyond means and ends, that it's good in itself. It's what I've learned from you over the years. Meanwhile, we do everything the crew asks us to do—and always a bit more. Then when the day comes to select the landing party—and I am likely to have a say in choosing them—the best must be our candidates. Best by any measure. Best in ways not even a commander like Rawls will easily recognize."

Claudio sat silently, looking now at Andromeda, taking his time, musing on the plan. At last, he sighed again. "Passing over a hundred questions that are not essential just now, how will you influence the development of these youngsters?"

With so much at stake, so much danger, so many contingencies to anticipate, they remained quiet for a long while using the heavens as thinking space. It was Claudio who eventually broke the silence.

"My friend, you are thinking like a scientist again. Do you think you can program free beings and foresee what they will do? This will be harder than herding cats! Cats aren't known for imagination. What makes you so optimistic about education? I know how much time we've spent on the curriculum over the years and with what success, but . . . "

Akira interrupted, "That's arguing from what we can't know. We can't know in advance what will result from such efforts. It's a gamble. It's life!"

"Yes, but what we can't learn by looking, we must learn by thinking. Don't overlook the fact that some of the best products of our schools die on the vine like the best grapes, for reasons unknown. They close down, go to seed, become dead wood. How do we overcome the tendency? Not to put too fine a point on it, what allowance do you make for old-fashioned 'sin'? The word will startle you, but I've learned from Elena Bart, who has learned from Hannah Jaeger, who learned from St. Paul, who made the purely secular discovery, that there is a wide gulf between knowing what's good to do and caring enough to do it. What is the secret of care?"

Akira chewed on this speech for a good while before replying. When eventually he did, it was largely a concession. "I don't dispute your point. It needs to be examined closely at another time. I do sense its immense consequences for all political life. For now, I'll only ask what alternative we have but to trust rationality and persuasion. We must hope that these kids will come up to the mark."

"We're together there. I only say that you aren't trusting rationality alone. You're trusting love, and you're betting the future of the species on keeping a deadly secret for years. What are the greatest risks?"

"One is that we're playing God . . . "

"Or riverboat gamblers."

"And there are the usual risks when real education causes the young to start thinking. They may figure us out, even begin to agree with us and start making noise! But no one need know about the invisible hands behind it all. That would precipitate a crisis, and the cause would be lost."

Akira got up as though he had said what he needed to say and had met no counterarguments strong enough to dissuade him. "You know I'm open to every argument, any alternative or mutation of the plan as we go. I count on you for criticism."

"How do you propose to begin?"

Akira smiled and tapped him on the wrist as though this part were the greatest secret of all. "I have an idea how it might be done and I'll tell you, but there is one other thing I must do first. Give me twenty-four hours."

And thus ended what may prove to have been the most fateful conversation in the history of the mission.

BEGINNING WITH WORDS

WHEN THE ELDERS gather each week in the Council Chamber at the top of the ship, people tend to arrive early to enjoy the casual company of friends, usually in front of the great window along one wall of the room. Most outside rooms on the ship have portholes rather than windows, but here, and even more on the bridge and the Observation Deck above, the views are incomparable, though to the naked eye, the points of light in that panoply of black hardly change from one week or one month to the next.

I often wonder what kinship draws us to that window and the populace to the Observation Deck. It's mesmerizing to stand before the expanse of deep space, bedazzled by the "nothing" that in a sense encapsulates "the all" without limits. In a limited way we know from gravitational forces that the black is not empty. There's dark matter and dark energy and who knows what else. It's just invisible. Is it the invisible real that enchants us? Divided beings, are we? Craving security, in love with the boundless?

On the occasion that I want to tell you about now, it was not the boundless that held us at the window. It was a different uncertainty. The Chamber was abuzz with chatter about the command to reassess the schools. The topic had come to engross us all. Who knows how many private exchanges there had been on the subject? Even now groups of two or three stand with their backs to the window, occupied with history and the political rather than the glories of the heavens.

To tear us away from our preoccupation Clive Dennet-Jones had to call the session to order, and we began to drift reluctantly toward our accustomed places. Kashimoto opened by reporting two developments: First, that our formal reply to Commander Rawls had been delivered as planned and received in respectful silence. Second, that the review of the science curriculum was underway.

As these points prompted no discussion, all eyes turned to Dennet-Jones as the designated moderator for the evening. He sat up in his chair a bit straighter, if that's possible, and spoke deadpan. "Tonight, we are to continue the modest project of reinventing education. I don't imply a criticism of Kashimoto's excellent suggestion that we start over. If we needed proof of the good sense of beginning again, we got it in Hunenko's criticism of liberal education. I want to begin with his remark if he will kindly restate it."

Dennet-Jones appeared to have changed his tune. Our stiff Englishman is usually condescending toward Hunenko's critical mode as though it violates his Anglo-Saxon sense of decorum. Or perhaps he's like me: It takes him a while to catch the motion of a keen mind.

Hunenko swallowed his impatience. "I raised two issues. As Claudio said at the time, they are best dealt with as we consider specific topics. Otherwise, my point is simple. I presume we aren't trying to train well-read tourists, however finely honed their sensibilities. Personal satisfaction is a by-product, not an aim, and certainly not a measure of success. The aim is to help develop thoughtful people of wide-ranging mind and imagination." He paused before adding, "Since we put language first, why don't we follow Ava Sarosh's suggestion and begin with the stories we tell the children?"

Gwendolyn Burgess endorsed that. "Yes. And first the stories our children hear—or should hear—at bedtime." As a social scientist, Burgess is a champion of acculturation. In fact she has gotten about as far as the notion of acculturation can take her, which, in this case, is pretty far. "Here's where we acquire the habits and the habitat of the tribe. Identity takes shape in these narratives."

As Dennet-Jones took a breath to respond, she held up a hand and added, "Before you launch your boat, Clive, I want to mention a related issue." The red hair that stood out around her head like a circle of fire might have suggested a volatile temperament, but the impression would have been false. In fact she's a considerate person, irascible only with dunces and far from timid in advocating her own ideas.

It's a long Council tradition to resist putting thinking in a straitjacket. Discursive thinking, directed toward solving problems, moves to a rhythm different from the leisured mind engaged in contemplation. We refuse to force a conversation toward preconceived ends, and since on this night we had time and to spare, Burgess' digression went unchecked:

"You know I have always disagreed with the way we separate children from their parents at age three or so. I understand the danger of parents passing on narcissistic habits, but I take exception to the notion that the schools do better. Some of you think this is sentimentality, but I still insist that the family provides a refuge for children of tender age. It protects them from the sharp cruelty of their peers and from public indifference. Meanwhile parents provide essential subliminal acculturation."

She then spoke of how manners and mores are instilled in the infant every moment of the day by drawing the child's attention to one thing after another, laying the foundations of character. Especially words—and the music of the words— expanding the inner space for receiving a world and the tone of that world. The lesson that one thing is beautiful, another ugly, that one is true, another false, that one is effective and another not so effective. "All these pass into cultural habit in ways so complex that even the philosopher can't process it all consciously. In stories," she concluded, "possible worlds are planted whole and unanalyzed into the child's imagination."

Hans Rückert intruded to add a further implication of what Burgess' remark. "Then on your account Gwendolyn, the narratives we imbibe with mother's milk set us on *a path* of life. Not a *correct* or *true path*—but each an exemplary path among many possible ones, however rich, fragmentary, or frivolous they may prove to be. These paths will return in the future as analogies or parables or paradigms or ways of life."

As an aside he added a remark to his neighbor at the table: "I grew up believing that it was a good thing to wean the three-year-old from the family. But I think Burgess has just convinced me that at that age the task requires individual attention that parents can provide better than school, especially when the parents are people of understanding."

Burgess clapped her hands in slow, ironic tribute to this unexpected conversion. "Then I've been wrong!" she replied, "Apparently even men—if you get them young enough—have some capacity for improvement!"

Nacho Rojas, who likes Burgess, especially her combination of a serious mind with a light heart, responded to her in brusque analytic detachment as though what she actually said was less interesting than what remained unspoken behind her words. As though he didn't have strong convictions on the topic, he asked, "Since selections must be made, what stories would you have us tell? What books should be read? And who gets to choose? Or should the shaping stories perhaps not be deliberated on, written down, and consciously instilled at all? Just let the 'truths' people hold to be self-evident pass along in the process of everyday life."

Dennet-Jones did not care much for such "underground" stories and was ready to prescribe the reading list. "It's the classics we need. It's what 'classic' means."

Rojas' penchant for exposing assumptions was still new to us as a group so there were a few titters when he responded in devil's-advocate mode. "Then the trick is to get on the committee that chooses what's classic!"

"It gives me great pleasure," Dennet-Jones replied wryly, "to appoint you to that committee, Rojas, since the ones who know best must decide." His irony, once provoked, has a way of getting sharper. "If, however, you're implying that the choice is a matter of prejudice, then you're not qualified to serve. The judgment is made in the best possible way, by what readers through the ages keep returning to."

At that point Akira did a peculiar thing. I don't know why a levelheaded man of science should have intervened energetically on the philistine side of the topic, but it's what he did. In his innocent way, he said, "Hunenko raises a good question: Are we starting from tradition or are we starting afresh? Isn't insisting on the classics just a conservative effort to repeat the past as we know it? Even the *trivium*—grammar, rhetoric, and logic. Is accepting them as founding disciplines a historical prejudice favoring charismatic education over the rigors of knowledge?"

"No to all that!" cried Elena Bart, springing suddenly to life. "It's a far-reaching question, but here's the alternative view. It isn't repetition for two reasons: First, because repetition isn't possible. We're no longer the same people in the same world as the stories that inspire us, so when we repeat them, we translate them. Second, it isn't repetition because we have only shreds and clippings of the past. Artifacts that spring up unbidden as artists catch inspiration on the fly. In honoring the past, we don't respond to a body of knowledge we respect. We respond to analogies that arrive like energy charges and encourage variations. Ground the young in stories, and you make them imaginative."

During this speech I, Kahn, was watching Rojas and comparing his rhetorical manner with Akira's. He might not have credited a word Bart said, but he took her in full seriousness, like Fyodor's analyst behind the couch. Akira's way differs entirely. His rational criticism of fiction as misleading the young was an ironic subterfuge. He played the double agent, champion of positive knowledge over imaginative fiction, as a way of bringing the issue vividly to light. I suspect he and Rojas were largely supporting Bart's point of view.

I don't usually say much in these discussions, but as a writer of a sort, I have a keen interest in storytelling, and by this time I was getting a bit impatient. "I'd like to get back to how we select stories for the curriculum. Alexandros is filled with classics. We can't teach them all. So which do we choose?"

Dennet-Jones is a fiddler with words, and he fiddled a bit before deciding how to answer. "To experience a forest, you don't have to climb every tree or smell every flower. Better to learn a few stories well by hearing them or reading them repeatedly." Fiddle, fiddle. "To change the metaphor, it's like soaking in a Turkish bath."

He didn't stop there, and we didn't stop listening. Clive may be a bit pompous, but he isn't shallow. On matters like this he's an ambulatory encyclopedia. He went on to remind us of what we were and were not trying to accomplish, until Kashimoto, still speaking for the devil's party, objected.

"I see that childhood stories teach us who we are and how we relate—and might relate—to others. Such underground narratives provide the colors and coherences of a world with all its furnishings. We don't so much learn the narratives as absorb how living is done."

Then he appeared to lapse into his philistine argument. "Even so, shouldn't truth rank above fiction? Why should we learn myths rather than facts? Why plant the false idea that Earth—which we've never seen!—rests on the shoulders of Ajax or on the back of a turtle or that it's embedded in crystal spheres? Perhaps the ethical version of the question is even more pressing: Are we to include stories that celebrate rape and pillage, genocide and revenge? Should we give children leave to model themselves on events that are contrary to everything we believe to be civilized and good?"

Dennet-Jones knew the answer to that one too! "The short answer is yes, other criteria being met."

But before he could explain, Hunenko, the political historian, intervened. "Kashimoto makes a good point. *Your* view, Clive, is even more dangerous than he says. Take his example of the tale that celebrates genocide and compare it to a humanistic story of equality and individual rights. If stories shape people to the degree you think, then what happens if half your city passionately believes in eugenics while the other half believes eugenics is the devil? Stories convey ideals, but ideals can also be prologues to war!"

"Or to political life!" Young Rückert muttered to me under his breath.

Bart leaned across the table and glared at Hunenko until she gained a head of steam sufficient for another eruption. "You're missing the whole point, Oleksiy! You're talking about propaganda, not education. Conditioned mice in a maze, not free citizens in a city. You can't program the behavior of free agents. We don't say 'Go forth and be Achilles or the Buddha or the Prophet Isaiah.' We show how people function and what commands their respect with what consequences. We don't make a moral lesson of it. You're imagining little behavior machines who don't make waves because they have crippled imaginations." She went on for a couple of minutes longer with examples about how we need to understand the suicide bomber assembling his vest and the saint sitting in the monastery praying her life away and the philosopher who spends his years contemplating unanswerable questions. By this time I was in grave danger of forgetting what topic we were supposed to be discussing. I suppose her point was that inconsistent stories, false as well as true, evil as well as good, provoke invention. She certainly wanted to defend both invention and morally suspect—even violent—fairy tales as passing down essential wisdom.

When, finally, her enthusiasm waned, she concluded with one of her arcane literary references: "I rest my case," she declared, "on the seventeenth-century Christian poet who championed the fortunate fall from a perfect world to a blighted world. John Milton said, 'I cannot praise a fugitive and cloistered virtue, unexercised and unbreathed, that never sallies out and sees her adversary, but slinks out of the race . . . '"

At that point Rucai, the old classicist, cried out in jubilation, "Hear, hear" and rapped the table thrice. "And since the subject tonight has been the poets, I'd like to paraphrase another: Our poets find us mute and give us speech; our painters find us blind and give us sight; our musicians find us deaf and teach us to hear."

Those two enthusiastic outbursts were enough to sink whatever else might have been said in this session. And so, since the point in recording the colloquies is not to collect answers but to show the Elders at work, I end this account here.

RECRUITING PAOLA

ON THE AFTERNOON of the day Akira met with Claudio on the Observation Deck, he descended by elevator to the bottom of the ship where few but workers are allowed. The elevator door opens on vast greenhouses extending the full length and breadth of the ship. It's a series of diverse environments where much of the food supply is produced. A worker on a small vehicle rather like a golf cart conveys him a full half mile to the laboratories where he hopes to find the person he is looking for. There, bent over a microscope in a white coat, is a slip of a girl whom he knows well but has not seen for many months.

"Paola?"

The girl turns on her lab stool. She is a plain-looking person of ordinary height, square in build, with rather nondescript dark hair a bit unkempt. Incuriously she lifts her head, revealing an intelligent face and dark eyes. As her gaze crosses his, hers turns defensive and she answers in an acerbic tone, "Yes?" The eyes say she recognizes him and that she would rather not. After all, he is a friend of her parents, whom she has known all her life. Whatever may have intervened, as a young botanist she would naturally admire the most distinguished scientist on the ship.

"I'm Akira Kashimoto."

"I know who you are." She keeps her eyes on his. "My father sent you!" She shakes her head in controlled frustration.

Akira advances, leans against a lab table just behind her and speaks in a solemn but affectionate voice. "Your father did not send me. I'm sorry to say that he has not spoken of you for a very long time."

There is a history here that colors every word, though the history is known only to her. It is this: Paola Rucai, now fifteen, has been estranged from her father since puberty. That much Akira knows, but he knows only as much of the story as Claudio lets himself know. Until the girl's early teens she and he had been inseparable, a learned man and a precocious daughter. She was not close to her mother. From the earliest years there was an undercurrent of competition for the father's attention, and she knew without knowing that he favored her. Where most children on the ship are removed from home so as not to dilute their education, she spent as much time at home as possible. Between visits Claudio often waited for her in the playground after classes where she would sit beside him, tell him about her studies, and be rewarded with a story. He knew all the great tales and she loved hearing them repeated in his deep, resonant and comforting voice.

The daughter's precocity extended in every direction until the thing happened that shook the foundations of her psychic order and was never spoken of. One afternoon she found him at home with a woman, not her mother, in bed. She slipped out unseen but the wound festered, and after a stormy period—"I don't want to know you! I never want to see you again. I can live without you!"—she severed relations with him and left the Rucai apartment. Not only did she retreat to suffer in private but she was strong-minded enough to hold to her resolution. Given the limited environment of the starship, it took caution to avoid meeting one of its most prominent citizens.

From that day forward she put all her energies into the biological sciences as though to stake out her territory as far as possible from his literary and historical interests. Now at fifteen, still a student, she is a fully accredited researcher in the botany labs, where she already has several important research achievements to her credit. It is this profile of her character that convinces Akira that she might be the very person he can trust in the crisis he has spent the morning discussing with her father.

He repeats, "Your father doesn't know I've come. I'd like to talk with you on a subject that has nothing to do with family and friends. Forgive the directness, but my purpose is much more urgent than anything personal. It has to do with the future of the Galatea mission."

She stares at him warily, long and hard, then replies, less to convey information than to clear the air, "It's about P2314, isn't it? I've just been given the analysis of its environment. I'm assigned to begin work on plant material that might be adapted to the planet." She looks around to assure they're alone. "Would you like to come to the office? No one else is there."

The invitation shows a slight relaxing of her guard, so he does. When he sees that she has accepted their relation as one scientist and one citizen to another without reference to her father, he explains in broad terms the political threat inherent to any new colony. Without mentioning Claudio, he relies heavily on instincts she has inherited from him. He knows that politics and the historical disciplines are more native to her than to specialists who acquire them by study, as he knows that she has acquired the sciences by hard work rather than by birth and breeding. Knowing so much, Akira proceeds cautiously. He does not speak of the potential for trouble between the rival visions of the Elders and Starship Command but only of preparing the way for a healthy colony.

Since he says nothing about what he wants from her or why he's taking her into his confidence, it leaves her to draw it out and piece it together. Far from being annoyed at his interrupting her work, she is flattered by the visit. How could anyone not be? And yet it puts her on guard against her own disposition to do whatever he has come to ask as, ever so slightly, she retreats again. Seeing as much gives Akira a fresh observation of the strength and direction of her imagination. When that shadow of fear concerning his motives falls across her face, dimming the first more generous impulse, he waits as quite different ideas begin to take shape.

As her father's daughter, Paola has a more than casual grasp of the politics of the starship and is careful *not* to ask questions too sensitive to be spoken of. Only after the air has been cleared between them and the affection of past years re-established does she come around to asking what he wants of her, cautious still not to speak hastily since words at such a juncture can influence the rest of life.

However young this woman may be, Akira reads in her silence and her caution the instincts of the philosopher.

"What would you answer, I wonder, if I said I wanted to enlist you as a secret agent to stand watch against the dissolution of the mission?"

She stares at him without answering.

"Not to act against any person or persons or to take any negative action whatever. Just to keep your finger on the pulse of a situation that could lead to the ultimate disintegration of humanity itself if precautions aren't taken." He stops with that obscure remark and watches how, if at all, she will take it up.

"You must think I'm blind." There's a tinge of indignation in the reply and a trace of the belligerence that has infected her life too early. "I may not want to see my father again, but I did grow up in his house. Don't think I'm stupid!" The youthful brashness in the tone may demand credit for her cleverness but it also shows strength of character.

"I'm sorry. It's not personal. But we are entering—*we*, if you decide to come with me—on treacherous waters. You mustn't underestimate the stakes or the dangers."

The intense face holds him in a laser-keen gaze for a few seconds until, deciding something within herself, she looks away and asks almost casually, "What am I allowed to know?"

He studies her in turn, the self-control without self-consciousness. How in the order of nature does it happen that a face so plain, so indistinct at first sight, can grow in depth of character with every subsequent glance?

Slowly he answers, "First you should know that Claudio and I share the analysis of the situation. If you agree to work with me, he will know it, but the relations between the two of you, however regrettable, are not my concern. I am approaching you without his knowledge at the very beginning of events no one can foresee. We do not propose to act *against* anyone or anything. If you think of it as subversive, it's subversion of an unusual kind." He allows himself a somber smile. "Passive resistance is a better term, but not by much. Between ourselves we've begun to call it *La Résistance*."

With a complicitous chuckle that shows her warming toward him if not his idea, she accepts the allusion to the French movement. "I'll need to watch *Casablanca* again."

He goes on to offer a sense of the slant he and her father are giving that name. "When we receive an order, we think of it as a packet of energy. We don't try to defeat it with counter-energy. We go with the momentum and increase it, trying to direct it toward unintended consequences. The object is not to *do* anything but prepare the political imagination of the colony. We are not trying to dictate, or even to imagine, a political structure. The point is to provide the conditions for the colony to morph from an efficient machine into a political community. If what I'm proposing has the aura of a cloak-and-dagger operation, it's only to avoid open strife between two cultures. Even as we *do* nothing, we must not lose!" Akira pauses to let the point sink in and take another sounding of her depth.

Growing less tentative, she remarks with amusement, "I remember my father telling me about a Chinese classic that advocated action by inaction. That's what you mean, isn't it?"

"Probably. I learned this peculiar lesson first from Elena Bart. Do you know her?"

At the name, Paola's whole demeanor changes. Her eyes blaze out at him in open hostility. Her body goes rigid, arms stiff at her side, and her face turns paler by several shades.

Akira sees all that and a little more but says nothing. Merely looks around at her workplace, absorbing the ambience of her life as the name Elena Bart visibly sinks back into oblivion under the weight of some mental restraint. And yet that critical moment has revealed something essential: Somehow Claudio and Paola and Elena make a trio, and it wouldn't be surprising to find that that ménage stands directly in his path.

As though in summary of all he has said, she replies, "Here's how far I can see: Once the technicians are on the ground and under control of Starship Command, the Elders' influence, especially their care for the young, will end. So the only thing to be done is infiltrate the colonists with people well educated in both cultures. Even so, such people will be a minority and under the influence of the power structure." At the end of this short speech the expression on the face of this gifted young woman bears more than a trace of self-satisfaction. But that too quickly passes as she adds, "What I don't see is what all this has to do with me."

Akira smiles. "I'd like you to stand watch with us."

She raises an eyebrow. "Stand watch with you and my father?"

Recognizing that the innocent mention of Elena Bart has lost him ground, Akira ignores her tone. "You have already grasped the essence." He shifts his discourse into a slightly conspiratorial key used between trusted allies. "I need you to circulate among the young students and help me identify the most likely candidates in the physical sciences and technologies. We should wager on people in Level One. The demands will be too great for the rest. We have several years but no time to unseat narrow prejudices. There's much to be done. Our candidates must be imaginative, hungry, and educable. The best will be people like you, inclined equally to the humanities and the sciences. Whatever they surmise, they must know nothing about our intentions. Any word now—or ever—about our purpose, and everything is lost. Some of the bright ones may eventually figure it all out independently, but it must remain a guess. There will be no organization to join. No chain of command. The risks are too great."

"And you want me to do what exactly?" Paola's words may still be tinged with irony, but Akira sees that his work is done.

So he slips into future tense and watches for evidence of her tacit consent. "Your task will be purely social: to identify potential recruits, size them up, and report your findings to me. Then we can begin quietly supporting them by enriching their learning environments and using friendship to stimulate their political imaginations."

She can see how it will work . . . if it does. Her role will be a bit like the salonnière of Enlightenment Paris. Bring a group of bright people together and meld them into a community of interests that will overreach the boundaries of specialization. Her recruits will be discreetly introduced into Akira's circle. That would flatter ambitious young people.

But there are obstacles. Except for school and the lab, she has secluded herself from social life, and reticence on this front is strengthened by the wish not to cross paths with her father. Now she's being asked to do the very thing she has the least taste for and that will likely throw her into his path.

Akira concludes, "We must get as many of our people in the landing party as possible, because the colony is likely to grow out of that group. No one need ever know that we had a hand in shaping it."

"What are the odds for success?"

"Ah, now you're trying to read the end in the beginning. I'm not a statistician or a prophet. I can only hope."

THE KLEIN BOTTLE COLLOQUY

THERE'S MUCH OF THE Galatea you have yet to see and still more you need to feel. Before giving you a brief tour, I'll try to convey something of what it's like to live inside a generational starship. In a totally artificial environment, where every space is measured and every material fabricated, reality itself is limited to quantification. The difficulty is to help terrestrial creatures feel at home.

You will already have grasped the source of anxiety where people live in a self-sufficient machine amidst a mind-numbing order of systems that exclude uncertainty, where all discord is harmonized and where lethargy and discontent follow. Everything undefined, dark, subliminal, or unexpected—whatever might provoke wonder and inspire invention—has been examined under the bright light of computation and marginalized if not dismissed as unreal. In one sweep imagination, fiction, and art are swept into the dustbins of "entertainment," "magic," or "superstition."

But I must abandon these imponderables before someone accuses me of being a philosopher. So back to the description of the ship.

You know something already about the Academic Deck where the schools, preparatory through university, are located. The next deck up houses advanced studies and most research facilities, except for biology, in the bowels of the ship near food production, and cosmology, in the dome at the top. These research spaces were assigned in the original plans as though by a symbolic vertical code. Research in other fields was brought online gradually, remaining dependent, meanwhile, on the mother planet.

I haven't yet mentioned the ample facilities for gymnastics. Physical health is always a priority where the point is survival, but much less thought was given to leisure pursuits until Ulro Year 2170 when the first epidemic of starship anxiety threatened to cripple the mission. At that time the Elders consigned one deck to "creative" and leisure activities. Many people still preferred idleness, but a significant minority took up ancient skills with enthusiasm. Instruction flourished in things as diverse as cooking and watercolors, bookbinding and violin making. You can imagine what an expanding investment of imagination was required for developing even the infrastructure to support such "hobbies." The point always was to encourage creative ventures that would give healthy form to life.

Next I want to show you where the fine arts are located, one deck up from the crafts. People who weren't born on a starship may not easily imagine how much we need beauty. I've mentioned the performance spaces for music or dance and the coffeehouse where people gather for reading poetry and other literary work. What I haven't mentioned is our relatively new museum. That comes with a story all its own.

Originally there were no provisions for practicing or teaching the plastic arts, as though the future of humanity could spare painting and sculpture. Who would have thought of sending a Rembrandt portrait into space instead of a spare toilet? Would any sane person on a technological mission or in a colonial outpost in space spend his life in a painter's smock with a palette in hand? All that's obvious, yet it's tinged with the implication that art is entertainment and not essential to life. Interesting, then, that we should have developed an appetite first for representations of natural scenes from terrestrial life and later for the play of pure color and form. It showed up first in residential spaces.

Most of the domestic cubicles on a starship have no outside view and where there is one, it's little more than a peephole on vacancy. So, acres of dead wall space cry out for relief. Somewhere along the way, that cry began to be answered, initially by the crafts and eventually by art. First came photographs for empty walls, then wallpaper with copies of terrestrial scenes reprinted from Alexandros and, finally, prints from our complete visual record of the Ulro arts. Slowly we learned to give blank walls the illusion of open spaces, lush gardens, and cityscapes, and this answer to a vital need expanded from representation into a passion for art. The purpose was never the shallow aesthetic of décor or design, but turning anonymous parametric spaces into habitats and, as people once said, "making a house a home."

By means of an old process of 3D printing, it all began in reproducing works so realistic that students could learn the subtleties of color and brushstrokes all the way down to the canvas. From that grew the idea of producing art for public display, which also answered to the hunger for the open in an enclosed environment.

The result was dramatic. The quality of life was so enhanced and people's spirits so improved—for a while!—that static representations of nature in private living quarters made way for moving images where you seemed to step into the green spaces, though for some reason I don't understand, these didn't offer the same enduring satisfaction as "the greats." Again the evidence of the dearth of sensory experience in an artificial environment led to boundless desire for the beauty beyond knowledge and utility. Like the hunger for music in a deeply silent environment!

As art became common, we dedicated space for a museum. The capacity for reproduction being unlimited, the collection soon overflowed into public spaces, and the museum is surprisingly well used. A curator manages the collection, changing exhibits to keep the experience fresh, and even stages exhibitions of works produced on the ship. At this moment, for example, you can see two paintings by Akira's wife, Atsuko Kashimoto.

Of course controversy and even disappointment followed on the heels of success. I won't go into it here except to mention three points that show the direction minds can take when they're not preoccupied with necessity. There is a rule, fiercely debated among the devotees of the arts, that precludes private ownership of works on the principle that art is a public heritage and cannot be genuinely *owned* by anyone. I don't know why this should matter in an environment where ownership of property is negligible and where "original reproductions" are available in unlimited quantities, unless it's that "value consists in limitation." If not limited, the greatest treasures become clichés. That, as much as ownership, is part of the debate.

The second debate is over the difference between "originals" and "reproductions." Never mind that no one now living has ever seen an original from the hand of an old master and that our own "original work" is, to put it kindly, not always up to the mark of a Giotto, a Rubens, or a Rothko. However, it's reliably suspected that if you could set one of our reproductions next to an original, the differences would be accessible only to the technical examinations used for dating and reading *pentimenti* beneath the topcoats of paint. To my way of thinking this fact makes the purism and the purists look puerile. In any case, to the benefit of everyone, young painters can now learn by copying works as was once done in the great museums of Ulro.

An arts topic of still greater moment burst into the center of our review of the curriculum as we began the return to Planet 2314: music. I may not have said yet that the Council typically settles on the topic for discussion a week in advance so we can begin turning our reflections in that direction. One evening the announced topic was the science curriculum, but the discussion got sabotaged before it began and resulted in a session destined to become legendary.

The situation was a bit like a scene in an old film: You pack your bag for one destination then, at the ticket office, seeing a poster advertising some place you've never been, you end up buying a ticket for it instead. Here's what happened:

Before we sat down and put our heads together, so to speak, chemist Yu Wang and Akira Kashimoto were chatting quietly about the mysteries of student interest, when one or the other of them was overheard to remark, "I wonder why it is that two bright and curious youngsters with similar gifts and training go in opposite directions. One develops a hunger to learn all about dark energy or the history of Renaissance architecture, while the other remains completely indifferent and turns away. Why is that?"

"Teach them music!" A voice from the other side of the table said eagerly.

Both men stared blindly at the woman opposite. Presently Yimou leaned forward and asked, "What did you say?"

"Teach them music. Teach them to care!"

That was the inaugural moment of one of the most extraordinary sessions of our generation. The remark came from Aurélie Lefèvre, who represents the arts on the Council. You may not remember Lefèvre. She usually attracts little attention in this lair of the high-verbals. Tall and straight-backed as Dennet-Jones, borderline anorexic, not aging especially well. Except the hands! They are as expressive as a Hindu goddess and as elegant as a Russian ballerina. The long fingers of a pianist. (Sometime I must tell you about the resurrection of the piano on a starship, if the chance ever offers.)

Anyway, whenever the topic touches on the arts, Lefèvre undergoes a metamorphosis before our eyes. Her whole body comes alive: The face and voice, hands and head work in perfect harmony with the rhythm of her words as the eyes move from person to person, adding force to her words.

During this evening I found myself not looking *at* her but *through* those mesmerizing grey eyes. She glowed with inspiration so compelling you'd think the muses themselves had descended Parnassus and taken up residence among mortals. And that's saying something for the muses, since we mortals are about three millennia and I forget how many light-years from Parnassus.

Kashimoto grinned pleasantly in the direction of her obscure remark. "Would you care to explain?"

"You're puzzled because you overestimate analysis and underestimate our saturation in mood. Your student will respond to the unpredictable thing that addresses him in person and seduces him. When a summons comes to him alone and demands his response, he will catch fire."

Akira stared at her as though searching for some sociable reply to words that made little sense until she added, "It's Eros, you know. From the sex appeal of the inorganic to the beasts of the field, from the loves of the plants to *Le Roman de la Rose*—it's all about the kindling and ordering of desire."

"And all this is related to music . . . how?"

By this time, the rest of us had forgotten whatever we were doing and begun gathering around the peculiar exchange.

"It's all to do with how music works on the human spirit. When we discussed how stories provide templates for who we are and how we might live, we said that the aim is not to invent rules that dictate the 'contents' of a life, but to awaken us to our powers of invention. I'm only saying that, where logic provides conceptual order, music—art—makes us *care*."

One of the two men asked, "By 'care' you mean feeling, emotion?"

"Something like that, though I'd say passion rather than emotion, since it doesn't originate in us." She answered hesitantly, even ambiguously, as though unsure how to put it. "Imagine a child hearing a piece of music, a simple march, say. Unselfconsciously, she dances, sings, and parades up and down to the beat of the drum, *possessed by* the martial spirit. The sounds may be new to her, but they aren't alien. She's attuned by the sound as an instrument is tuned. Ordered by a rhythm akin to bodily rhythms: the peristalsis in her gut, the beat of her heart, the waves of her brain, but it's much more than physical.

"Now stop the march and play a waltz. Because she is too young to resist, the shimmering, diaphanous tones of the dance immediately reorder her in an entirely different mode and expand her responsive range. Her caring isn't just a feeling she has. It's more like 'caring for.' She's *affected* from outside, formed and reformed by a stream of feelings, moods, or affects. We might call it enchantment!"

Before Lefèvre could finish her thought, Joseph Kern intruded skeptically. Kern's extensive literary culture should make him a natural ally of Lefèvre—or a formidable opponent—but I can never predict which it will be.

He began ironically. "In addition to communication with spirits," he said, "I don't see that you're saying anything more than that music expands our capacity for responding to auditory stimuli. That's a good argument for the utility of the arts in the curriculum, but where's the news?"

"That, Kern, is because I've only just begun! Along the way we might discover that the 'spirit' of music is essential to the well-being of creatures like us."

Since by this time we had all taken seats and become attentive, Lefèvre accepted as given that the topic for this meeting had shifted. Reaching down to the floor beside her chair, she brought up a piece of glass as though she had been preparing this spontaneous performance for a long while, awaiting the propitious moment. Even now I wonder how she happened to have that object at hand!

"I'm circulating something you're all familiar with but don't see very often. It's a bottle. An unusual one. It's to look at as we talk about listening." Without further comment, she passed her strange exhibit to her right where Gwendolyn stared, bemused, as though confronted by a three-dimensional koan.

Yu Wang had not tuned out as he often does when a line of discussion yields less than it seems to promise. Ignoring the bottle, he raised Kern's irony to a higher degree. "I do hope you're not teaching that poor child to indulge the caprices of pleasure that we've regularly warned against?"

Aurélie acknowledged the remark with a smile. "Yes and no, to you and to Kern. We don't exclude aesthetic pleasure. We try to locate its proper place, as an effect of art, but not its source or its purpose. When we concentrate on our own pleasure in listening, we erect a barrier between us and the music, blocking its effect. That's why the child is a good example."

Without interrupting, I heard Elena Bart muttering under her breath, "Except you become like little children, you may not enter her kingdom."

Aurélie Léfèvre was continuing, "Music is certainly one of the joys of life, but my effort is to contemplate its power to give intelligibility to disorderly feelings."

Dennet-Jones asked, "How heavily do you lean on the analogy between logic and music? Logic belongs to the primary curriculum—the *trivium*—because, as it gives order to thinking, it also makes an orderly mind habitual. Does music have such permanent effects, or is it more transient?"

"That's a good question, Clive. I think the analogy may be extended as far as forming habit. As we become habituated to well-ordered thinking, so the experience of orderly transitions in our affections can prepare us to expect a similar ordering. Music encourages what I like to call an interior economy of feeling or an 'economy of affects,' even an 'economy of desire,' though the term 'desire' may seem to miss the consensual character of the experience. In fact, the experience is doubly a summons from beyond ourselves as individual auditors and an objective bond with others in an audience."

This was her main point. You could tell from the way her eyes moved from one person to another around the table, not stopping at the face but reading each of us in turn, guiding our conceptual motion by the precision of her words—her music!

When no one volunteered a further response, she continued: "This musical 'economy'—this 'ordering of our subjective house'—works by evoking disparate feelings in one moment then, in a second moment, organizing them. We're familiar with the speculation that when citizens on Ulro lost the capacity for governing their feelings, it became a planet teetering on the edge of a nervous breakdown. This may be related to starship malaise as well, but I'm only suggesting that music encourages coherence in a dimension of experience that, as often as not, makes victims of us all."

Having first inspired the discussion with his question about analogy, Clive Dennet-Jones had now lost that small advantage and joined the ironic tone already sounded by Joseph Kern and Yu Wang. "So please, Madame, lead the way into this dark realm."

So she did. And began by singing a simple melody, the Marseillaise, of course. The first and last time anyone argued a point by singing to us. "Now we might think that that tune is constructed piecemeal by adding one note to the next. But no. No more than we add an infinite number of points in drawing a line. Melody is the movement of sound in the process of forming a whole. The per-*form*-ance that the moving-form passes through and *in-forms* us. We are shaped, as it is shaped, by participation."

She stopped there, and silence descended on the room as happens in the concert hall between movements when we're given a few moments of quiet to digest and prepare for the next wave of sound.

That reminded me of one of her inscrutable definitions of music as "silence made audible!" But by now I was quite lost. In part because I enjoy her warbling too much to care about the rest. Seduced by the wrong thing, I suppose.

Meanwhile, Elena Bart had been listening with her mouth closed—may God be thanked!—until she could no longer resist the silence and broke into speech: "Would you say more, Aurélie, about this ordering of our affective houses? Is the parallel of music and logical thinking only an analogy, or are you implying that they appear as distinct and rival faculties because they have become dissociated, to the detriment of both?"

Aurélie replied, "I hear two questions in that. First, the one about a musical economy calls for more complex examples.

We've mentioned how the simple song lends itself to a variety of distinct moods: the physical exuberance of a dance, the melancholy of a funeral dirge, the joy of a jazz tune, the sentimentality of a love song, or the emotional density of joy-in-suffering, the blues. The song form, being small, is typically limited to a single disposition. More complex forms—like the concerto or symphony—evoke a sequence of moods, like an intelligible configuration of the vicissitudes of life. Such ordering of diverse affects, abstracted from physical conditions, suggests that we're no more victims of shifting dispositions than we are of incoherent ideas. Through the stresses and strains of tonalities arriving and departing, our affections are evoked, explored, and recomposed across an expanse of musical time."

This answer was addressed mainly to Bart, but the next was addressed to us all. "As to Elena's second question, about reason and feeling as conflicting forces, my answer is that common sense has missed the mark. We're treating a historical dissociation as though it were natural and universal. When we misunderstand ourselves as conceptual beings through and through, we relegate our feelings to an incoherent solitude that cripples experience."

Burgess interrupted. "Now let me see if I've got this right, Aurélie. You're denying that reason and feeling are different software packages. I suppose you mean that thinking requires us to care enough to think whatever we think—otherwise we'd be androids. And feeling requires us to think what we feel—otherwise we'd by animals. So a person whose *reason* is undeveloped wallows in feelings and may end up as a slave to animal drives, while a person whose *sensibility* is undeveloped may kill affect and live with a withered heart?"

Lefèvre admired that summary and replied, laughing. "Excellent! And both pass though practice to habituation. But I'd make one small adjustment to what you just said: Our being-affected or attuned comes before thinking. Structurally first and chronologically first. We're always saturated by some mood. We must actively care enough to think, but we don't have to think our way into feeling. We live in the residue of moods. That's what intellectualism misses: Attunement first; thinking second—even when they're simultaneous! As our Council meetings require a community of mood before a real conversation can occur. That makes the ritual dimension of our weekly schedule important and even these otherwise useless robes we wear by tradition." With a finger she lifted the fabric of one sleeve in illustration.

"We can see why it's essential to kindle the passions of the young, so they won't live with constricted sympathies or encroaching apathy. Feelings are not simply wild things that depend on reason to impose a discipline from afar. Desire is not the enemy. The enemy is deformed desire. The idolatry of some affections out of harmony with others—and with thinking. Without an experienced heart *and* a strong head, their capacity for loving the world *and* for understanding it will be weakened. As Gwendolyn says, one produces a fool; the other produces a monster."

Only one person in the Council Chamber was *not* absorbed by this line of thought. The boyish Hans Rückert was absorbed in tracing with one finger the twists and turns of the Klein bottle.

But Joseph Kern compensated, if compensation was needed, as he caught Lefèvre's idea and her fire. He raised his eyebrows in her direction: "If you're right, then this has consequences on our schools."

"You may be ahead of me there, Kern," she replied. "I'm not proposing practical expedients, you know. Only trying to understand. My point is that music teaches us to care as in 'taking care.' Played in that key, care is another name for love. But why do you set it at the origin of language?"

He pressed on with the novel idea. "Intentionally or not, in establishing the parallel of logic and music, you've evoked an essential correspondence between language and music at the source of a curriculum centered on acquiring language. We don't really understand language until we've caught the spirit in the voice! As you said, a line is not the sum of its points, nor a melody the sum of its notes. Nor is language the sum of its words. To speak, to hear, even to read aloud or silently, requires first the music. Language originates in sound, and, as you've said, it's never originally *my* sound."

This time she responded with a degree of astonishment. "Of course, we know from poetry that music is an element of language. But why do you put it at the *origin*? To understand the command for reforming the schools, did we need to hear Allison Rawls' voice? Couldn't she just have sent that piece of paper?"

"Yes! We would have understood the brute signs, but not the full banality of what we got. That came in the melody of the voice. Language has as many moods as music because *it is music*."

"Why do you insist on 'the origin?'" Dennet-Jones repeated.

"Because language begins in pure sound. A song without words. The cry of the wolf in the snow-covered forest. The sound of the wave on the seashore. The human baby in the crib, alarmed by the voices of its quarreling parents, will search the faces and begin to cry, or under the tranquilizing effects of a familiar melody be lulled to sleep by the lullaby—either, without understanding the words. Proof that he's growing into the sensory register —the affect—of language before the sounds convey semantic references. Music first, signification later."

Then as an afterthought, "Just incidentally, Aurélie has expanded your *trivium* into a foundational *quadrivium* parallel to the specialized languages dealing with knowledge of nature: first music; second, grammar; third, rhetoric; and fourth, logic! Then on to the languages of nature where music was traditionally about number."

By this time Lefèvre's strange exhibit had passed to Kashimoto, who sat smiling at it, turning it slowly round and round on the table. The satisfaction on his face suggested recognition of some relation between the bottle and the discussion that certainly missed me.

Meanwhile, Hunenko, sitting next to him, was staring at the tabletop as he often does when an idea puzzles him and he's trying to form a question. Except this time he, too, was thinking about the mellifluous voice and the riveting gaze. Eventually his head rose and he looked earnestly at Lefèvre.

"If the arts are prologues to care and care is some kind of love, what does care care for? What directs it?"

The two philosophers, Hunenko and Rückert, had said little in a discussion that they might well have dominated. But now Hans responded to Oleksiy's question:

"Care is care for nothing, no-thing. It's directedness without object. Care cares-for All. Limit it to an object or a goal, and care will be care for the wrong thing."

Lefèvre, who had listened raptly to these exchanges, sat a few moments gazing out the window across the room. She might have been waiting for some muse from the void to show her the way forward. More prosaically, she might have been evaluating whether she had done justice to her inspiration. I say "inspiration" because, call it what you will, no one present would have denied that she was inspired or that she was passing the inspiration on to us.

Eventually she added: "An old maxim, traditional since Plato, says, 'Let me write a nation's songs, and I care not who writes her laws.' That's because our first opening toward reality is through mood, affect, love. Then all this gets expressed in language and concepts. If music provokes listening as universal attentiveness, then it teaches love even of discord as the possibility of harmony, in life as in pure sound. 'Properly'—which means 'in itself'—it's a disposition of welcoming and participating in latency. Sound may come with alluring beauty or as the chaotic noise of an industrial city or the lonely silence of cosmic space. We wait for wherever the performance may lead, in confidence that all that turmoil will finally come to rest. It's no accident that music is *played*. It's *play* rather than work; *use* rather than possession; *cooperation* rather than dominion. It teaches love of the latency of being."

"So," Hunenko added as though in a footnote, "music on this account is next of kin to ethics. The formation of character, so perhaps the city."

Rückert replied, as though in summary: "The phrase 'economy of desire' reminds me of a famous remark by someone: 'Love and do what you will.' So long as you love 'the whole' and not just a part, for loving in part would be to ignore, resist, even hate the whole on which the part depends!" He laughed and added ironically to Hunenko, "If you want timid citizens who give their highest allegiance to stasis and the state, keep them tone deaf. If you want them to be politically imaginative and open to All, teach them music."

At that point Bart added another of her provocative asides under her breath yet audible this time to the whole room. "The sacred and the profane. Music is praise even when it's barbarous."

That remark, I can tell you, dropped like lead and drained the life from the conversation. To me it was utter nonsense, and I'm recording it only because it is the only instance I ever witnessed when no one in the room made any sense of something Bart said, Claudio Rucai being absent that night.

When it appeared that the discussion had reached a full stop—as though the high-verbals were ever in danger of that—Burgess suddenly cried, "Wait! What about this bottle? I don't see the point."

Instead of speaking to the question, Lefèvre merely asked, "What's in the bottle?" The abruptness, and its apparent irrelevance, threw a bolt into the gears of the exchange and no one answered. She merely repeated, "What's in the bottle?" Then waited until we all began to feel uncomfortable.

Finally, Yu Wang, who might have known better, answered, "There's nothing in the bottle. It's empty."

"No!" Akira said, turning it around and around on the table in front of him. "A Klein bottle is constructed like a Moebius strip so that there is only one surface. Inside and outside are the same; everything in this room is 'in the bottle.' In fact, everything in the universe is in the bottle or at least addressed to it. Like a living mirror or an echo chamber."

"Exactly!" Lefèvre exclaimed. "What's inside and what's outside are concurrent. The difference between them is neutralized, rendered inapplicable to the case. Now"—she pointed to the object in the middle of the table—"our job as teachers is to polish that responsive, transparent membrane so that its reflecting and resonating capacities are enhanced in all directions."

"But," Dennet-Jones objected, "the bottle is only a metaphor."

Bart cut in again. "As is inside-outside! Everything's a metaphor, Clive—or even less. Metaphors are like horses. The trick is to ride one until it gets tired then trade it for a fresh mount. Aurélie has just revised our habit of taking a person as an isolated object with an inside facing outward into a black hole. Hence the Klein bottle."

"Oh, God!" exclaimed Burgess. "So we are wrong-side-out bottles, and music is a bottle brush!"

At that Rückert groaned. He understood Lefèvre's point and had caught her inspiration. "Yes, Burgess, except that it's about participating in the tune. Falling in love. Eros. Beauty lures us out of our empty selves and toward the good. We *fall*—there's the point, the falling—helplessly falling into an abyss of love, being perpetually reborn . . . and loving the risks."

Thus ended what forever after would be called the Klein Bottle Colloquy. I include it here because this conversation planted a seed that grew like a rhizome underground, subtly altering our perspective on other topics. Now, long afterward, I would say that, music aside and probably without even recognizing it, Aurélie Lefèvre had reoriented all our questions by showing that thinking is saturated in advance by prior states of mind. The difference is as subtle but decisive as a tiny shift in the axis of a planet around its star.

LURING THE YOUNG

THE FIRST COMPLICATION in Akira's secret plan testifies to the notion that ideas are not invented by thinkers alone but arise in their own time and for reasons unknown. The difficulty surfaced when Claudio Rucai asked to meet Akira again in the observatory.

Entering the Observation Deck late one afternoon, Claudio sees his friend standing as though at attention, facing him across the large room. Akira's Japanese posture is unlike the starched and stretched rigidity of Dennet-Jones. He appears to stand taller than his actual height, yet perfectly relaxed and balanced in mind and body. He crosses the room with unhurried steps, confident, open, alert, as Claudio comes to meet him from a quite different physical culture. His hands are clasped behind his back, elbows slightly extended to the side, open in disposition, without a hint of Akira's natural reserve. Claudio is taller by half a head than his younger friend and, though at home in himself, wired to a higher voltage. As the one bows formally, the weathered face of the other breaks into an amused smile.

Claudio lays a hand on Akira's shoulder. "Thank you for seeing me on short notice. Life is becoming complicated."

Akira gestures toward a glass enclosure recently installed for a new project, offers Claudio a seat on one side of a small

123

desk, and waits quietly for the urgent news. Claudio's hundred wrinkles gather into as urgent an image of anxiety as can be accomplished by a person who somehow cares carelessly.

"I asked to see you because I have had three unexpected visitors and learned two things that you must know immediately. The first is that Hans Rückert is on to us. The second is that we may have a traitor in our midst."

These announcements have no effect on the smile with which Akira welcomes all news, favorable and unfavorable.

"A few days ago Rückert and Hunenko came to see me. They wanted to discuss something 'too sensitive,' as Oleksiy put it, to bring up in Council. It seems that Rückert went to him first and asked what to do. The short of it is that on his own Rückert has arrived at almost exactly our reading of the political situation, including the necessity for acting and keeping mum about it!"

Hans Rückert's precocity is not surprising. As part of his advanced studies, he had read ancient philosophical texts with Rucai and political theory with Hunenko. Both know the energy and range of his mind. In fact it was on the strength of their recommendations that he was lately added to the Council.

Kashimoto asks, "What exactly did he say? What was his general tone? Or did Hunenko do all the talking?"

"No, Oleksiy let Hans talk, since it was his idea. He wasn't impassioned or indignant, and he certainly wasn't gloating like a teenager over his own cleverness. The only concern seemed to be the sensitivity of the subject."

Akira takes his time and eventually replies with characteristic reticence. "Not surprising. When you look at the generation between us and the kids we're trying to recruit, it's hard to find his equal. What does he think he sees?"

Claudio's smile shows a degree of satisfaction in Rückert's acuity and his foresight in not raising the subject in public. "He sees that any possible colony will inherit all the advantages and all the limitations of the starship. His term for it is 'bio-politics,' political life reduced to management of biological needs. That, he says, will end in benevolent violence and counter-violence. He sees that we can't let that happen but sees no way to prevent it. The subject is too dangerous to discuss openly, so he confided in Hunenko, who brought him to me."

Akira gazes thoughtfully into the cosmic distance before replying. "So what do we do about him?" Recognizing that Rückert's independent account confirms their own reading of the situation, he goes on to ask, "Did he speculate at all on what might be done?"

"No. I'm reasonably sure that his anxiety has led him only as far as this analysis. But for him, thinking and acting are the same. It's only a matter of time until his kind of intelligence begins to invent courses of action."

Though neither Akira nor Claudio shows any alarm, both sense the danger of being unintentionally compromised. "We can't confide in him. That would include Hunenko, who would be sympathetic but less sensitive to the risks."

"Then," Claudio concludes, "you go about your business. Put this out of mind. I'll commend Rückert's foresight so he doesn't feel isolated and say we must be attentive but keep quiet until some course of action turns up. Meanwhile, you and I can't risk confiding even to our allies. I don't doubt Rückert's trustworthiness, but with every person who knows, the risks multiply exponentially. A verbal slip could be disastrous."

"All the same, having seen this much, he will begin to see more. Especially what's going on among the students!"

"He didn't let us know just to amuse himself. I think he understands that the tension between the Elders and Command has reached a critical point. Understanding that much and knowing that we know he understands, he won't dare act on his own. When he sees more, he'll offer what support he can while remaining silent."

"Well," Akira says with a shrug, "These are risks we're obliged to take." Then a moment later, "You said you'd had two visits. Who was the second?"

"Rojas. My health was the excuse but we both knew that was a social fiction. Just before leaving he dropped Ang Yimou's name and, in the most casual fashion, mentioned Ang's relation to Talib Nasser."

That gets Akira's attention. Even throws him off his verbal stride. Without an intervening reflection he shoots back, "What relation?" He stands up and begins slowly pacing back and forth in the tight space of the research cubicle, hands clasped behind his back.

Claudio grins at the impulse Akira doesn't bother to suppress, then answers, "It appears that they were boyhood friends. Not surprising. But what matters—and what Rojas knows matters—is that we didn't know. Not to know about a colleague's old friendships on this tiny ship smacks of concealment."

Akira nods. "So the question is: What is being concealed and why?"

Claudio's reply is indirect. "There are mitigating circumstances, of course. Ang and Talib are the same age, old schoolmates, but both have been absorbed in other things since graduation."

"I know you're not accusing Ang of treachery."

"And I don't think he's consciously playing the spy. Certainly not on our scale." Claudio indulges his characteristic chuckle. "At most there may be an unconscious sympathy with the technological vision of the crew and a degree of blindness in Council deliberations. It's detectable in his conversation. But that's fine. We ask for imagination and criticism, not unanimity or loyalty. It's just that as a showdown becomes inevitable, unconscious opponents and allies could be equally dangerous."

"So if Ang were on to us . . ." Akira doesn't finish the thought before another intrudes. " . . . As you think Rojas may be and you know Rückert is . . . "

Claudio waves the suggestion aside. "With Rojas we'll never know. He's no firebrand. He's a man of wisdom and experience. Knowing nothing or knowing all would be the same in him. It's a professional habit. You only learn where he is by watching his interactions with other people. If we had to tell all our secrets to one other person, he'd be my first choice."

Akira silently ticks off the ones who are not Claudio's first choice—even Elena Bart, strangely, given the old and curious friendship between them. Then he almost but not quite laughs. "It's beginning to feel crowded around here."

These sobering topics done, Akira reports—without mentioning Paola—that he has been reading the credentials of students, looking for recruits. "What I need now is to make the first good connection and let things take their own course."

"Why not look up Paola?"

Akira stops with his mouth still open. It's Claudio's day for surprises.

"She always loved you. You know a little about all our past trouble, but she would respond to you if you didn't mention me. I have no idea what her state of mind is. The last time I saw her she was still angry. I hear she's working in the botany labs. It's worth a try, at least, but keep me out of it if you please."

"I won't mention you, though once we assemble a few people, it will be important to include you. But that's another matter. One day at a time."

And on that note the conversation ends.

On the last day of the school week Akira goes down to the Academy Deck to pick up little Yori and walk him home for the weekend. By habit they always stop off at a park for children on the Activities Deck that's more like a small gym than an open-air playground. Yori likes to play on the gym set as Akira watches from a park bench, but only after the boy has told him about his week in school. It's a ritual moment of intimacy between father and son. Akira takes a lively interest in the details of his studies, using every opportunity to encourage his sense of wonder.

On this afternoon someone is watching these two from a distance. Paola, who has not seen the boy since he was a baby, studies the intimacy between Akira and his son with a pang of nostalgia, tinged perhaps with guilt. Her most precious child-hood memories are of afternoons just like this shared with her father. When Yori goes off to play, she approaches Akira.

In his first conversation with her, he had said nothing about meeting again. That he left to her invention. If she were willing and up to the task they had discussed, she would see the implications of modifying her present way of life and even encountering her father. So his idea has been to wait and see where the proposal would come to rest in her mind. Either she would come to terms with the risks or she wouldn't. If she sought him out, it would mean that she had accepted the sacrifice and was committing to the cause. As it isn't very difficult to find anyone on a spaceship who's willing to be found, the meaning of this encounter is immediately and mutually understood.

As he gestures for her to sit down, the curious boy returns. He doesn't recognize her, and Akira formally introduces them. "This is Paola Rucai," his father says. "Do you remember her, Uncle Claudio's daughter?"

Yori studies her with quiet, thoughtful eyes, much older than his years, perhaps even understanding that this is not a chance meeting.

Accordingly, Akira gestures for her to wait until Yori goes off again to play. Then he smiles kindly and remarks, "He's like you were. Already he understands everything around him."

Yori soon leaves, but she doesn't answer promptly as might be expected. Just stares into the distance until she's ready to deliver her message in one flat phrase. "I'll do it."

Akira nods and waits for whatever she wants to add.

A few more moments pass before she begins the conversation, at an entirely new place. "I cannot help you—and my father—unless I talk to you first . . . about him."

Wherever she's headed, one thing makes it easier. Neither has to look at the other. Both watch, or seem to watch, Yori climbing and swinging on the bars beyond the sound of their voices. With a slight wave of his hand Akira invites her to continue.

"You must know about my father and Elena Bart." She begins, waiting this time for a reply.

Surprised again. But seeing that she's gambling on his response, he speaks guardedly. "I heard some rumor several years ago, but I've never had time for rumors. Rumor is a blank sheet other people write their passions on."

When she doesn't follow up, he modulates the tone to set the topic beneath him without making her feel that her confidence is unwelcome. "Don't you find that the more accurate gossip is, the more false it is? Truth is in the unknowable context. Gossip has no appreciation of that fact."

He has read her well, but it takes her a moment to decide to continue. "I need to get this out of my system, so I'm just going to spill the whole thing this once. Three years ago I left school one afternoon and went home because I felt ill. My mother wasn't there, but I found my father and the Bart woman in bed together. They didn't see me, and I snuck out without their knowing, but I was devastated. Since you came to see me in the lab, I've been trying for the first time to understand. If anyone was betrayed, it was my mother, but I wasn't thinking about her. I felt personally betrayed, lied to, violated. After that I went home only once. There was a terrible scene and I left." Even now her voice trembles and she stops, expecting no response.

Akira has the good sense not to appear over-interested in this information, attentive while treating it as ordinary. And so he waits for her to decide how far she needs to go. When she continues, the passion in her voice has diminished as though just saying it to another person has drained the poison from the wound. Besides, the man next to her is not just any other person. He's her father's best friend, a formidable paternal figure, and a distinguished man of learning. His turning up suddenly in her world, asking for her help, has broken through the fortress of her resentment and enabled her to face the trauma.

She continues, "I see now how little my response had to do with the love affair. It exposed something in me that I don't understand." Then she backs away. "Do you think this is on the right track? You know your plan will throw me in my father's path sooner or later, and I can't let that get in the way of our work."

As the momentum of her confession slows, Akira gambles on the personal side of the issue. "It sounds like the quandary is, if it wasn't the love affair that disturbed you, then what?" Then, as she doesn't respond, "You must know that I am not qualified to offer advice. If I had your questions, I would know only three people who might be helpful, and they are the last ones you could consult."

"Which people?" she asks with a bit more than curiosity.

"Nacho Rojas, your father, and Elena Bart! Each has forgotten more about the dark side of psychic life than I will ever know. The intellectual interests that she and your father couldn't share with anyone else on the ship may even be the root of the relationship."

To that she makes no answer, but she pursues her own line of thought with renewed vigor. Even her face becomes more energetic than before. "I know I cannot know their circumstances, or even the reasons for my own response with any certainty. But aren't there things that we have to give some account of just to go on? Just for coherence? Even if the accounts are fictional, they may help us hold ourselves together. Otherwise, we're paralyzed."

Instead of trying to formulate an adequate reply to that speech, he remains impassive, yet wondering at such insight in a person so young.

After a time she continues without having moved a step from her last remark: "Isn't it more than possible that I used this as an excuse to break with my father for reasons having nothing to do with jealousy of the Bart woman? And yet I have no idea why."

With the fewest possible words, Akira makes the effort to keep her going. "If you don't know *those* reasons, what can you make out of what you do know?"

She doesn't respond to that because she's still trying to integrate her troublesome experience, despite the uncertainty. It's the way she thinks. What she says is, "You've made me see that dwelling on my wound until it becomes an open sore will make me useless. I must get over this thing and move on. I can never know what brought those two together. If it was a fault, it wasn't *my* fault. Loneliness perhaps. Except for you, me, and his books, my father's life has been rather lonely, though I don't think he sees it that way. He'd say that his best friends live on his bookshelf. But as you say, he doesn't have many peers on a starship."

Then she recurs to the idea of the moment and adds, "When that stands alone, it dominates my landscape, but if I can give it a context, it will be less formidable."

To that Akira replies, "It may be more promising to look for Claudio's strengths than for his weaknesses. He is a wise man, but I'm sure you remember the story of Thales falling down the well while studying the stars."

"I don't need to know what his weakness for Bart was, if it even was a weakness. I need to develop some view of why it affected me as it did." She pauses, leans against the armrest of their bench as though considering the point while staring gloomily at the ground.

Both parties to this conversation have talked while looking away into the distance where the child is playing, rather than at each other. But now Paola fixes his gaze with her dark eyes, searching for answers. "If we're trying to encourage recruits to become citizens as well as scientists, then we have to help them put collective interests ahead of individual interests. Either *I* do that now or I'm the wrong person for your assignment. That's why I had to bother you with my problem."

Akira takes the question of her participation as settled and moves beyond the self-analysis. "Shall we talk then about how to proceed?"

She nods. "Tell me first what you have in mind, then I'll tell you what I've been doing."

He chuckles. "I need you to identify likely candidates we can cultivate without making a stir." And he takes some time to list the special skills that would be needed among the first explorers.

"I've made a start with three people whom I've known forever." She adds aside, "Don't worry. A start not a stir! The first is my friend Bahram Sarosh, an engineering student. Bright, serious, mature, and completely possessed by the history of architecture."

"I know who he is. Ava Sarosh's younger brother. I recently visited a physics class he was in. Interested in structural engineering, if I remember. Good start!"

"Then there is Kwan Shi Wa, who is beginning to study medicine. You'd like her. She's quiet, even shy, but watching her eyes is enough to show there's depth there. Her friend is a biology student named Edward Hamilton. He's more the extrovert than she but no less accomplished and mature. His interests are not narrow, but he leans toward zoology and will make a good researcher if he's selected for that path. I've known them both forever. They all started school together, but I was a bit younger."

Akira gives her a long, affectionate glance. "I was right to search you out, wasn't I?" Without leaving space for a reply, he adds, "Why not start with you four and see what develops? When you feel comfortable, you should resume your place as an intimate friend in my family. You might find it convenient to stop by our apartment casually some evening with one or two of these friends. You can introduce them, and we'll have a drink together."

"Would I find my father there? I'm not sure I'm ready for that. That will take time."

"You're right, there is a reasonable chance that it will happen sometime but not by my doing."

"I understand you. We let things find their own direction in their own time."

Akira says no more, but Paola lingers as though there's something else on her mind. To ease her way, he asks, "How difficult do you think it will be to get your people to begin imagining what life in a colony might, even should be like?"

To that she responds with a detectable measure of enthusiasm. "The problem will be restraining them. Whenever I skirted the idea, they rushed in like water into a gulch."

"Why do you think?" He leans forward with his arms on his knees, hands clasped, watching Yori in the distance. "What's their general disposition?"

"There is little on a starship to anticipate in the way of risk or action. This kind of security makes bright people either sluggish or restless. The idea of being engaged in something important is seductive. The risks may be hypothetical, but if they were real and in a worthy cause, my guess is that they would welcome that too. The subject's never been mentioned, but I suspect these three would love to be in your landing party."

"Then all we have to do is lightly nudge the topic in a political direction."

"Yes." And for the first time there's a trace of a smile on her lips. "We scatter words like gumdrops along a forest path and wait. Soon enough these people will learn to think outside their disciplinary boxes and begin dreaming of new ways of living."

Her face reflects the satisfaction of having anticipated him. "You're trying to prepare something like a Council of Elders for the colony, aren't you? You—and my father, I suppose— are hoping that some of the people eventually chosen for the landing party might become permanent settlers."

Instead of endorsing all that, Akira suggests a limit. "We may give little prods in promising directions, but we're not trying to determine the future."

"I understand. You're not trying to 'make' something; you're trying to 'let' something occur. You want to assure that citizens of a new world are capable of finding their own way by making good choices."

With that Paola seems to know that all has been said that needs saying for now. She stands up, shakes Akira's hand, throws one last glance toward little Yori on a swing, and walks away.

ARGUS' EYES

IT IS TIME TO describe how a teenage girl became a hero in a movement so secret that neither of the contending parties knew it existed . . . until the end! My philosopher colleagues never tire of showing that what I'm about to do here distorts my intention. They say that when you try to present a thing by tracing its causes, you distract attention from the thing itself and end up obscuring it. I suppose they mean you can't explain the effects of a firecracker by explaining its origin. Well, they may be right. Perhaps Paola Rucai is one of those rare people who is continuously transformed by events. Still, what can I do but fall back on her story as I came to know it? If I can't explain her, I can at least fill in a little of the context of a life that contributed—tragically contributed, as it turned out—so much to the Galatea mission.

Part of her story you already know: that she was the daughter of the revered Claudio Rucai, that she was a gifted student in the starship academy, that she became a talented researcher in the biological sciences. In a school system where the highest possible achievements are expected and rewarded, her boundless energy and liveliness of mind were a perfect fit.

Then there's her father. It would be hard to overestimate the effects on any child who came to consciousness within the scope of Claudio Rucai's mind and the nuances of his language. Imagine being native to that field of reference! Then add the fact that the two of them, father and daughter, were completely devoted to each other. Until she reached puberty, they spent endless hours talking together. In light of the profound truism that we become what we love, it's hardly too much to say that Paola was on track to become another Claudio.

And yet amid such riches there can be snares, not least in the intensity of the relation. Paola's snare was that she worshiped her father. And why wouldn't she? He loved her more and was more attentive to her than anyone else. He spent innumerable hours with her during those placid childhood years as she passed from discovery to discovery. It was as if she were crossing a dark lagoon, skipping lightly from one bountiful word to another until his world became hers. What better guide as center of her affections, seat of all wisdom, god of her universe? How was she ever to overcome dependency on such a figure?

Now be forewarned. The second snare, Claudio's, is my own speculation. It results from the force of such a bond and what almost certainly would have happened when Paola reached puberty. It could only have been complicated by the shock of her discovering him with Elena Bart. But of that, Claudio knew nothing. We're not speaking here of sexuality in any narrow physiological sense. There was no hint of the incest theme that titillates the bored readers of popular fiction.

No, I start from the ancient recognition that the force that binds all things together is best understood as erotic. A man of Rucai's wisdom, if he hadn't recognized it in advance, would have been quick to discover the need to put a certain distance between himself and such a daughter. Who knows, his way may have been, consciously or not, to transfer some of that erotic energy elsewhere. Is it too much to imagine that it contributed unconsciously to a new intensity in the long friendship with Bart? If so, then at puberty Paola may have become jealous of her, and that might have prepared the context for the trauma that followed. To whatever degree Claudio retreated from her, her resentment grew. I don't insist on the point, mind you, but when Paola confided in Kashimoto and he saw—but declined to say—that the eavesdropper cannot know what he's hearing or the voyeur what he's seeing, he may have been dead on.

What could possibly sever the bond to such a father and let her judgment mature? Nothing less than exposing the clay feet of her god! That, in sum, may prove to have been Elena Bart's contribution to this threesome. Paola's eventual response was to shift her interests as far from Claudio's as possible by rejecting everything associated with him. Having banished him from her life, she as precipitously moved from the human sciences to natural science. But she had yet to learn that opposing a thing doesn't eradicate a thing. Quite the reverse. It raises the intensity and the stakes. She didn't leave behind for one moment her inbred angle of vision. How could she? Witness the way she instantly saw what Akira foresaw in the prospect of a colony divided between Elders and crew. None of us can by conscious decision throw out the world as it is given to us. We may choose blindness over vision in the first instance, but, having seen, it's not so easy to reject sight.

By retreating from everything but her classes and her lab, she hadn't escaped her trauma. She had made an issue of it and brought it closer, until it dominated her idle moments. Nothing mysterious, then, in her following in her father's footsteps even after her love assumed the negative intensity of hate. You've heard the expression, "Tell me what you hate, and I'll tell you who you are"? Well, the young Paola became a starship version of the inside-outsider. In rejecting all, she negatively embraced all, and—if what finally happened hadn't happened—she might have become a philosopher, the very thing closest to Claudio.

Enter Akira with his summons to action. The distinguished man whom she had known and admired all her life might have become a substitute father, except that there was no room in his project for minions. It would have wasted time and been too risky. He needed a partner of mature discretion whose faculties were running at full tilt moment by moment. So he made his proposal and gave her time to consider before responding to his call.

"Call" is the right word, since he called and she answered as clearly as if she had pointed to herself and asked, "Who me?" In accepting, she left the resentful Paola behind, unresolved. She saw at once that to answer the summons to action she would have to surrender a resentment that would limit her usefulness. Hence, that confession in which she dedicated her loves and her hates not to a person but to a worthy action.

The practical consequences that followed may be exemplified in two instances. First, she agreed to identify the best and brightest science students and introduce them into Akira's company. When later she dropped in at the Kashimoto apartment one afternoon to present her friend Bahram Sarosh, she was a bit uneasy since both men were important to her. She mentioned that Sarosh's hobby was the history of Renaissance architecture and remarked ironically to Akira, "Feel free to send him down to the planet. Architects are not very useful on a starship."

Unintimidated by the great man, Sarosh responded playfully, "There's not much to build, but that will change, won't it?" Then to Akira, "I enjoy making sketches of buildings for an imaginary colony. We don't know what the conditions will be but it's exciting to think about."

"I'd like to see those sketches sometime," Akira replied, immediately interested by an idea that had barely crossed his mind. "What do you imagine as the best physical shape for a colony of several hundred settlers in a desert landscape?" And from that moment on, the way was open for discussing colonial life in ever-expanding scope.

Paola repeated the social call with Edward Hamilton, the biology student with whom she was working on an obscure project having to do with balancing the flora and fauna in speculative ecosystems. Then with medical student Kwan Shi Wa. And from four, her circle of influence grew into an amorphous movement without membership or agenda. The effect is understandable if you consider the phenomenon of starship anxiety that had so much occupied us. Whenever she started chatting with one or another person about an actual colony, he or she was mesmerized. Why? Because in the context of "nothing to hope" it was irresistible, this possibility of being part of the first real event in their lives. They couldn't find time enough for discussing such a future.

Meanwhile Paola took care to connect the recruits one by one and then, except for her three closest friends, to retreat. A result of this "Olympian" detachment was that her influence flowed through the movement invisibly. Like the good undercover agent, she never hinted even to Bahram that there might be anything ulterior in all this new sociality. Nor did she mention any relationship beyond family friendship with Akira. In truth, the relation with him was a bit like a clandestine love affair never spoken of—love of a political idea, not romance. They didn't even meet except when necessary or by chance at one of the ad hoc gatherings that she rarely attended. But then, one occasionally hears it said that the profoundest loves feed more on absence than on presence. Thus was she transformed.

Yet anxiety hovered still in some recess of her mind, for any day, rounding any corner, she might meet her father, as eventually she did. And when it happened, it happened like this:

There is a coffee shop on the Food Deck—for what we call coffee, anyway—where the students in her circle sometimes gathered after classes, and it became a kind of center for conversation among those preoccupied with the colony. Though she made a general point of avoiding such encounters, one afternoon she agreed to go there with Bahram. When they arrived, a dozen or so of her recruits were assembled around four tables that had been pushed together. Her entrance made a stir and not only because of the vaguely comic sight of the tall, good-looking Bahram in the company of the short, commonplace girl at his side.

While the seating was being arranged, she failed to see one person sitting just beyond her line of vision, until a few moments later when she turned around to accept a chair. There, not ten feet away, was her father!

More than his presence startled her: He was much older than when they last met. Vigorous still, but all that wonderful hair had gone nearly white, and the lined face had become more deeply creased. For an instant, before Claudio's gaze crossed hers, she hesitated, considered a quick retreat, and chose to stay. Then eye to eye, each weighed doubly on the other with the effect of seeing and being-seen. They remained for a long moment face to face across the length of a table, each like the fish in an Ulro film, caught on the fly fisherman's hook as he feeds just enough line to let the other decide.

In the middle of all this, a handsome stranger arrived whom the others didn't know. Paola remembered him only as a lively young student who used to come to their apartment when she was a child. She didn't recall his name, only that she had liked his thick blondish hair and his energetic spirit. Without looking at any of them, he took a seat at an isolated table beyond the perimeter of the group. Paola saw that her father both knew him and was surprised, even a bit unsettled. So she began keeping tabs on Hans Rückert, who spent the afternoon observing inconspicuously from a distance without speaking.

I must pause to insist on the sum of ignorance in this gathering of intelligent people. You'll remember that aside from whatever Rückert may have guessed, at the time neither I nor anyone else on the Council knew about Kashimoto's plan.

I only got the story of the plot from Claudio much later—after our hopes were dashed and success had turned to ashes.

On this occasion a rambling conversation eventually focused on political authority in the new colony: If—or when—there was no Starship Command, where would authority reside? Paola paid less attention to what was said than to the participants themselves and the current of hope that ebbed and flowed like a tide among them. She said nothing until much later, and then she spoke only once. After every possible way of establishing authority and every possible danger of sustaining it had been proposed by someone and overthrown by someone else, she asked a startlingly simply question: "Can the same person who can make a law be controlled by that law?"

She knew that was not quite what she wanted to ask, as though she had an intuition but couldn't find the right place for it or the right words. Something was fundamentally wrong in starting with a sovereign something or someone. She knew that much. And yet, without a sovereign authority somewhere, chaos would come again. No one wanted that, or automatons. And so she lost her way.

So no one responded to her question. Yet it gave the conversation a new turn. After an awkward silence, the partisans appealed the question of sovereignty to Claudio.

As is usual with him, instead of providing an answer he burrowed so deeply into the roots of the question that no one at the time saw the pertinence of his reply. He was never one to mistake the noise of "communication" for language. Rather than choose one answer over another, he made a cut on the diagonal across all their issues. And when he spoke his manner matched what he said. This time, too, the modest grandfatherly figure with the affectionate face spoke words that were destined to survive in memory long after the speaker had passed and the world had changed.

He began like this: "I will tell you a tale. You have heard of Argus Panoptes, the all-seeing Greek giant with the hundred eyes? It's all to do with the loves of the gods. Hera, Zeus' wife, set Argus to watch Io, one of Zeus' lovers. Then Zeus responded by sending Hermes, messenger of the gods, to put out Argus' eyes with the charms of his speech before killing him with a rock. This is the story of those eyes. It's a myth of subtraction: Hermes luring Argus to sleep, a few eyes at a time."

Claudio is the most engrossing talker I have ever listened to. It's not just what he says. It's his physical presence. Typically he sits with his feet flat on the floor, knees almost together, and speaks what I can only call two languages at once. The voice and the bewitching words, of course, but then there are the gestures! Not the flamboyant waving of arms and hands of his Italian ancestors. Instead his hands move sometimes like an architect describing a structure, sometimes like an Eastern wise man weaving the auditors themselves into the Argus myth.

At first the hands were at rest on the edge of the table, tips of the thumbs and index fingers touching, the other fingers straight. If you know the Buddhist "mudra of discussion," then you have the picture. Written here it may sound affected, but to appreciate the arresting effect you must visualize it in the smiling white-haired man with the face of a hundred creases.

Here's what he said. "It all began, this story of love and wrath, in an age when mortals knew little about the extent of what we would call the Real. What they could see—what reached them—was an almost unintelligible diversity of images like figures in a deep mist. To these images they gave names and formed legends about the play of gods at cross-purposes. That was as much of a tangled reality as they could take in."

He paused to breathe freely for a moment and looked across the room, where he found Paola not so much looking *at* him as looking *through* him, and he seemed to draw inspiration from her gaze as he continued:

"So Hermes began to lull Argus to sleep just as the mortals began to sort disorderly phenomena into orderly concepts. With this new skill they could replace contingency with causal connections—but at a price. Whatever exceeded rational consistency—the beyondness of things—they largely jettisoned as mystical, misleading, and worthless.

"The result?" The hands spread in the gesture of open consultation. "Where mortals had been minor participants in a play without rules, they became spectators of a universe of objects observed through the lens of ideas. Especially the idea of an impersonal, orderly nature. Under this regime of verification, the gods retired to the heavens where, so far as is known, they ate their ambrosia and drank their nectar in eternal, uncreative silence."

Claudio's storytelling was like the wandering rhapsodes of the ancient world singing the songs of Ilium for provincial courts, gathered around evening hearths. I don't know how much of what he was saying was understood at the time—how much of a myth ever is?—but his audience was held in rapt attention. The room was so quiet you'd have thought no one dared breathe.

When he came to Argus' blinding, he raised his left hand to his brow in what the Samurai called the "knife-hand strike," index and middle fingers straight with two fingers and thumb making a fist. Then the strike or the hand descending.

"Hermes' magic wand put Argus to sleep eye by eye and art by art." Claudio marked the stages by knife-hand strokes in the air. "And the mortals, who for security had '*leaned on heaven before*,' became sufficient to themselves. They dubbed 'real' whatever could be reconstructed in a chain of causes. And so down the ages, as wonder dwindled to certainty and the remainder was dropped, the heavens were emptied of all but the scraps of matter in motion."

He stopped to see if anyone in the silent café was still conscious and found every eye on him, most intensely, Paola's, glowing with an intellectual brilliance that let him know that someone—the most important one—had understood.

"Soon enough, with the invention of the telescope, the planet of the mortals became a speck in interstellar space, and they understood themselves as a natural species liberated from the appearances of things by substituting their own subjective maps of reality. This dawning age of humanism had its glories, of course, though as the human became the measure, things were left out that shouldn't have been."

Another silence. "Hera's revenge and Zeus' retaliation were not quite over. Argus still had eyes enough to keep watch as lived certainty turned to rational doubt. Sleep begot sleep and what was called Real morphed into what could be verified by taking measurements. The love affair with reason turned into a crisis of reason, and reality shrunk to appearances as *'reason called for aid on sense.'* Anything that didn't give itself as an object to perception—imagination, for example—was deemed suspect and discarded. So by a rash overestimation of consciousness, mortals took themselves for the owners and masters of nature."

He smiled with welcoming arms open. "It was a great success! One of the greatest in history. But as the success—and the attendant amnesia—grew and nature was replaced with those mental maps, the masters, ever more ambitious for further mastery, began to dwindle into slaves of their own computations. They wished to be 'free.' Free from need, free from labor, free from time and space, free to please themselves." As Claudio's words spread up and down the assembled tables, his eyes rested for an instant on one person after another.

"To that end, the real became the virtual, progress turned the world into a machine, and the machine became so powerful and so complicated that it undermined security and threatened to destroy their planet."

There was a long pause as the planetary disaster sank in. Then the terrible climax:

"Eventually in this long descent from the eyes of the gods to an age of anxiety on the planet of the blind, people began to dream of escaping the prison-house of object-nature and the slow suicide of the human world. Without suspecting that the cause lay in themselves, they built an artificial paradise on a flying island and incarcerated themselves in it. No more earth; no seasons; no weather; no day or night. Nothing to do but read gauges and push buttons in their mechanical womb. At what price?

"Lost, the sense of place and ground. Lost, the memory of drinking from a pure Alpine stream or walking among oceans of lavender in the meadows of Provence or wandering in the forest of the Cedars of God. Enamored of simulation and dissimulation, impotent to create, they lounged like the immortals, depending on technical processes as mysterious as the old gods themselves. Now, anxious and bored, they wait to die. Death—as was once said of Proust—by 'no longer knowing how to light a fire or open a window.'"

Claudio ceased and dropped his head. The silence in the little café was sepulchral. No clock could measure, and no scale could weigh the long moment before he half-raised his head and exchanged a searching gaze with the long-estranged daughter become secret ally. Then, by way of epilogue, in words almost whispered that would be remembered long after he and his world had passed: "We must never forget the origin of this tale of lost wonder. All began with the loves of the gods. Love suppressed till *'universal darkness covered all.'*"

A CITY WITHOUT WALLS

On THE EVENING OF Rückert's "maiden performance" as leader of a Council discussion, he took the moderator's chair, leaned his elbows unselfconsciously on the table, and ran the fingers of one hand boyishly through his blond hair. He may be a talented thinker, but he's also a good-looking lad who often appears more disposed to mischief than deep thinking. I wonder if that's why, in retrospect, the women seemed to have dominated this meeting! But that's another matter.

He began with a grin. "I'm going to disappoint you tonight," he said. "The topic was supposed to be teaching philosophy: what exactly, how much, when—that sort of thing. Well, I'm not going to do that. Something more interesting has turned up. I want to tell you about a conversation I heard a few days ago among a group of students. It was about colonial government after the starship becomes irrelevant. They, these students, take for granted that the ship will disgorge its colonists and eventually move on." He leaned back in his chair, elbows on the armrests, tips of his fingers touching, continuing to grin as though playfully daring us to object.

It was a bold beginning for a young member, but that only piqued our curiosity. "I'm bringing this up for two reasons," he said. "First, because it will become an urgent practical matter for a colony that isn't likely to have the time or the political imagination to deal with it. So it's up to us to try to develop political wisdom in eventual settlers.

"The second reason for scrapping my plan for the evening reflects the history of this Council. It has—we have—talked about political topics off and on for nearly two and a half centuries, but the discussions have been abstract, without practical urgency, and in a sense, parasitic on the status of life on a starship." He added with a confident shrug, "And why not? We were born and have necessarily lived in an authoritarian military structure where governing was rarely the main issue."

The astonishing thing about this preface is that Hans was essentially repeating what Command said about the Council: that we are a bunch of dreamers, always talking, doing nothing! He continued, unfazed by the solemn faces around the table and even by the inexplicably grave expressions of Kashimoto and Rucai. "These students," he continued, "are arming themselves for what would once have been called political action. In their view the time to prepare is now!"

His eyes sparkled with excitement. "I'll come back to this later." This was no casual moment for him. It was daring, and we could hear that in the tension of his voice as he continued:

"In the conversation I want to tell you about, one participant had taken the trouble to inform himself very well, and he formulated the question of governance like this: Given our peculiar history, where will sovereignty likely come to rest in the new colony? It's a question that has always already been decided in this room. But the students whose history is about

151

to be broken in two are urgently asking where colonists *should* place their allegiance and their faith."

He leaned back again in the challenging pose, this time only half-playfully. I hardly need to say that by now we were buckling our seatbelts for a rough ride. This would not be a casual session for passive observers. We'd have to work for it.

"The question of sovereignty translates, in Humpty Dumpty's words to Alice, as 'Who's to be master, that's all.' In any imaginable colony sovereignty might reside in a person or persons, in an institution, in a code, or rest on some supreme worldly or otherworldly principle. But here's the critical point. This young man perceptively described sovereignty in terms of opposites: those who are 'in' versus those who are 'out.' His age-old examples, which exceeded the city, were between people on the 'inside' and people on the 'outside.' If the Greeks were in, the barbarians were out; if the Jews were in, the gentiles were out; according to the religions of the book—the Torah, the Bible, the Koran—the pagans were always out. The same for the Japanese and Chinese in the East. In modern political contexts, too, it's curiously either/ or. In the West, colonialism set 'civilized' white Europeans against 'primitives' and people of color.

"The nation-states also worked by inclusion and exclusion, friends and enemies. In his most dramatic example, the Nazis secured their identity as a superior race by destroying people who were mentally defective, people with congenital weaknesses, gypsies, and especially the Jews. The heinous acts were not his point, mind you. He was interested in the underlying structure of these binary relations: inside-outside, white-black, good-evil, up-down, and on until the universe is bifurcated. His provocative claim was that the principle of political sovereignty, so powerful in the age of humanism, shares this dual structure."

At that point Ang Yimou, often Hans' opponent and not given to lightness, asked almost playfully, "Did the other students understand all that? If they did"—he looked around the table with a grin—"then the schools must not be in such bad condition as is sometimes alleged."

That lightened the tone for a moment as everyone chuckled and Rückert replied, "They didn't understand at first, but they gnawed on it like a pack of hungry dogs. As the haze began to clear, first one then another saw that a static organization based on some ideal like unity or peace would always divide the world. As an antidote, others proposed making strife inherent to the political order, as in the eighteenth-century Constitution of the United States, before it was overwhelmed by other forces."

He stopped for a moment then added with enthusiasm, "But listen to this. One young woman who had not said a word so far suddenly asked, 'If you're right, then what would put an end to the either-or and overcome both sides at once? That might be a different kind of political possibility.'

"I can tell you her question opened a speculative free-for-all."

"And where did it get?" Ang asked skeptically.

"To two different answers. Both intended to disrupt unity (the one) and binarity (the two) at one stroke—by welcoming plurality."

In an editorial sidebar Rückert added, "I would rather call plurality 'the third' because if you can count to three, in principle you already have infinite multiplicity." Then waving all that aside, "But back to my story. Some people immediately equated multiplicity with democracy, which quickly led to self- or class-interest and popular opinion. And so that option vanished."

Occasionally Dennet-Jones can be relied on to ask the right question at the right time. "So what is the point of this interesting report?"

Rückert didn't appreciate the question as much as I did. He stared at it for a full half-minute before collecting himself sufficiently to answer. "I want to put their question to you in a different form if I can. My quandary is about the difference between two people: one who makes a law from outside the law, where of course laws are made, and one who is irrevocably inside and bound by the law."

There he stopped, uncertain whether that formulation advanced the question. The interval was just wide enough to give Yu Wang an opening. I may have told you that Yu is a quiet, middle-aged little man whose virtue is not quickness in mind or speech. His virtue is thoroughness: slow, laborious, mind-numbing thoroughness. He hovers over a subject—in his research as a chemist, as in everything else—taking care to define every term with more precision than it needs and tracing the history of every topic back to Methuselah before letting a discussion get off the ground. I'm sure it's the secret of his scientific achievements, but I'm just saying that it drives me up the wall and over the edge. On this occasion it seemed to have the same effect on others.

In a characteristically external approach to the political question, Yu said, "Why not limit the field . . . uh . . . review available . . . uh . . . forms of government?" Since he was unusually halting this night, I won't subject you to his actual words, but in a characteristically literal-minded way he did what he promised: said that a colony would be loyal to Starship Command at first, then gradually change as conditions changed. Ultimately people would be loyal to whatever worked. Then he waited for Rückert to pick up the suggestion. When that didn't happen, he did it himself, describing how governance eventually would be exercised by one person (like a governor), a competent few (as on the ship), or by everyone (as in popular democracy).

Rückert nodded respectfully. "It's a good point, Wang. Those are age-old forms we have constructed for locating responsibility and the power to make and enforce law. And if our passion is for security, there may be an appropriate time for each of them. We tend to be loyal to whatever machinery can guarantee our safety. It's part of the question of sovereignty that has been important since the Renaissance."

Dennet-Jones interjected, "The high priest is the one who can keep the machines running. Most people don't care how it's organized so long as it works."

Rückert shifted a bit uncomfortably in his chair, conspicuously uneasy with the direction of the topic toward popular opinion. Gwendolyn Burgess, always quick to grasp what's at stake in a question of organization, observed his discomfort and came to the rescue. "Then technology isn't the root of the matter either. Political loyalty is about the instinct for survival. Animal instinct is supreme."

Seeing her point if not her concern for him, he responded politely. "I see that, but if all politics is about biological

survival—as this ship is about the survival of the species—
then it isn't political at all. But I'm still not getting to the
essential question. The topic of sovereignty is somehow leading
in the wrong direction."

In a remark ambiguously situated between assertion and
question, Claudio tried to put the conversation back on
Rückert's track: "You think we're capable of something better?
We could say that if all the Galatea mission has been about
is biopolitics, then we might have saved ourselves the trouble
and died comfortably in our Ulro beds."

Rückert received the remark with a grateful smile, and the
twinkle of mischief returned to his eye. "Let me tell you one
other thing that happened in that student conversation. After
they had prosecuted the notion of sovereignty until it began
to feel like regicide, someone switched directions with a story:
the blinding of Argus. At the time I felt a distant relevance,
but even now I'm not seeing it clearly." Then, addressing the
rest of us, "Let me just remind you of Hermes' putting out
Argus' hundred eyes."

And so he did. Without knowing where it might lead, he
retold it straightforwardly, unselfconsciously, without interpretation. Such stories are always fascinating even if his purpose
in repeating this one was obscure, but that merely caused us
to listen more closely. Only much later, after Claudio had
told me all, could I see what was so striking, even daring,
in this performance. Having already let Claudio, and hence
Akira, know how acutely he had read our political situation,
he had turned up uninvited at the coffeehouse where the
students were meeting more or less clandestinely. From the

gathering itself and the unusual political sophistication of the students—especially from their enthusiasm—he would have surmised enough to make him suspect subterfuge.

Now here he was, repeating Claudio's myth to his face with Kashimoto sitting down the table listening! True, he kept the compromising specifics out, but they couldn't have known where he might be headed. What do you suppose was passing in the minds of those three as he spoke? Knowing what I know now and considering how much was at stake in the underground operation, I can't help wondering if he even knew how audacious he was. Maybe. One thing I did see: From the moment he began the Argos legend, he spent the rest of the evening—rather discourteously, as I thought—avoiding the eyes of two of the most prestigious people in the room. How could they not fear that he might expose them to charges bordering on mutiny and putting their whole scheme at risk? And for what? Not for mischief surely. That would have been a childish prank.

So here's what I think: I think he knew exactly what he was doing and deftly omitted any detail that might compromise them. He was taking a page from their book and giving the Council the very lesson the two of them were giving the students. It's what they would dearly have liked to say to us themselves but couldn't risk. Whatever the truth, there was high drama right under our noses and none of us suspected a thing.

After rehearsing the blinding of Argus, Rückert asked, "Now what's remotely political in that story? The only thing it says about power and maintaining order is Hera's unsuccessful effort to keep Zeus out of Io's bed, and that only ends in collateral damage to Argus' hundred eyes."

"Then why bring it up?" Dennet-Jones inquired sardonically, and I remember feeling grateful to him for the second time in one night. At least I wasn't the only one who was wondering why rehash an obscure tale that was irrelevant to boot.

Hans was visibly annoyed by the dismissive remark but still more annoyed by his own failure to formulate the issue he had come to explore. "There's something wrong with the sovereignty question itself. Is governance about establishing and managing power? Maybe what we need to get in focus is ourselves. Our peculiar ability to imagine *any political order whatever*. That's not a pedestrian fact. It's a miracle! And somehow, the Argos myth is key."

As he paused, Bart seized the moment. "It's wonderful that we're sitting here in the place of all places where myth has no place, listening to the story of Argus. A starship is the place for the alphanumeric bias, where all that matters is the knowledge that comes as facts or numbers. Hans is reminding us that myth works in the dark where facts and concepts fail. That may be why Aristotle says, 'The lover of myth is a lover of wisdom.' Myth may avoid shallow rationalism, yet I still don't see anything political in Argus' eyes."

At that, Hans sat up straight and exclaimed, "That's our point of departure. I'm struggling to see where it leads! Argos as a paradigm of transition between two ages. From an Age of Wonder to an Age of Anxiety. Some such story is essential, because from either point of view we lose sight of the other and whatever their unexpected coincidence may bring to mind."

For the moment, the exchange continued between Bart and him. "Then you mean to read Argus as a transition from the age—and the loves—of the im-mortals to an age—and the insecurities—of mortals. Not being mortal, the gods weren't threatened by contingency."

"That's helpful," he answered with delight. "Apparently, the Olympians loved the way everything kept shifting like a kaleidoscope against the background of an ordered cosmos. They amused themselves eating their ambrosia and responding like Aurélie Lefèvre's young student absorbing music! At home with themselves, playing their games of love and revenge like children in a universal playground. There's strife enough, but the denizens of Olympus dwell in wonder without agenda, forgiving the past, welcoming whatever comes in their peculiarly amoral way. Not like us then, spinning alternative worlds out of consciousness, lying awake nights wondering what, if anything, it all means or where, if anywhere, it's all going. The gods dwell without agenda, in wonder. Until that vision is lost, and the deathless gods disappear."

"Just a minute!" Ang Yimou cried. "Once again we're wandering off into the jungle of fiction looking for truth."

In this discussion the young biologist and the older chemist Yu Wang were apparently destined to defend knowledge against fantasy. "What sense does it make to consult a legend instead of the facts of political history?" He frowned at Bart. "You'll have to forgive my rationalism! I'm just a humble scientist."

Ava Sarosh's interest in anthropology gave her some sympathy with Ang even as she struggled to keep up with the topic. You would never have known from her demeanor, smiling affectionately at Rückert, just how exasperating she found his penchant for romantic tales. "Why," she asked, "does this sound like nostalgia? You and Elena enjoy imagining a world that never was. An impossible age of gods who loved flux—as well they might, being immortal! But I find that mortals tend to have a penchant for stability. There must be a center somewhere, however transitory. Even if we accept your reading the myth as a piece of political imaginary, what does it prove?"

"As usual, Sarosh, you're missing the point," Bart answered. "We've already learned that these narratives serve as the inexistent *but necessary* source of the present. We're not looking for things that materially 'exist.' We look about like archeologists for provocative images, insinuations, echoes, the barest scent of political possibilities that may feed imagination. These are richer than the consistencies of knowledge that give us back images of ourselves."

"You're being very hard on us, Madam." It was Akira's voice, affectionate, even if it did seem to come from Olympus.

Bart threw him a long, serious glance that slowly relaxed into a familial grin. "The cosmologist constructs a story about a universe cooling enough for electrons to combine with protons, making a cosmos possible, but all that paraphernalia is a theoretical production—a fiction—to save the phenomena around us from obscurity. Theoretical stories exist to help understand the human condition. What happens in a supercollider is like an Argos myth from a world that never was. To make sense of the life-world, we all consult things that, for our world to be as it appears, had to happen whether they did or not."

Then, frustrated, Sarosh added, "I suppose this is horribly literal-minded, but I don't live in a world that never was."

The cheerful tone of that remark came over us with the balm of comic relief.

Until Bart replied, "Then you live in this world blindly."

Rückert beamed with admiration not at his more prolix ally but at the recalcitrant Sarosh. Though you would hardly call her middle-aged, there is something in the tone of their relation that reminds you of the affection between the older woman and the talented boy responding to the mother figure. I don't mean to trivialize a perfectly mature relation, but you could feel the affection in the intensity of their interactions just as you felt indistinct crosscurrents among the women in these exchanges.

Hans replied, "I'm not saying the story is *true* in the sense of a thing to be verified, Ava. Nor that we should imitate a purely imaginary pattern of life. Of course we need stability. I'm not trying to prove anything. I'm looking for alternatives that may clarify dark places and open our eyes to what we need to understand. Argus is a figure out of time whose unintended coincidence with our situation may make things thinkable that would be unthinkable without it or something like it. Since it doesn't claim to be empirically 'true,' we can read the tale freely just to see what turns up. It helps me see that constructing a way of life by deliberating on means toward ends, as though we were building a machine—that procedure differs radically from living well as a good in itself."

This time it was Bart who doubted. "Even if we read Argus as a descent from vision to blindness, what light does all that darkness shed on sovereignty? So, there's a top-dog god on Olympus who goes around making love to everybody in sight, but Zeus is not sovereign in any modern sense. And it's Hera's hatred of Io that unintentionally results in Argus' blinding . . . to death! Sovereignty of what, then? Conjugality? Hera's holy family?"

In another liberating moment Dennet-Jones covered his face with his hands. "Oh my God! It would be a relief if we could pass on to the Age of Anxiety."

Rückert smiled. "And so we will." He leaned back in his chair in a manner that reminded me of hitting the refresh button. "The myth as I'm reading it contrasts the synchrony of the immortals and their contingent world with the insecure mortals of a later age. The historical dimension is important, because we're leaping over intervening centuries when developing religions encouraged a new self-consciousness that the ancients would not have recognized. Remember, Hermes puts out the hundred eyes sequentially, historically."

Gwendolyn Burgess usually has little sympathy with what she calls "the mystery-mongering mythologists among us," and in the speech that followed it was unclear whether she was feeling generous toward Rückert or just keeping up the female competition in befriending him. "I'm not sure what profit there may be in comparing humans with Greek gods, but if it's alternative dispositions you're looking for, please explain the relation between wonder and anxiety."

"But before we do that," Hans interrupted, "let's recall two seminal events of the early modern era that illustrate the alleged second age. The first was Galileo's telescope. Centuries earlier, Archimedes of Syracuse had imagined a point beyond the earth which, used as a fulcrum for a lever, could enable one to move the world. But with Galileo's 'spyglass,' anyone could see that the earth was not a special place at the apex of cosmic order or that its inhabitants sat enthroned at the center of reality. Zeus may have dismissed mortals because they didn't last long, but the telescope let us see ourselves as extraneous and homeless mites on a random piece of cosmic rock, living without purpose or security in an illusion of grandeur."

"And the second of your encouraging events?" Burgess asked, frowning.

"Second is the rage for certainty. Once they had become suspicious of the authority of tradition and common experience, the mortals replaced all that with the authority of their own judgment. Under the surveillance of universal doubt and with pride in their own powers, they instrumentalized the world and revamped it as required by fear, desire, and inner conviction. Reality justified by faith replaced wonder with anxiety."

Rückert opened both hands as though laying something on the table. "And here, at last, is the meaning of sovereignty!"

"With the addition of one footnote, please," Claudio joined in playfully. "What better paradigm for wonder reduced to calculation and utility than a starship? The human maker has measured all things by his own capacity to fabricate a world filled with tools for construction projects without end. It's the new ideal: To be human is to make! Never mind that when we alter the world as given, there will always be collateral damage. In a contingent world nothing goes as planned or unpunished." He gestured with one hand to indicate our "handmade environment." "Every detail is calculated, and two and a half centuries later the consequences remain incalculable!"

"By the way," Dennet-Jones added facetiously. "Whatever happened to the political? We seemed to have mislaid it."

Hunenko made an inarticulate noise that sounded like a grumble or growl. "The implication in the air is that the immortals and the mortals offer alternative political paradigms." He scratched his head. "Yet how could I live like the gods, as though I weren't dying? And if I could, what difference would it make to my life as a citizen?"

Bart: "You're missing something, Oleksiy. Argos is a story of gods, but it's told by humans. Since it's our story and we can understand it in a variety of ways, the immortals in it must delineate possibilities that we can receive, however tentatively. It's true that where the gods appear and disappear, we are born and die. But not always! The heroes and saints have often lived more like the gods than like the rest of us, and the philosophers have often exhorted us to *live like* the immortals. So both ages configure human possibilities. If that's so, then all along we have been discussing alternative modes of being, even political being."

For some minutes Rojas had been looking off into space, puzzled by Hans' rejection of sovereignty. Sensing that the discussion was coming to an end, he asked almost passionately, "May we go back and briefly revisit two important points in the comparison between the age of the gods and the age of men? On this account the gods and men obviously differ on the axis of mortal-immortal or life-death, and that difference is a version of contrasting dispositions toward time. Odd, isn't it, that the gods should be named by their lack of capacity to die! Contemplate their almost nil disposition toward what lies ahead, and you sense the distance from our anxiety *toward* a blind future in which we will surely die. And yet, like the gods, we are here until we aren't. We, too, might live the day without nostalgia or guilt for the past and without anxiety over uncertain futures. The idea is that if we can imagine, we can cultivate living 'like the gods.' Isn't that how the heroes of old became *im-mortal*? We don't have to wallow in our finitude. I'd say the myth presents the possibility of living the pause between past and future rather than lamenting our brevity. Zeus was wrong in finding us insignificant because we don't endure, but we may be right in finding him limited because he does. His time unlimited loses its value, and he fritters it away in fickle love affairs."

"There you are," Bart replied. "And that's why the idea of sovereignty in the colony was the wrong direction: Building a world, whatever the model, is a subjective projection of useful ends and means of constructing them. But the political issue is the life worth living as an end in itself. All other goods are ancillary. That's where the political question begins!"

For Oleksiy Hunenko these summary speeches opened new political insight. He turned to Rückert and asked, "Then what kind of citizen would the gods make? The Greeks may have invented politics, but apparently their gods didn't admire them for it. What kind of city would you have where the people in it lived like gods?"

Rückert, passionate now: "They wouldn't fritter! They would neither resent time and change nor be completely at home in presence. They might be comfortably *included* in a city but with capacities too wide-ranging to *belong* to any city. Beings in surplus, exceeding all measures. Subjects without fixed outlines."

Oleksiy: "Then the students formed their question poorly?"

Hans: "I don't see what you mean."

"If we're on the right track, then citizens cannot be constrained by organizations and rules. They simply deliberate and act together on what's to be done here and now. Unbound by any sovereign power. The force of law would be pedagogic: 'This is how we do it.' Law would be as flexible as situations allowed, and fostering common-sense understanding would replace enforcement by violence."

Rückert took that in slowly. "Then the proper place for citizens who are inherently exceptions to all rules would be a city without walls. Or put it this way: Where law names the outer limit of acceptable action, then it is the power to discipline and punish; but if 'limit' marks the boundary at the beginning of action rather than its end, then to acts follows authority rather than the power of restraint. The City without walls is not an establishment organized by rules and constraints. It's an open place where people dwell together and where all available modes of action are considered and settled."

Oleksiy: "Then the last thing I want to know is what's left, in a city without walls, for the ruler—who wouldn't exactly be a 'ruler'—to rule?"

And Rückert's last reply was, "There you're ahead of me, Oleksiy. I seem to have made rules and rulers obsolete. And yet I'd say that the ruler, who is also one among the citizens we're describing, is critic-in-chief of the *status quo*. First the ruler holds himself courageously open to infinite possibilities, then he stands ready to inaugurate whatever the time requires. Meanwhile, he faithfully executes the provisional order. Bart would probably call it 'fidelity to the word of the last god!'—as he waits for the coming of the next."

He stopped, and for a considerable time there was silence in the room. As a common mood slowly took shape, tentative glances passed back and forth. Then the whole room broke into applause! That had never happened before, and I can't tell you what it meant. Not total approval of what had been said. I'm sure of that much. And, except in Dennet-Jones' case, not relief that it was over at last. But whatever it meant, there was electricity in the air. Instead of hanging casually around for a few minutes then wandering away as usually happened, little groups milled about the room for the better part of an hour, continuing the feverish talk before anyone thought of going home.

THE LANDING PARTY

TWO HUNDRED FORTY YEARS and eight generations
going nowhere with nothing to hope. Another six to return to
Planet 2314 in expectation of a new world. Is it any wonder
that the public spirit of the Galateans should leap from dullness
to exuberance? By the time the sun of the target solar system
has rendered its planets visible to the naked eye, people begin
to gather in the Observation Gallery. There's little to see, and
what there is has been seen before: an anonymous piece of
space rock, surveyed, rejected, passed up, and forgotten. But
now? Well, we too *are such stuff as dreams are made on.*

The public decks are also filling with people moving rest-
lessly about, chattering to one another like birds approaching
their nest. There's nothing to know save a few statistics about
distances and speed, which are nothing to the purpose. And yet
the walls of the Galatea can scarcely contain the enthusiasm.

In the middle of all this ado Akira Kashimoto is
summoned to the bridge. The request is not surprising since
he is sometimes consulted on technical issues. When he arrives,
however, Commander Rawls is not there. She has delegated the
assignment, whatever it is, to First Mate Talib Nasser. Akira
doesn't know Nasser. Oh, he knows who he is. Everyone knows
the name and face of everyone else. In a mass society that may
pass as knowing another, but hardly in a space village. What

Akira sees directly is an appetitive, passionate nature stamped into the flesh of the man before him.

Once they have taken their seats in the conference room behind the bridge, Nasser reports precisely and needlessly to an astrophysicist the exact position of the ship in relation to their destination and how many days until they settle into orbit around Planet 2341. Anyone with a taste for human folly would be amused by his tone, equally mixed of bureaucratic self-importance and sycophancy. Yet there is news here, even as he continues speaking like a person using an unfamiliar language, putting the emphases in all the wrong places.

"Today I am instructed to ask you to prepare recommendations for personnel for a landing party. There will be a flyby or two as landing craft are dispatched to confirm our prior readings and photograph the landing site targeted earlier. That should give you more than enough time. There will be a maximum of twenty people—all young and healthy—covering all the skills agreed to earlier. Those selected must then be given a crash course in survival based on updated readings of surface conditions."

Akira receives this terse speech with the formal dignity and diplomatic smile he wears on all occasions, but its content gives him much to think about. Months before, he had headed a task force of technicians whose assignment was to determine what skills and specializations would be necessary for exploring the equatorial region of the planet. The exact size of the party had not been specified until this abrupt demand for a list of twenty. It raises questions enough about where exactly he stands. Is the selection left to him alone because selection of personnel is an administrative detail? Or has he lived with suspicion so long that he hasn't noticed how well his strategy has worked? The Elders have acted openly during the return journey, complying promptly—and exceeding—whatever instructions Command has given. Is this a test of loyalty then? Or is it a trap? And if so, what kind of trap? Subversion is always a double game, and Claudio has never failed to admonish him to "assume nothing; expect everything."

Now, denied the chance to take a reading of Commander Rawls, he must continue to assume that he has been led on a fool's chase and is about to pay the price. Faced with an event as significant as a planetary landing, the best case would be that the practical people have dropped their suspicions on the assumption that the Council lost the initiative at the beginning. What, after all, can a band of old fogies do once a landing party leaves the ship under strict military authority? Meanwhile, what can he, Akira, do but what he's told?

First, consult Claudio.

Everyone, including the Elders, is now to be seen consorting in the public spaces or crowding into the Observation Decks, so Akira arranges with Paola to use the botany labs for meeting her father and sends him a message mentioning the time and place. Claudio hasn't been so deep in the ship for a very long time, and he enters half expecting to find his daughter there. Looking around in the dim light of the abandoned lab—for the plants it's night—he detects Akira sitting on a lab stool in a dark corner. He pulls up another and they sit, knee to knee in the tight space, as Akira recounts the meeting with Nasser and his instructions. Then he enumerates once more the skills they have spoken of many times: a medical officer, a communications specialist, geologist, botanist, water engineer, building engineer with architectural skills, people to set up and maintain a camp, and so on. Then he presents his list of choices which, having been a preoccupation for years, has taken no time at all to assemble.

"But I do have a couple of surprises for you."

Surprises from Akira are routine. Claudio just opens his eyes and grins. "Knowing you has been an uninterrupted stream of surprises."

"I'm going to suggest Paola for the landing party."

Claudio stares but not, as might be supposed, out of paternal pride or fear for her safety.

Akira continues matter-of-factly. "There is no young botanist better qualified by training and experience than she. More to the point, she has the comprehension of what it takes and what it would mean to turn that rock into a green and pleasant land."

Claudio doesn't take the suggestion seriously. He replies almost casually, as to a whim, "There you are quite wrong. You can forget about my daughter. I know how generous you've been in including her among your acolytes, and I hope she's been useful. But you don't want her. She's like Ang Yimou. She belongs to the enemy party without knowing it." A deep sigh expresses the sorrow of a disappointed father.

This time Akira smiles with a warmth of affection that has no place in his public persona. "What you don't know, my old friend—what you have never known—is that your daughter has been the key figure in our conspiracy since the first day you and I spoke of it. I've never said anything to you because of your private difficulties. It wasn't my place to intrude on all that, though I have long wished for your reconciliation."

Claudio offers no response, but his face shows that the conflict with Paola has brought great sadness to his later years. It's enough to make Akira wonder why the one extraordinary meeting with the students had not brought the two closer. He hadn't been present, but he could see it all: Father and daughter, the most important people in the world to each other, almost face-to-face across a table, communicating globally without a word. What would have kept them apart after such an exchange?

Without further comment on the subject, he continues, "Another thing."

Impatiently, "What thing?"

"*I* need to be in that party."

Again Claudio is speechless. After a few moments the white head shakes gravely. "No, my friend. First, you will never be selected. None of our kind will. Command may have ignored the Council and looked the other way all the while, but they know we're not like them and can't be trusted. They and we were born on this ship but have lived our lives in different universes. Without understanding how or why, they know—at least Alison Rawls knows—that from this point on we're enemies. If they really are giving you the latitude to choose the landing party, it's because they think we were outmaneuvered long ago."

When Akira doesn't respond, Claudio goes on opposing the impossible. "Your credentials are ideal, of course. But the explorers will face unknown hardships. They must be young and strong. Besides, consider the life here. Whatever the difficulties of living on a starship, when we few stand together looking out at the cosmic void, we see the moment after creation. We feel kinship with it all and gratitude for being here. Not to mention Atsuko and little Yori and your friends whom I know you love"—his face wrinkles into a mischievous grin—"even if you don't make a show of it. You know what the chances are that the explorers will even survive. They're young. They will imagine that their friends and family will soon follow them. That hope will sustain them. But you would have no sustaining illusions. No, my friend. You can't go. Fortunately, you won't have the choice."

Bypassing this truth too, Akira continues unimpeded, "There are only two or maybe three advanced physics students who together can do what I could in that group. Of course I know you're right. I would never be chosen . . . willingly. So at the last moment and under some urgency I *must* get myself substituted for one of the others."

Claudio sighs heavily. "But the person you choose would have to sacrifice his position willingly. How likely is that after you have seduced them with fantasies of a new life? You can't forget that this is the most important thing that will ever have happened in these kids' lives, and they know that!"

Akira goes on musing nonetheless. "It would require some kind of emergency. A sudden illness or an accident. Otherwise it would mean an immense sacrifice for a greater good. I wonder if that is more or less likely in the young than the old."

"The young have often shown themselves more heroic than people of our ages."

The two men chew on that remark before Akira concludes, "Well, there it is anyway. There's nothing else to be said today."

Neither moves, and Claudio looks around the unfamiliar environment of the lab. "Where does Paola work?"

"Right there." He points to the stool Claudio is sitting on. "That's where she spends her days."

Claudio looks around carefully at the tools, the plant specimen on the table, even picks up a pair of work gloves and examines them longer than gloves require. Then he gets up and leaves Akira in place, so they won't be seen together.

The following day Akira returns to the labs in the bottom of the ship, looking for Paola. He wants to vet the list with her before taking it to the bridge. When he arrives she is reviewing the work of several years on the ecosystem of P2314. It's the first time they've met in her work space since the day several years ago when he proposed she join the Résistance, and he now takes the time to inquire how she imagines planting might proceed in a desert landscape without surface water. Eventually they move into the little cubicle that serves as an office, and he recounts the recent meeting with Claudio and his opposition—without his reasons—to her being included among the first explorers.

When, on the matter of her father she makes no comment, he goes on to review the names on the list they have long been discussing. Name by name and skill by skill, all goes as expected until they come to the two cases where Akira has proposed a first and second choice. He watches with amusement for her response.

"I see that in these two cases"—she points to the two positions—"you're baiting them. But why? We both know that the second in each case is better qualified."

"You're right. It is bait." He answers solemnly. "I can't bring myself to believe that Commander Rawls is leaving the selection in my hands. I need to see what they do. They might turn down our whole list and substitute one of their own. In that case we will have lost most of our work and they will have opened the war. At the other extreme they may adopt our recommendations without a second thought, judging us powerless to obstruct their plans. The two names are invitations for them to remind me that they are not asleep and have the power to do as they like."

Paola, having long been his agent and much more, understands his caution. Still, she holds the paper in her hand and runs her eyes up and down the sheet as though in a quandary.

"What's wrong?" he asks after some moments of watching.

"Now that I see the whole list, something seems to be missing." She studies the problem a bit longer while Akira watches in silence. "When I see these names together, it looks very different somehow. It's thin. These are all young people, highly competent, and in varying degrees inclined to view the prospect of a colony in a political light. But there is no center of gravity. These people will be at odds with Command within weeks, and there's no one here who could temper their passion or mediate disagreements."

Akira takes the paper and appears to study the problem from her perspective. "So what are we to do?" he asks.

"Your name should be on this list. There's no alternative!"

"And you think Alison Rawls will approve that?"

"Of course not. And yet you have the respect of all these people and long success in working with Command. If conflict arises—or rather *when* it arises, because if we do our work well, conflict is inevitable—we will be seen as insubordinate or worse. Who could deal with such a situation as well as the one seasoned person trusted by both sides?"

"But that isn't the issue, is it?"

"I know. Putting you on the list would ruin everything. So it will have to be subversion as usual. We have gotten rather good at it!" She smiles with youthful satisfaction and continues to stare at a problem without a solution.

Neither speaks until her eyes brighten and she bursts out, "I have an idea! You may have guessed that Bahram and I have become a couple. I think our conspiracy—yours, my father's, and mine, if I may say so—our plot has been the glue that bound Bahram and me in a common purpose. Since we've been together our fondest hope has become to go on this mission together and remain in the colony. And I don't mean the technocratic colony Command may not even know it intends to establish!"

What strikes Akira in this speech is the quiet dignity Paola has gained during their years of their work together. More than dignity, she is centered like the world tree at the navel of Middle earth. In place of the gloomy self-absorption of the Bart-Rucai confessions, she has become all poise and maturity, even in love.

He responds, "I'm happy for you and Bahram. I hope the world of your dreams may come into being." He pauses. "But I don't see where that gets us. This list has to go upstairs almost immediately."

"Give them the list as it is," she answers offhandedly, then adds one of her wry, assessing, Paola looks. "Meanwhile, what if I persuade Bahram to back out at the last minute and you arrange to be the only person who can take his place? Ostensibly it would be an emergency expedient—until he had recovered from . . . oh, I don't know . . . some illness, say. Later you could exchange places, though if we succeed, you might find it hard to give up your role. Once authority has gravitated to you, replacing you won't be easy. But you could have him added as others inevitably will be." She watches his face, hardly expecting the prudent man of science to accept such a crazy idea.

Akira remains opaque, as though neither dismissing the idea nor accepting it, while trying to decide some different question.

She adds, "I see how unlikely this sounds, but think about it."

He decides. "You may be surprised to hear that I have just discussed such a possibility with Claudio, who, of course, opposed it as madness. It's a long shot, but your idea of a last-minute substitution might work. A fictitious illness wouldn't get past our medics, but something of the sort might. Bahram couldn't just back out. That would be unbelievable and permanent. But something very simple might be believed. Even so, I don't see how *I* would ever be accepted." He grins at her. "Even *I* would not believe I had not engineered it." He pauses seriously over the idea. "There would have to be some scientific urgency that made it obvious to everyone that it was the only solution and a temporary one."

A long hiatus follows in which both ponder how a mad idea might become a sensible plan. Meanwhile she shows him some of the plants she has been nurturing in environments that simulate the planet. Then, returning to the topic of the moment, they talk through it once more, looking for a solution. Finding none, the matter is suspended but not forgotten. And he leaves.

His next task is largely pro forma. He has a private interview with each of the people on the list of personnel, first to inform them, discuss the risks, and take a final measure of their commitment. The second reason is undefinable. In a sense it's putting his ear to the ground, taking seismic readings from a distance. Listening for nothing particular but trying to divine what concrete difference his own presence or absence might make in each case, testing how it might be received if it came at the last minute and came as a shock.

This done, he reports to Command. Both Rawls and Nasser receive him on the bridge, and the reception is a bit on the cool side but amiable enough. As they pass through to the conference room, he watches for what art historians call the Morelli effects, the unconscious revelations of an artist's hand in inconspicuous details like fingernails or ear lobes. He takes a seat on one side of the table as they sit opposite, shoulder to shoulder, like judge and jury ready to deliver a verdict.

"So what do you have for us?" Commander Rawls asks in a calculated, neutral tone.

Akira passes a single sheet of paper across the table. "Here's a list of the people who will in my judgment make the best landing party. In addition to the distribution of skills and the competence of each person, I have tried to assemble those who will work together harmoniously and faithfully execute their instructions."

He is alive to every movement and every blink of the eyes on the other side of the table as Rawls slowly, silently, studies the names, not sharing it with Nasser as she easily might. Her perfectly even and noncommittal demeanor leaves Nasser adrift. He can't ask Akira questions or make small talk lest some unwarranted opinion escape him before receiving instructions on what opinions he's to have. He can't even find a place in the room to put his eyes. So he stares at the table in front of him, varying his gaze by simply opening and shutting those dangerous little organs. When Rawls has finished examining the list, she passes the paper to him and says nothing until he has finished deciding what he's expected to say.

"Now," she says, "talk us through it person by person." The comfortable formality of Akira's voice dissolves the air of reserve as he comments on each candidate. When he comes to Paola's name, Rawls says, "Isn't she the daughter or something of old Claudio Rucai on your Council?"

"Yes," he answers, noting that her attention gravitates toward any connection between a name and the Council. "You may know that they have been estranged for some years."

Rawls allows herself one raised eyebrow in response and passes on. "And this Sarosh boy, he's related to Ava Sarosh how?"

"Her brother, but almost a generation younger. He's trained in structural engineering. He also brings an extraordinary knowledge of the history of architecture. That may prove useful as your project develops."

The review, start to finish, is thorough and balanced. No one on the list is rejected. At the bottom where he has proposed alternatives, Rawls selects his second choice without any sign of interest in the individuals or their competence, and Akira treats the whole matter as perfectly routine. Judging by appearances he might have been given this task only because he was the shortest line between two administrative points, and the substitutions were nothing more than a reminder of where the power is and will remain.

Personnel questions settled, Commander Rawls picks up the paper lying in front of Nasser and scans it once more. She pushes her chair back from the table and asks in the most business-like tone, "Now which of these people will make the best leader of the mission?"

Akira hears Claudio's voice echoing in his ears: "When you don't know what to do next, wait for the impossible to turn up."

He answers, "I have given a little thought to that but not enough to make a positive recommendation. Off the cuff I'd mention Bahram Sarosh. He has all the personal qualities: quick, articulate, reliable, well-liked, a good leader. The points we've already discussed about him would seem to support the idea. One reason for recommending him in the first place was that his knowledge of building structure and design can give you a head start on eventual construction projects. Since there will be nothing to build on this mission, he would have more time to oversee technical development than any of the others."

At that, Nasser glances spontaneously at Rawls. For some reason she, who never acts without sufficient reason, meets his glance and erases his worst fears. To Akira's evaluation of Sarosh, she replies simply, "Good. You can train him for the additional duty. You may think we are asking a lot from you, keeping you from your research and all, but you are better prepared than anyone else on board to digest all the data and help the project leader understand what he will be up against. So think it over, and if your view doesn't change, talk it over with Sarosh. Talib will provide all the data you need to bring him up to speed. Confirm your choice as soon as possible, and let's push this project ahead. If the surveillance craft find no surprises, we should be able to confirm our readings of surface conditions, pinpoint the landing spot, and get this job done."

Despite Akira's perfectly composed exterior, the rhythm of his heart has been responding to every word and every gesture in this meeting, racing to keep up with every trace of disposition and hint of motive that might have implications for his protégés. He and Command have been circling one another for years, wary or aloof. Now they stand, face to face, together or apart, poised on the threshold of an event that will, for birth or for death, make a fissure in history and rewrite the human story.

ANIMAL-HUMAN-CYBORG

"ANIMAL-HUMAN-CYBORG. Interesting title, but whatever does it mean?" The question came from Aurélie Lefèvre, who usually "keeps the silence" before the music—or the words.

Oleksiy Hunenko replied in an unusually playful spirit. "We have been sitting here forever talking about hundreds of problems, rarely noticing that every one of them is based on an unasked question. That question is: What, who, or how are we? How do we understand ourselves? It's a mystery, and we'll accept a ten-cent fact anytime to avoid a million-dollar mystery. Why would I actively avoid inquiring into my most effective ways of being? Even refuse to hear a question on the subject?"

When he didn't go on, Nacho Rojas, the analyst-psychiatrist, casually volunteered, "I'll hazard a guess, Oleksiy. Except when it's sloth, maybe we're more intelligent than we think we are. So intelligent that we know instinctively to avoid questions that might destabilize us. We know it with a kind of animal sense that doesn't reach consciousness. Not that we *can't* know ourselves. We don't *want* to know. The garden-variety passion for ignorance."

I was arrested by the shift that Rojas' short speech made in the mood of the room. Hunenko's witty, even playful topic had suddenly turned dark and a bit ominous.

Earlier Lefèvre had opened the question of our willful ignorance of our affective capacities, but this time she fired back, "Why should that be, Nacho?"

To which he responded, "Maybe not knowing is my way of not losing my grip. If I admitted just how precariously my being is, fragmented and scattered in time, I might lose myself entirely. Maybe I need the illusion of solidity because somewhere in the back of my mind I suspect I'm less a finished urn than a blob of shapeless clay responsible for its own shaping."

Apparently Hunenko preferred to approach his subject from less risky directions. "Good, Rojas. And so tonight's topic, Animal-Human-Cyborg."

I, for one, saw no connection between this and the political topic, opened by Rückert with a promise to continue.

"Earlier, Hans described human being as an operation rather than a thing. 'A verb,' he said, 'rather than a noun.' That makes a big difference. If he's right, then when we treat ourselves as objects present to reflection, we're likely to overlook our most intimate capacities for making good use of ourselves."

"Right, Oleksiy!" Elena Bart added with her usual enthusiasm. "That's our history in a nutshell. It's why the two cultures on the ship only *seem* to be in static opposition to each other. All along, the Council has been conjugating verbs while Command sorted its nouns. And, both standing our ground, we've been moving away from each other at warp speed without anyone noticing."

But before Hunenko starts building bridges from Rückert's phrase "living in the open" to his own "animals and cyborgs," I, Kahn, have a bit of what people call "human interest" to relate—the good, the true, and the beautiful being non-human! It is the special relationship between Hunenko and Rückert. Beyond teacher and student, the relation of the older mentor and the younger disciple is reminiscent of the ancient Greeks. These days they even live in side-by-side apartments and spend most of their time together. I'm not implying that they are lovers in an erotic sense. Nobody cares enough even to gossip about that. But what does affect us is the rigor of two keen minds engaged in perpetual dialogue. It's not unusual to find them, between Council meetings, one week to the next, having developed a topic so far beyond where the rest of us left off that it takes a while to catch up. Nothing strange, then, in Hunenko's undertaking to extend Rückert's line of thought.

Oleksiy resumed—or tried to: "I'm not going to classify or describe the human among all the other beetles in our box, because I'm looking at another angle on the political being beyond the animal. I want to clarify it differently, by reference to the boundary cases—if they are—of animals and machines. I think this approach may interest you. So take the animals first."

Claudio Rucai chortled, "Good. I've been waiting for years for someone to talk about animals." The topic somehow touches the mischievous side of his disposition. "I've always wondered why, in a place where no one for nine generations has seen a living animal, we love to watch them in films, read about them in stories, and study them with concentration. Why are they so important to us?"

Then as Hunenko was about to introduce his topic, Claudio smiled cordially and continued. "Have you noticed that when the gaze of an orangutan in a documentary seems to cross your gaze—not to mention the gaze of the actors in films when nobody's there—you feel you're being seen? Watch a family of monkeys acting like precocious children or an ape using the opposable thumb to turn a stick into a tool, and you feel kinship. Like the child recognizing itself in a mirror. The naturalists are ready to tell us how little we differ organically from the primates, but whatever the similarities we may have in the desire for food, water, sex, or shelter, there's a mysterious surplus. Or a vast difference of category. Is it that we are the animals who recognize that we aren't?" The idea seemed to fill him with delight, and he laughed merrily.

Hunenko frowned a little, then abandoned his own direction and accepted Claudio's. "We may be animals driven by our instincts, but you're right, there's always a remainder that doesn't yield to computation. For example, we can also answer yes or no to any situation whatever. That's not an addition. It's a discontinuity, a moat, between us and the beasts. One is *a being* while the other is—or is also—a *way* of being. The difference is between the *what* and the *how*. This unaccountable juxtaposition of biological life and consciousness often leads to the notion of the human *against* its animality, spirit *against* flesh. Perhaps it would be better to say we mark a place *between* these dimensions. The 'spacing' between. The 'place' where nature and culture are knotted together. Or maybe we *are* the knot!"

"Or *not even* the knot!" Rückert chuckled.

Dennet-Jones, who would not have even tried to understand Oleksiy, much less Rückert's remark, sighed deeply and stumbled into a pun, surely unintended, "Could we get back to the animals please?"

Meanwhile Ang Yimou vigorously protested Hunenko's point. "You're starting with an unwarranted conviction that the human is not a natural species. That's a philosophical prejudice against the axioms of science! Whereas philosophy— what positive knowledge has that field ever given us?—is all metaphysical mystery-mongering. How can we know without knowing or think outside the rational paradigms of science?"

The point may have been peripheral, but serious enough to cause Hunenko to accept the digression. "Not quite, Ang. I start with the everyday observation that humans are not *only* a natural species. Not to see that we are more than natural would be amnesic. The devil in our term 'positive knowledge' is that it idolizes verification and casts suspicion on the remainder. Verification is essential, but it's not the whole business of knowing, nor is knowing the whole business of living. As for the paradigms of science, they have a limited life expectancy, and when they outlive their explanatory power, they're forgotten or become dogmas."

"You're blaming science because it's incomplete," Yu replied. "Think of how the Human Genome Project and the sciences of the brain have narrowed what you hastily call discontinuity between organism and consciousness."

Rather than quarrel, Oleksiy hedged, probably to save his topic for the evening. "It's a salient point, but let me ask this: If you and I had just met and wished to get better acquainted, which would be the more effective way: to exchange our organic and medical histories, including complete genetic codes and maps of our brains? Or to share our experiences: the stories of our relations with others, our anchoring in a world, our habits, loves, aversions, hopes, fears, our whole incompletable biographies? One of these gives us an organism, the other gives us a human being. An object versus a performance, so to speak."

Ang shrugged. "Your argument from the incompleteness of science just isn't valid."

Claudio intervened to check an all-too-human contentiousness and return to the tranquility of the animals. "Meanwhile, back in the zoo, what's the difference between the animal's *behaving* as a captive of stimuli and our *responding* to stimuli?"

Hunenko welcomed the question as a substantial advance on the topic he had been trying, unsuccessfully, to discuss. "Thank you, Claudio. We know what it's like to be hungry and to look for food as the beasts do. But *we* can also decide to eat or not to eat, to give the food away, to fast, to diet, any one of these for a thousand different reasons. The animal lives as a captive of stimuli, but we don't. Or we don't *have to*. We have a say. And let me add one small point that is forgotten by an I-can-do-anything culture that can even go to the stars in a biscuit tin! We can say 'no' to what we can do, but we can also say 'yes' to what we can *not* do. Under the illusion that we can do everything, we risk losing our capacity to act at all. Where everything is possible, nothing is."

That last remark caused Rückert to laugh aloud. "Your small point is small the way a radioactive isotope is small!"

"Perhaps," Hunenko said, grinning. "But I wonder whether, in neglecting who we are and letting our gifts atrophy, we can slip back into animality."

Rückert suggested, "Wouldn't 'slipping back' be to retrace a path?" You could tell from the tone of his voice that he was on Hunenko's wavelength but wanted to avoid another endless debate with Ang.

"If we got here by interruptive evolutionary mutations rather than by *pro*-gression, then *re*-gression explains nothing. One mystery to explain another. When Claudio Rucai recognizes his own image in the animal, he doesn't see a barrier to be crossed or something to be overcome. He sees discontinuity, a non-coinciding. Himself as kin to the beasts *and* radically different. We need the animal to show us what the animal will never see: itself first, then ourselves as exceptions."

Sarosh, for one, was making a genuine effort to understand, and what she wanted to know was this: "If there's no regression to the animal or even further to the inanimate, what happens when we let our powers deteriorate? Is it a bit like what was once called 'post-history'? When work becomes unnecessary and the struggles over class and inequality are over, when there's no more expansion, when there's nothing left to desire and energy wanes, then where will we be?"

"On a starship!" Kern answered mischievously. "Wall-to-wall comfort. Nothing needed but maintenance. It's like . . . "

" . . . a retirement village on Ulro!" Burgess completed his analogy sarcastically.

"Boredom," added Rojas somberly. "Escapism!"

188

Rückert's satirical response sounded more optimistic. "Then, according to Bart, there's hope. Animals and androids don't get bored . . . "

Bart: " . . . and have no use for myth!"

"Maybe we should give up. Settle for the last man and the end of history."

" . . . or become theologians."

"What's the difference?"

"That makes boredom sound like paradise."

I don't know who said what in that flight of fancy, but it encouraged Hunenko to pull the discussion back together. "Post-history never was about a time when things stopped happening. It was a speculative time when the myth"— looking significantly at Ang—"or the *axiom* of historical progress had run its course. But the interesting question still is, can we 'slip back'—not quite devolution, Rückert!—toward animals in a comfortable zoo? Can the soul die and leave the organism behind? Is one still human who is affected only by his nerve ends like a fish in a pond, or does some new being emerge after the last man?"

Kern objected (not very coherently, thought). "The difference may be between the fish immersed in water but not knowing it, and an amphibian who, seeing and feeling water, knows it to *be* water. If I can't see that I differ from the animals, maybe I don't."

"There's your answer, Hunenko," Burgess cried. "After the last fish comes Kern, the super-frog."

At that point Dennet-Jones did his thing: He indulged a private satiric moment by implying that nothing of importance had yet been said and that it was high time we got back to the topic. "I must have missed something. Why do I need to understand the animals to understand myself?"

"Because, Clive," Kern snapped impatiently, "we don't know what a thing is until we know what it *isn't*, its boundaries, what it excludes. The animal is a mirror in which we can see ourselves as *not there*. Otherwise I might be the very thing I'm *not*, or no thing at all, as Rückert seems to think!"

Through all this, the good-natured but often skeptical chemist Yu Wang had said nothing. That wasn't unusual, but I noticed he was all ears and eyes this time. Quite suddenly he raised a strong protest with a vigor that almost cured his halting speech.

"Stop!" he cried. Then snickered, bemused. "We've lost our way in this talk of a surplus in the organism. Ang was on the right track. You say when science anticipates a total organic explanation of the human, it projects a fiction. In a sense that's true, but the same is true of you. You're supplying a speculative chasm between body and mind, nature and culture. At least we've known for centuries that Homo sapiens shares origins with the other species in the phylum. Whatever else gets added along the way"—he looked at Hunenko sharply—"the *base* is biology. You can't deny the continuity. We have the traits of the animals, and we know the history and mechanisms of natural selection."

"Right!" said Rojas unexpectedly. "*And* we have known for centuries, the collective experience belonging to persons but not to animals. Hunenko's point is that neither positive knowledge nor the heritage of wisdom can do without the other. And first we must appreciate the difference."

Wang waved his hand a bit impatiently, dismissing something Rückert wanted to add. "Yes, yes, here comes the argument from language, so I'll quickly add that the animals also have primitive communication systems. Then you'll say they don't use metaphor for saying what's between two words as we do. And I'll say, give them time, and full language skills will follow. After all, that's how *we* got them."

"Is it? Did we?" Another of Rückert's ironic responses that came like a bullet as he leaned back in his chair, arms akimbo, and sniggered.

Kashimoto, the physicist, had been another silent presence at the table until this contentious point arose between the "humanists" and the scientists. He stepped in, for truth perhaps, but also to protect the conspiracy we didn't know he was fostering on the ship even as we disputed this arcane point. He addressed Yu in his calmest diplomatic mode.

"I understand what you're saying, Wang. DNA is basic, though it's less clear what it's basic to."

He delayed just long enough to break the momentum and disrupt the high spirits of the exchange. "The issue here is not anyone's being for or against science. Science is physical reality as objectively understood so far. It's part of our common heritage. But the sciences, historically and especially at every 'paradigm shift,' reveal their own origins in the imaginary. At such moments we drop back to consult in wonder the prescientific web of human experience where science begins."

Akira cast a long glance in the direction of Aurélie Lefèvre. "Recently we had an illuminating discussion of the universal role of care in experience. When we reflect on our ardent wonder at the stars, you might think we'd been shot by Cupid's arrow and infected with a passion for the unknown. We find kinship with them long before we discover a chain of cosmological events. From the initial moment of quantum fluctuation—or whatever the Big Bang was—through cosmic inflation, nucleosynthesis, the forming of neutral atoms, the first stars, and on and on, immensely complex systems of inquiry and verification followed on the heels of wonder. Our love of the unknown keeps the fires of research burning and eventually finds paths to demonstrative truths. It's what makes us scientists wake up in the morning excited about the day's work. Wasn't that Aurélie's point about music and affect: love—or care—inspires all our ventures?"

Kashimoto knew that you can't bludgeon a man into enlightenment, though he might not go quite so far as to say one could be seduced into truth. Only the female Elders and Socrates might go that far.

Hunenko also tried to draw Yu back into the conversation. "Here, Wang, is another way of looking at the imaginary as the seedbed of systematic investigation, still holding in mind that our central point is the nexus between animal and human. When we study a troglodyte or a mouse, we can proceed from part to whole. From simple elements to complex objects: atoms to molecules to cells and complex systems beyond. But when you study an Englishman . . . "

"He means *even* an Englishman," Clive suggested to Yu in good-humored irony.

Oleksiy chortled. "You find that, whether you want to or not, you have to talk to the bloke. We might say there are two ways of knowing an Englishman: Begin part-to-whole and end up in mystery. Or take him all-at-once, as he's given in experience, and try for consistency of the whole. The first starts with the metaphor of a person 'as if' he were an isolated object and tries to reconstruct him from the simple elements, as though to know a thing is to be able to build a thing up from its elements. The result will be an instrumental fiction, until the moment you succeed in constructing a Shakespeare in the lab who demonstrates your success by writing a new play! In the all-at-once procedure we interrogate the human being as it performs."

"Exactly!" Rückert insisted. "Proceeding whole-to-part is what Plato calls 'preserving the appearances.' The point of science is to understand a person or thing in action, not to substitute computational models that lose the thing itself."

Oleksiy: "Of course we could move in both directions at once, circling from the Englishman to his presumptive organic elements and back again until we either close the circle or fall into the gap between."

"You know, Wang," Kern intervened, "that immense consequences follow the leap of faith that interprets the human as organic through and through. In ethics, governance, jurisprudence, and much more, the naturalistic thesis alters everything in sight. Think of slanting of genetic research toward socially desirable traits and favored patterns of behavior, or toward 'cures' for unacceptable habits. These contaminate a research environment that prides itself on objectivity, disinterestedness, and value-free investigation."

He paused to judge whether Wang was listening or had tuned out. Then continued. "On what basis does a science assume that survival is a virtue, that the fit are better than the unfit, or that social conformity is better than revolutionary opposition, heroic sacrifice, or retreating to a hermitage? Which mutations are good and which not so good? Why the ecology of a planet should be preserved? Or even life? I'm not answering these questions, just asking what capacity any science has to decide such essential questions in ordinary life."

Here, I hasten to inform you, was a topic I did understand, and the reason is that I had an example at hand: the secret of the lifelong friendship between Rucai and Kashimoto, the historian joined in friendship with the naturalist. In my eyes their relationship fully illustrated the synchronism of scientific rationality with all its necessary causes and abstractions, with understanding grounded in historical experience. And what makes the meeting of such minds possible is not knowledge. It's their respect and care for each other. That's Aurélie's 'economy of affect,' and its real name is love.

While I was distracted by this idea, another bee had lodged itself in Elena Bart's bonnet. For some reason—or none—Kern's remarks about science and technology had reminded the strange little woman of the Babylonians' effort to reach Heaven by building a tower.

"Isn't it ironic," she was saying, "that a city, rife with stories of heaven and the gods, should fall into confusion trying to reach Heaven by their own ingenuity, piling up stones until they all came crumbling down?"

"As in the myth of Argus' eyes," Rückert added, "and this starship! The Babylonian project, at the heart of all our woe!"

I, Kahn, so rarely contribute anything relevant to these proceedings that I'm proud of having been able to add: "Except that on Ulro the tower was already falling, and the starship was a salvage vehicle."

Then poor, exasperated Dennet-Jones, with great show of humility, asked if we might please get back to the unanswered question of the animals.

"Don't you see, Clive," Bart replied with equal impatience, "the question has been answered. We may have taken a long way around, but we've been speaking of the animal and the human all the while. The issue arises from what empirical research omits: the surplus in the creature who lives in desire for *what is not.*"

That was hardly the first speech in this session that left some of us feeling like drowning divers struggling for air.

Burgess caught her breath first. "Well, now, I sincerely hope all that brings us to the topic of the cyborg at last. If, contrary to appearances, we don't become animals, then maybe at least we can become efficient androids. That would be an improvement on several people I know." She looked down the table at Bart.

In fact, that did *not* bring us to cyborgs, but I feel sure you'll thank me for pulling the plug on two more hours of talk that still never got as far as our beloved machines.

PLANET RISE

"At 08:00H TOMORROW the Galatea will begin its first approach to Planet 2314. The Observation Gallery will open to the public at 06:00h and all events will be accessible on personal monitors." This unexpected announcement came last night and caused euphoria on board. There was an eruption of joy more like carnival than the orderly routine of a starship. People rushed impulsively into public places to share an excitement out of all rational proportion to the real situation. It's like what occasionally happened on Ulro when an armistice was announced or when a public disaster occurred.

The astonishing transformation in public spirit is difficult to describe. To understand what happened we must imagine what it feels like to spend all one's life passing through indifferent space at no matter what speed toward a hypothetical destination.

That's the epidemic of public lassitude in a nutshell. Stasis. Aimlessness. Time-space stretching out behind us to a nearly mythical home planet and forward toward nothing. At least that had always been the case until the decision to turn back to P2314. Then monotony was eclipsed by the lure of a new world. We were going to a place!

For what seemed an interminable period that morning, there was little to see and no information about where exactly we were. But our impatience was interesting: The promise of a destination gave us a sense of time and location that we hadn't known before.

Then suddenly last night, a contagion of eagerness at the news that we would see our new home in a few hours . . . more or less. Enthusiasm not dampened by the fact that we would park in orbit while manned landing craft performed flyby tests and surface mapping.

That's what all the scurrying and chattering has been about during a sleepless night and again this morning in the lines of people waiting for the Observation Deck to open. Sharply at 06:00 the doors open, and hundreds of people flow in under the great dome until the space is filled and the doors are closed. The air remains filled with indistinct voices. Nothing is known but that one announcement of less than fifty words, and yet it grows into a story reaching back more than sixteen years to the first exploration of P2314 and forward into an imaginary future. For all the talk among the adults and all the excited squealing and pointing among the children, there remains nothing to see but a nondescript object suspended in the dark globe of the heavens, marked only by an electronic pointer on the dome.

I happen to be in the company of Kashimoto, who has brought his son Yori and Yori's little friend Lars Hanssen. At a gesture from Kashimoto we take the boys back into the research area, where he gives them a close-up view of the planet and the presumed landing site in an equatorial desert through one of the smaller telescopes.

Meanwhile some disembodied technician pours a running commentary into our ears. It's all in quantities,

of time, velocity, and distance that add little to our understanding. But all it does, that voice, is supply the background
music for a piece of dry cosmic rock beginning to grow ever
so slowly on our vision. So slowly that if we were not told,
we wouldn't know the descent had begun. But this is not a
visual or even a rational event. It's visceral. Seduction, even.
As though the planet had us in *its* line of sight, stealthily
materializing before our eyes, bearing down on us, altering
us. Rationally, we know very well that few will ever set foot
on the ground. But we, weary and homeless wanderers, live
already out there in a beautiful new world. Drawn toward
home with the force of a poet's dream or the promise of
health after a long illness we hadn't known we were suffering.
It might be rational to ask why? Why, beyond curiosity, we
should care? But "why" comes too late: in cool retrospec-
tion after the agitation of experience. For us, heads leaning
forward and eyes staring in wonder, it's the first morning of
creation. People forget to breathe as the bright spot, nameless
but no longer anonymous, fills us with a joy like being drunk
on a new wine.

The planet slowly becomes a great brownish giant with
wondrous geological striations until it fills a whole side of
our transparent dome. As the ship banks and moves around
toward the dark side, we can see mountains and plateaus
in the "evening light." Someone in the throng mentions
water! The very word flows through the eager crowd as
fingers point out dry riverbeds threading their way across
the dimming surface. Fossils of water where, we are assured,
there has been none for eons. And yet imagine, if you can,

the thrilling magnetism of those traces of the elixir of nature, more precious than jewels to people reaching out in hope across a galaxy of darkness and fire.

We circle the planet once then move away again to "park" in a lower orbit from where the landing craft will be launched. If all goes well, we will sit here for some months while twenty brave souls discover whether P2314 can sustain human life. If so, we will sit here for several years during the design and construction of our new home.

Two days later we learn that the landing party will depart for the surface within twenty-four hours. The public will not be admitted to the launch area, because the U-shaped shuttle bay at the bottom rear of the ship has only narrow quays on the perimeter of the docking area. Beside members of the ship's crew, only Council members will be admitted, though the event will be broadcast to all. There is no room for spectators on the loading side of the bay, so we few observers watch from the quay opposite as technicians scurry about under the watchful eyes of Commander Rawls, First Mate Nasser, and Kashimoto. The moment we await is the arrival of the landing party.

Launch time is set at 07:00h so the shuttles can reach the planet floor before the midday heat. At 07:00 minus 30 minutes the twenty young adventurers enter the bay in double file and proceed along the platform to the waiting craft. Once they're on board, the hatches close and a voice from the speaker system resumes the countdown: "Minus 15 minutes to launch." At launch minus 5, two medics enter the bay and board one of the landing craft.

Without explanation, the count stops and nothing happens for some minutes. On the opposite quay Commander Rawls, speaking to someone inside the shuttle, becomes visibly agitated. A few moments later a person is brought out on a stretcher as the voice on the speaker announces, "The countdown is on hold." Otherwise no explanation.

Later we learn what happened. During the boarding process Bahram Sarosh had sprained an ankle—severely, according to the report from inside. Team medical officer Kwan Shi Wa examined him on board and, after consultation with Commander Rawls, summoned the medics who carried him off to sick bay. Somehow it happened that Nacho Rojas was on duty as the attending physician! Much later I learned from Claudio that he entered the landing craft and, with a silent exchange of glances between him and Shi Wa, examined the already wrapped ankle and reported him unable to walk, hence useless to the mission.

At the time all we could see was Rawls, First Mate Nasser, and Akira huddled together, apparently discussing alternatives. I had never seen the Commander so flustered as she paced up and down, up and down for some minutes without any visible concern that commanders don't behave this way in public. As it turned out, it wasn't "behavior." It was "real." And eventually I learned what was said as the three tried to decide about the launch.

Nasser said to Rawls, "You can't send a cripple to the surface of an alien planet!"

"Thank you for that observation, Talib!" She stopped in front of him, gave him a look of undiluted contempt, and resumed her pacing.

Then suddenly she stopped in front of Akira. "So, Professor Kashimoto, what do we do now?"

He answered with a shrug. "We postpone the mission until someone else can be prepared to take his place. That will take time."

She cried, "The mission can't be postponed!"

"Then send Talib," he suggested.

She stared at him with a degree of incredulity that seemed to say, "And I took you for an intelligent man!" For more than a minute she studied the surface of the deck, shuffling from one foot to the other. Then her head snapped up as if confronting the enemy: "For a hundred reasons this mission can't be postponed. Not now!" She pointed a finger in Akira's face. "There's no one else. I'm sending you!"

Without waiting for a response, almost forbidding one, she exchanged messages with someone in charge of the launch, then ordered that the countdown be interrupted for exactly two hours, "and not one moment longer."

Within a few hours the shuttle landed on the north edge of the plateau floor just below the first line of higher ground. As soon as further readings of the atmosphere had been made, the door opened onto a scorched and rocky surface. It would be hard to picture a more inhospitable environment and yet to the eyes of space wanderers it was thrilling beyond words. A dead world perhaps, but a new world. Alive with possibility for people who had been preparing forever for this moment. The first step onto that terrestrial surface was a miracle repeated twenty times, as all—Akira included— moved tentatively around, stamping lightly on solid ground, testing the resistance of a dusty platform like nothing in their experience. One would stare at the ground while springing up and down. Another would walk a few steps then turn and walk back again. Still another kicked up a cloud of dust and pebbles.

I, Kahn, got these details thirdhand from Claudio and secondhand from Akira himself, but I am no less astonished at the drama. We have always lived with gravity equally strong, but "artificial." Always lived on surfaces nearly as solid, but fabricated. Here again it's not the facts but the global experience of the facts that begets wonders! For a full hour they did nothing but walk around, not so much testing repetitive perceptions as assimilating the percepts to their own sense of being.

And the heat! Twenty adults with no experience of extreme temperatures welcoming rather than resisting the adventure of a celestial oven. Once it was verified that the air was in fact breathable without masks, a new joy erupted. One after another deep breath of the first "natural" air they had ever breathed left them as dizzy as children in a new playground. Every sensation was a new experience, every person a new being.

After getting the "feel of the place," Akira set in motion the plan for the remainder of Day One. Eighteen of the twenty were divided into six teams of three persons each to make an initial survey of their surroundings. Three groups, led by Paola Rucai, Edward Hamilton, and Kwan Shi Wa, fanned out on foot into the nearby highlands north of the plateau looking for campsites. The three other groups, each in land rovers, set out across the greater distances to the east, west, and south edges of the plateau.

Those on foot had a strenuous climb, but to people well-prepared for reading the geology of those hills there were discoveries to be made at every turn. Using the small canyons and still smaller crevices that wound upward among the modest peaks, they quickly found traces of ancient surface water. Hamilton's group climbed an old streambed that had more stories to tell than they had time to read. There was history in the walls of canyons where channels of water had once flowed swiftly into the basin, now the desert floor below. While exploring crevices in rock walls Paola's group discovered a cave that, as it turned out, would serve as a refuge for the whole party from midday heat and freezing nights.

For the groups exploring the plateau, the scenery may have been a bit monotonous, but the day was filled with adventure. There was little to see besides a wilderness of rocks small and large. But navigating over and around and through the forbidding terrain, they saw with eyes of luminous possibility. Each group reached a farther shore of the primeval lake and observed the transition from plateau to higher ground. Though less dramatic than the hills on the northern perimeter, the swelling of the ground offered unique geological features. One group even collected a few scrubby plants to present to Paola in the evening, less for science than for fun.

At sunset—the first of those fiery red sunsets that are distinctive to the planet—they all returned to the landing craft. The reports from the south were thin, except for valuable information about the performance of the equipment, especially the land rovers on which so much would depend in the explorations to follow. The big news of the day was the traces of water and the discovery of the large cave. And so it was decided that on Day Two the cave should be explored. If it proved sufficient for shelter and relatively easy to access, they would move the landing site and their supply dump nearer that point and make it their temporary center of operations. With these reports and these few preliminary decisions, the euphoric first day of humans on P2314 ended.

That night they bunked down among the landing craft and surface vehicles like a circle of covered wagons in an Ulro film of the Wild West. Though well prepared for the plunging temperatures, another adventure was feeling cold for the first time by briefly exposing hands and faces.

The next morning work began in earnest. By plan, the party divided, this time into two groups. The first, including those trained in environmental science, were assigned to explore the cave in the hills. If conditions proved favorable, they were to transport the bedrolls and consumable supplies and establish a camp underground. That done, they would begin orderly evaluations of the environment with an eye to long-term monitoring procedures.

Yet another delight, realized more slowly, was the necessity itself. Here things had to be done right. At every turn there were contingencies and dangers to face. To strike out across this surface one had to take care. At the very least they had to be able to get back. There was nothing equivalent in their experience of centuries of "hibernation." The necessity for action brought an immediate sense of their own limits.

The second team began organizing technical surveys essential to a settlement. Foremost was water. Subterranean aquifers had been located by aerial survey, and some people were assigned to search out their accessibility. Others began the much longer task of figuring out how the water could be captured in what quantities and conveyed to which possible building sites. Meanwhile, some on the team studied possible locations for a permanent base camp suitable for planetary exploration. The number and complexity of questions involved in that problem were mind-boggling: Where to put it? What infrastructure on what scale for how many people? What physical structures? How indigenous materials of stone and sand might be conveyed to which sites? How to insulate a habitat from the extremes of heat and cold and for how many people? Every question begot a multitude of additional questions.

Thanks to the work of the first team, camp was moved to the cave on Day Two, and within a week the landing site was shifted to a more convenient spot. Amid all this bustle a decisive transition began that was recognized by no one. Having lived in the anonymous, interchangeable spaces of a starship, they had no experience of flesh quietly putting down roots in a natural environment. It would emerge, when it did, as a matter of orientation. The purely pragmatic act of moving camp literally *into* the hills determined that the explorers would be oriented to—and from—the highlands rather than the plain. They would *become* highlanders, and that fact would have far-reaching consequences.

In the second week the first group began the months-long project of installing permanent environmental monitoring systems. They tested for harmful elements, recorded what weather patterns there were beyond variations in temperature, tapped aquifers in the hills and tested water samples, collected botanical specimens, searched for arable soil, even discovered places in the hills sheltered enough from the heat for growing edible plants. To that end they considered how soil might be manufactured—all in preparation for a human habitat on this desolate rock.

Akira's task was to organize and coordinate, but it quickly became obvious that Bahram Sarosh was essential to the project as much for his architectural imagination as for his knowledge of construction materials and procedures. Since most of the issues to be settled at this stage depended on the location and design for a headquarters, Akira sent an urgent request to Command that Sarosh be sent down as soon as possible. There was no mention of how he was to get back and forth from plateau to the camp in the hills, only that a land rover would be available for his work. Remarkably, given Command's indifference to sensory details they couldn't imagine and their preference for information that came in weights and measures, all was done just as Akira requested. When there was no mention of his returning to the ship, he began to wonder if they might even be happy to have him separated from the other Elders.

So Bahram arrived and, aside from the happy reunion with Paola, was busy within days sketching an atmosphere-controlled headquarters built in modules that could be easily moved or expanded. In the weeks and months that followed he had the surface surveyed for building materials, determined what kind of support would be needed from the ship for constructing the first two units, and figured out how they might be fabricated and delivered to the ground for assembly. The first unit would be used as temporary living quarters while the second would house fabricating technology already under production on the ship. A major consideration was the strain the building phase would put on the transportation system. Then he and the technical team waded into the issues of how a comprehensive plan was to be reduced to a series of practical stages.

All the preliminary questions being interrelated, Bahram had to confer often with everyone else. One result was that the convivial evening hours when they had to retreat from the extreme surface temperatures became a general consultation of all with all. Consequentially he was soon ready to assemble a master plan of the construction. The ultimate aim was to reproduce all the Galatea systems except those concerned with flight. Thus, in a little less than three months, advance planning reached a crucial stage that required the consent of Command on numerous issues. Predictably, when controversy arose, it was about ways and places and means.

One issue lay at the root of the rest and became a source of controversy: location. Where was colony headquarters to be built? Sarosh, Kashimoto, and everyone else on the ground agreed that the best location would be the point that had attracted them all from their first week and would attract anyone else: the hills. They had come to love a landscape that offered variety and rest for the spirit and where several caves provided retreats from the harsh environment. The problem was that, except for the proximity of water, it would be the most difficult place to build, inconvenient for moving materials over rough terrain and inaccessible for the landing craft and land rovers.

This was the first issue destined to cause irritation between the landing party and Command. The thing that made it contentious was that, once the proposal was submitted, it got settled so easily and quickly from above. In response to the first exchanges on the subject, Command made the decision unilaterally and without consultation: The colony would be located on the desert floor where transport was most convenient. And with that, the matter was closed. No mention of quality of life in perpetuity. Material convenience dictated that the colony would be built on that blank table of scorched earth.

Question settled, the debate began. It was endlessly discussed among the young scientists, whose experience now exceeded anything that could be conveyed to people who had never had their feet on the ground or sat on a rock in the evening and spoken with a calm spirit about the human things that matter most.

In fact the explorers had slipped into an end-of-the-day habit that bore tangentially on the disagreement. The habit was little less than an ancient ritual that provided an anchor for collective life and work. It happened first like this: Someone discovered a place on a promontory where a crescent of wall around a patch of rocky ground overlooked the desert. Gradually it became their meeting place at the end of the day where they would spend the period before the deep cold set in. One evening someone had the idea of gathering a supply of dried brush and making a fire in the middle. And so they sat together with the pungent smell of burning brush in their nostrils, discussing the activities of one day and planning the next.

But the topics didn't stop there. The setting also encouraged long-range speculations. There was an implicit hierarchy of authority among the twenty—Akira as natural leader and Bahram as designated chief of the mission—but the authority that counted most was the person who knew most about the topic under discussion. One might call these conversations incipient, even natural, political events. Of course people disagreed on ends and means, and some points were fiercely debated, but the debates continued until some vision emerged.

Still larger and more contentious issues became "campfire topics," as happened when Starship Command became dissatisfied with their rate of progress. In the view from the bridge, where people sat in orbit waiting to get started with the thing they had come so far to do, three months had passed without anything significant happening on the ground. The regular reports from Bahram and Akira seemed more like temporizing than pushing the plan ahead on a schedule that, after two and a half centuries, required expedition. Akira saw that whatever Command was told, they paid attention only to what fit their disposition to send workers and start building something. In their view that should have happened within weeks. And so rather than acknowledge progress and discuss conditions, they sent instructions based on their concept of a colony that began and ended with technological competence in the service of survival.

As the contrary intentions of the young explorers became more sharply defined, Akira watched them becoming radicalized. There was something exemplary in the situation. Not differing theoretical or ideological views. Rather a radical difference in orientation. Even if Command had cared enough to pay attention to their communiqués instead of waiting to "see progress," the people on the bridge would have gotten only representations, and representations divorced from being-there could only misrepresent. The situation required that one feel the temperatures as boundary experiences of one's own flesh, that one smell collective thought and speech in the scent of burning brush, taste it in hot dusty and clean freezing air, hear it in the sound of rock loosened by footsteps and tumbling down ancient streambeds. Without these and a thousand other things received and perceived, what needed communicating was incommunicable. Meanwhile, the landing party was mutating in character under the influence of a different lifeworld.

On one such evening after a day of happy toil, they sat together across the smoldering brush fire under the open sky and a panoply of stars as the opaque earth returned the pressure of their bodies like a lover. In the cool of the evening the topic turned to Command's distrust and resistance. Akira recognized the dangers in twenty young people in a semicircle around a campfire murmuring against the only human order on this side of the galaxy. In his most diplomatic mode and by force of character more than by words, he tried to moderate the collective mood. His chief point was that they not let tomorrow's troubles destroy their joy in one of the finest nights they had ever known.

In the middle of that effort, he received the following message: "You are required to return for consultations. A landing craft will arrive at 08:00h tomorrow."

THE LOOKING-GLASS
COLLOQUY

I, ISHMAEL KAHN, am haunted by a ghost. Yes, I know that's nonsense. There are no ghosts on a starship. Still, my inexistent ghost gives me no peace. Here's what I mean. Mainly because of Bart's occasional references to a past member of the Council, I can't escape the name Hannah Jaeger. It—she—haunts my quiet hours. You might say I live with her, since my apartment was hers more than a century ago, but that wouldn't matter if she weren't such a potent character. It's all very quirky on my part, to say the least, since the apartment was occupied by several other people between her residency and mine. But say what you like, the fact is they never disturb me, and she gives me no peace.

It's not just her. It's the intellectual baggage she brings, crowding my space with unwelcome echoes of dead religions. Given her Jewish ancestry (and mine), Jaeger's passion for the explosion of thought in Ulro's "Axial Age" (8th-3rd centuries B.C.E.) makes a certain sense, but it doesn't fit in this little world where we congratulate ourselves on having replaced magic and mystery with "truth." The pivotal half-millennium of ferment that extended from the planet's Mediterranean Sea to its Pacific Ocean hardly seems relevant to twentieth-fourth century life in space.

And yet a succession of learned people on board have been strangely infatuated with ideas from these sources. The Elders may represent a kind of counterculture in the starship, but Jaeger belongs to a line of voices alien even to us. I have mentioned before that all information about the mission was wiped from our records before launch. The reason for the omission is as tantalizing as whatever it was meant to conceal. We can only assume that such elaborate precautions were to protect us from matters harmful to the ship and its people.

And here's the point: Though the original Council kept no records of their activities, we know a few things. We know that in the beginning there were no formal sessions or records of the deliberations. And we know the names of three original Elders who were part of the mission at launch. Their names will mean nothing to you, but I record them for what they may reveal about the intentions behind the Council and a certain perverse, if not revolutionary, "spirit" that extends from these three down to Hannah Jaeger, on to Elena Bart, and even to Claudio Rucai. I think you'll agree they make quite a menagerie!

First, an Argentine writer named Miranda Ribeiro; second, an Indian Buddhist philosopher named Abhay Gupta, both in their 70s at launch; and third, a middle-aged Orthodox Christian monk, Pavlos Demetriopoulos, who left his monastery to join the mission. We also know that the first "colloquy" was a lecture by Abhay Gupta just before his death on the topic "Much Ado About Nothing or The History of Zero." So you see, the direct link between Jaeger and Gupta is precisely "nothing."

Bart once put the conundrum like this: "You may make it to the heavens on a rocket ship, but you can make it to *Heaven* only on the wings of imagination." Well, I take no comfort in that. I'm not trying for Heaven, and I'm happy to leave technology to the technocrats. Still, I sit here night after night trying to write, unable to escape Jaeger's Germanic features and bob of unkempt grey hair, leaning over my shoulder, whispering messages in archaic languages I don't understand and don't want to hear.

In her generation my spectral roommate was the closest thing to a trained philosopher on the Council, which contributes to her legendary status. But there's more, much more. One of the most astonishing parts of the Jaeger legend is personal. She was a quite plain woman with a seductive power over intelligent men. You don't see it in the video record when she's up in years, but if you go back to her youth or even middle age, it's clear enough. Plain as she was, clever men found her charismatic and irresistible. It had something to do with the way she listened to others and with the extraordinary force of her concentration. She had several lovers in her time, though none lasted. A colleague would get into a debate with her on some arcane topic and, after hours of head-to-head combat, they would wind up in bed. Apparently once she had grasped their ways of thinking, she got bored.

For some reason—unless it's a fact without a sufficient reason—her inescapable non-presence in my life recently inspired me to review Council records and some of the colloquies from year 2170, when mental health was the burning issue. One of these dialogues I could neither understand nor put out of my mind. The one Bart had mentioned. It's about "negation" and, to my mind, sails uncomfortably close to mysticism. If we take material objects present before our eyes as the model for what is "real," then even to consider such nonsense may be to relapse into magical thinking. Is that what I'm doing? I wonder.

You will understand how serious this matter is for me when I tell you that I have sometimes sought medical advice for anxiety and insomnia. Eventually I learned that relegating an unpleasant symptom to the medicalized body, calling it a disease, and demanding a cure can be as counterproductive as anesthetizing your hand so you can hold it in a fire without pain. I prefer my symptoms to being dumbed down by tranquilizers. Besides, I blame Jaeger. (You see how dubious my "sanity" is!) My long relation to this woman whom I never met is intensely personal. Her astonishing words come with the authority of one who must be heard. Somewhere in the back of my mind I suspect she's only needling me to recognize a discredited part of myself.

All that aside, when I searched the record of year 2170, I found her listening in silence to several Council discussions of "starship syndrome." She listened, then pondered the problem in her peculiar way for months—in my apartment, of course! All that cogitating led her far afield from what her Indian colleague Chetana Dubashi had said about the starship malaise, with results that were to make a stir in her world and in ours.

I had already begun to see her ideas as foreshadowing Lefèvre's remarks on music's "tuning" our affections and on Bart's defense of mythology in an age of science—even on Rückert and Hunenko's accounts of "living in the open."

214

But there was so much more. So far-reaching, in fact, that I decided to share it with the Elders and, because it's so personal to me, to include it in my book. The performance itself has come to be called "The Looking-Glass Colloquy." So you can judge for yourself.

My presentation to the Council on the night in question began with an explanation: "We might have expected that the prospect of a landing would have raised the spirits of the people on board. Now we see that after the excitement of arriving and parking in orbit, people have slowly realized that establishing a colony is not as sexy as they thought. If it's possible at all, it will be a slow process and very few of us will ever set foot on the ground. Given the harsh surface environment many may not even want to. So now, public spirit, after briefly improving, has plummeted once more. For this reason, I want to share with you an extraordinary dialogue from a century and a half ago where this legendary woman interprets starship malaise as a disease of the human spirit."

As I pushed the play button and the video flickered, the Council Chamber opened once more into a prior age, where we were joined by the people we had seen before.

Jaeger, elbows on the table as if to hold herself up, began the conversation in a voice that sounded weary. *"Thank you for agreeing to discuss the anxiety epidemic once more. Parvaneh Sarosh's earlier report on the symptoms disheartened us all. Whatever the causes, it feels like a petrifaction of the spirit that calls for an altered disposition. Our own pessimism seems to confirm that people are right to have lost hope and that the best we can do is invent distractions to help them forget the reality of life in space. The idea is familiar in the phrase 'the opiate of the masses.' If not religion, then art or entertainment so we don't die of too much truth."*

The oddly charismatic figure of Jaeger, slumped in her chair, equaled in discouragement the glum faces of her colleagues. They might be discussing the suffering of others, but the obscure effects reached far down the room into our time. We, too, drooped like plants wilting in a hostile environment, and yet as she spoke—putting it in a story—her own sap began to rise.

"In our first discussion of the malaise, Chetana Dubashi remarked that a review of empirical conditions is not likely to help. That made me wonder: If not empiricism, then what? Tonight, I want to propose an answer by reflecting differently on the public mood of dejection."

As Jaeger spoke, I was distracted by how, in her sixties, exposed to the gloom we all share, she still radiated passion. And her contemporaries were anything but indifferent. At both ends of the room, in their time and ours, people were mesmerized. Even Dennet-Jones and Yu Wang had laid aside their woolgathering and were listening with eyes wide open. To me, her manner was redolent of the old, discredited virtue of piety. I mean piety in a non-pietistic sense of loyalty to what commands respect as most worthy, and duty accepted. Though she could be harsh toward parochial interests, even the people she annoyed never doubted her fearless devotion to what is true and good. Say what you will about Jaeger's manner and ideas, if ever our little city in space included a prophet, false prophet or true, it was she.

The next moment she pushed her chair back and said, *"Everyone come with me. We're going on a field trip. I want to show you a looking-glass!"*

Manuel Didière groaned petulantly as though he were being imposed on, but she calmly walked around the far end of the table toward the window and stood before it, pointing.

After hesitating, Didière and company followed as the recording camera panned so that, from our end of the table, we were looking at their backs lined up in front of the "virtual" Chamber window. The same scene separated by a century and a half and an angle of 90 degrees.

"What I would like to know is why are we mesmerized by the view of the cosmos from this window or from the observatory upstairs. Whether in awe or terror, we can't forget the sublimity of this view. I wonder why that should be."

When no one responded to the strange question, she resumed, *"So Didière, what do you see?"*

First you must know that Manuel Didière was essentially a technocrat, though occasionally a serious mind could be detected through the haze of residual French melancholy. In his generation, he performed a useful service as liaison between the Council and Command, rather as Kashimoto does in ours. But he was not an intellectual and there was no love lost between Jaeger and him, unless that's exactly what had been lost and what fed their evident antipathy for each other.

He answered her question peevishly. *"I see a bunch of inmates from an Alzheimer's ward staring at their own images and not recognizing themselves."*

"And Sarosh, what do you see?"

217

"I see myself flanked by the rest of you." She pointed down the row of images: Viktor Pastukh beside her, Dubashi next, then Robert Forsythe and beyond. Her hand moved back across those images to the table, chairs, and the wall of books behind them and even us who both were and were not there. *"They're all images. Not real."*

"What do you mean by 'not real?'"

"That there's more there than meets the eye. Something like the non-image implied in the mere image. We know from other sources that the points of light conceal more than they reveal. There's always more than we see, and we're drawn through the visible into the invisible. Those lights are only the radiation from the furnaces of stars reaching out toward us."

"And the darkness between?"

"The dark is the absence of light. In an expanding universe it's light moving more slowly than the expansion rate so that it never reaches back to us."

"Good. Now indulge me in one more question. Where does all this seeing begin?"

Ava looked askance as though it were a trick question, then ventured, *"I guess it starts with me. With my curiosity. Though it started just now with you and your provoking questions."*

"Yet shifting it to me doesn't really add anything, does it? That would locate the event of our seeing in psychology. But does either of us initiate anything here? Or do we respond involuntarily to a summons issued from beyond ourselves that is strangely matched with our powers? Though we know—or think we know—that these stars were shining eons before there was anyone to respond as we do."

Then Jaeger turned to Chetana Dubashi and asked what *she* found most unique in the scene on the other side of the looking-glass.

You could read in Dubashi's smile that she had caught Jaeger's line of thought. *"Once I stop admiring us,"* she replied, *"I, too, see nothing but points of light in infinite darkness. Emptiness. The void."* She stopped, as if hearing something else in her own words. *"The lights are given by the dark. If the sky were a great globe of fire, there would be light but it would be concealed."*

"And what first attracted your attention?"

"I see. You mean it's the scene 'out there.' For me it's the void. The infinite nothing constantly provokes my gaze, though there is nothing to see there. The stars—like pearls displayed on a dark cloth in a jeweler's shop—lead us beyond into the dark. The unchanging sight, defined by those points of light, should get boring, but somehow it doesn't. And I never tire of looking at it, searching it. It answers to something in me."

Jaeger continued to turn the idea this way and that, as though not to let it pass unexamined. *"Isn't the sense of awe remarkable? Instead of initiating the event of seeing, we feel ourselves looked at, addressed, called into the open by the void itself. Whether in awe or fear, we are lit up by an absence that conveys a sense of concealed possibilities. As though seeing ourselves seeing because of first being seen! Roused by wonder, even by ignorance, and surprised by a felt kinship with uncanny possibilities."*

By this time Robert Forsythe, the historian of science, was growing impatient. Forsythe was/is American. After generations in space, he managed to retain the unmistakable residue of Anglo-Saxon common sense and American optimism, as though the decline of his ancestors' country had not touched him. This sociable and unimaginative literalist was a unique figure on the Council, even a bit of a misfit who sometimes appeared dull.

He protested, *"I can't tell, Hannah, whether your disease is philosophy or mysticism. But the sky isn't empty. Never was. There was the zodiac and, after the telescope was invented, innumerable and wonderful cosmic objects including dark matter and dark energy. So why insist on emptiness instead of what's there?"*

Then followed a polite, halfhearted smile. Forsythe was not as brusque as Didière, but, having forgotten the provenance of the word "mysticism," was frustrated with Jaeger's appeal to things unexplained.

She answered with the usual cryptic directness. *"And yet I insist on the emptiness, Robert, because it isn't empty exactly. Nothing is not absolutely nothing."*

"Then use the example of the so-called 'black hole,' where the star that implodes on itself leaves a density of matter so great and so infinitesimal that it makes a hole in our field of perception. Almost nothing can escape its gravitational pull. Or use 'dark matter,' which must be there to account for gravitation but can't be seen."

"Good, Robert. There you bring us to the point. And isn't it remarkable that a fullness so great that it can only appear as empty lights up a corresponding emptiness in us? Loving beyond our reach. Notoriously desiring what can't be possessed. Threatened by void and amorously drawn to what it conceals.

Always 'calling spirits from the vasty deep,' *giving names and telling stories—true names and true stories—where 'true' speaks of provisional coherences rather than static proofs."*

With a gesture that seemed not to stop at the window but to pass through it, she continued. *"We sail into that dark on imagination, looking for the unseen, listening for the unsaid. We resume old words and legends that offer unexplored potential for new realities, opening the way for the labors of reason. As those pinpricks of light out there suggest kinship, give them names and fold them into the unwritten narratives that punctuate our lives. Whether the void terrifies or comforts, we go on and on, in dreams and myths, in philosophy and science, expanding the story that is more than ours into the dark, rendering it intelligible. Else, not to acknowledge the void, we live like Narcissus in an image of ourselves, enslaved by the certitude of our own convictions."*

At this point Didière joined with Forsythe by demanding peremptorily, *"What is your point, Hannah? Somehow I received the impression that our topic tonight was the starship malaise. What cure or comfort are we to draw from mystical speculations about insatiable desire and the great nothing?"*

Jaeger's grey hair shook as she snapped caustically, *"If comfort is your aim, Manuel, take a tranquilizer. If you're in a hurry, stop the ship and get off. But if you can spare the time to reflect on how we actually function, you may discover something extraordinary. The ominous symptoms of distress we count in the populace of the ship—as if we knew what we were counting—may show that we're facing the death of desire in creatures of desire."*

221

"Oh my God!" Didière lamented. He covered his ears histrionically as though to shut the madness out and preserve a tenuous hold on common sense. Then looked up and asked in a voice trembling with indignation, *"Then what, briefly if you will, is the cure?"*

In a chilly tone that visibly irked him, she replied, *"Without confirmation of a disease, the concept of a cure makes no sense. I'm saying anxiety is not a malady. It's a precious revelation of who we are and a foreshadowing of different modes of being."*

You see that Jaeger had no time for flattering idlers into thinking well of themselves or pandering to laggards who prefer amusement to understanding. Such intellectual poverty embarrassed her gods and put her world at risk as truly as would a captain asleep at the helm of the ship.

Meanwhile, what I, Kahn, marveled at was the spectacle of her audience of serious-minded people, including the protesters, standing there in a semicircle around her staring into the abyss of space, captivated by her rhapsody to infinition, contradicting their own assertions of indifference. Without understanding a word of what she said, I knew I, for one, was doomed to hear it echoing through all my midnight reveries.

She picked up the thread of her argument—if it was an argument. *"Now hold on to the guardrails, because what comes next may be still more alarming. It is this: Life on the generational starship is paradigmatic of the universal human condition, and it has everything to do with 'nothing.' We have said the starship is the right place for discovering essential things easily ignored in terrestrial life. Here"*—she tapped the window with one finger—*"there is no place to hide from the void on the other side of the looking-glass or from the total, mind-numbing security on this side. But to make sense of all this, I need to remind you of a bit of Ulro history."*

I saw Robert Forsythe smile with satisfaction as though he thought "a bit of history" might restore some sanity to this outlandish talk.

"One important element in the cultural mutation of Western Civilization that we call the Renaissance was a crisis that's not easy to recognize. Over nearly two prior millennia, we had learned to describe all experience as beginning in bodily sensations, then passing though the bodily juices or 'humours,' becoming vaporous fancies and moods, until they reached the place of imagination and, ultimately, reason."

She stopped short. *"Now, you can forget all that. If you want to go into this history, look it all up on Alexandros and spend the next ten years reading ancient medical texts and love poetry."* She chuckled. *"One benefit will be that for one decade, at least, you'll be too busy to suffer anxiety and boredom."*

Then, before anyone could obliterate her historical setting, she rushed ahead. *"What comes next is what matters. Late in the Renaissance the whole picture shifted. The demand for subjective certainty went* 'ravaging, raging, and uprooting' *the authority of imagination until it came into* 'the desolation of reality.' *Forgetting that we don't live by reason alone, what followed was the strip-mining of the human world for the ore of positive knowledge, until the procedures of religion, ethics, politics, the arts, even the earth itself were despoiled!"*

She paused, and Didière made a show of having paid attention: *"So?"*

"So I repeat: The Galatea is a laboratory for studying the unforeseen consequences of our forgetfulness and the mutation in our self-understanding in the loss of wonder."

Forsythe demurred. *"If we follow your lead, what do we learn from the void? Aside from negating our greatest achievements in history?"*

This time Dubashi took him up by addressing Jaeger first. *"We mustn't let him keep dragging the issue back to knowledge and our subjective standard! What we're discussing, Robert, is the history of being that sets knowledge on course. All the folklore, the myths, the religions—all that you would dismiss as mystery and superstition—are so much as we have been able to receive and be shaped by at given times and places. Nothing in that competes with knowledge. It's the springboard!"*

"Well said, Chetana," Jaeger replied. *"Whatever provisional consistencies people have been capable of living up to are disparaged at our peril. If we're attentive we can still be dazzled by the traces of Job's patience, by the love of Paolo and Francesca, or by the faith of Augustine of Hippo. Verification of facts is insufficient. Exemplary stories are 'true' because they shed light! We send our gaze out across this darkness like Noah's dove looking for a perch. But mark this: Success or failure, we end up restless and with a sense of something lacking because we, too, are compounded of nothing. That's our story of desire and of hope as the testimony to things unseen."*

Suddenly Claudio raised his hand to interrupt time past. I pressed the "pause" button, and he punctuated present and past with a voice from a still greater distance:

224

Hope is the thing with feathers
That perches in the soul
And sings the tune without the words
And never asks for more . . .

Looking around the table to see if we were ready to resume, I saw something remarkable: Every face was blank. No self-consciousness! All absorbed in digesting what we had heard, including Claudio's quotation. And so I waited for them to emerge from their reveries.

But for now, by pressing a button we return to Ulro year 2170, and a gleeful declaration from Parvaneh Sarosh:

"You've given a wonderful sermon, Hannah. I've never heard anyone say so much about nothing. However, most of us are more concerned with what is *than with* what isn't.*"*

"No, you aren't, Parvaneh," she replied gently. *"You understand more than you know, or more than you're willing to know. Having heard these words, you will not be able to un-hear them. They will return as an echo of your own experience until 'being' and 'nothing' occupy a single field."*

Meanwhile, Viktor Pastukh had been waiting for a chance to raise a different question. *"In the past, Hannah, you have said that we give objectivity—once you called it 'local habitation'!— to things more speculative than actual by giving 'true names' and telling 'true stories.' How do I do that? What is the standard of the true where correspondence or verification is lacking?"*

Faced with another question that showed a will to understand, Jaeger paused to relish the question and formulate a worthy answer. *"If names bring things into presence before us that are barely things at all, then the name we use must connect with a context we already understand. If you tell us there's a book under the table, we look and behold; you have made the book accessible. A 'correct statement' corresponds to 'reality.' But if you say there's an angel in the room, the task is to find a path to that name. To let it lead us to something behind the word. Otherwise, you're speaking nonsense. Withhold names, or give names that reveal nothing, and we remain in the dark. That may be why the mythic imagination has always been careful in naming the infinite: Because names are also placeholders for the inexistent and unknowable that nonetheless concerns us absolutely."*

"*Where do we find such names?*" Pastukh asks.

"*Follow the poet who, in a propitious moment, takes up old names and fits them to new contexts. That's when what was inaccessible passes to us in a new setting. All relations shift, so to speak, and make room for the inaccessible. And—this is essential!—in naming we celebrate and, in celebrating, we are assimilated to what commands our attention and concerns our mode of being by assimilating us.*"

"*And yet you say we must name truly.*"

"*As happens in a moment of myth-making: fortuitous names for fortuitous events. Maybe that's why the smartest gods withhold their names—or have none—so we can't take them as objective realities and become idolaters or be blinded by the light.*"

"*The gods!*" Didière exploded with incredulity once more.

"*Like the name of a nameless god who doesn't ex-ist. Maybe that's why Socrates, who says he knows nothing of the gods, also says he fears nothing so much as naming them. Isn't that strange? What's to fear? Except that foolish names may dim their light or conceal them entirely. So the poets strive to give true names, auspicious names that summon us from afar and rekindle desire."*

Beyond incredulity, this speech stirred embarrassment. No one spoke or even looked at Jaeger. You could see in the video the dumbfounded expressions on the faces of her contemporaries, and the words sounded quite as mad to most of us as a palpable wave of resistance united the two groups and the two moments of history. But Jaeger didn't care. She was in no mood to let her feathers be ruffled by any of us. I knew from experience that the event in 2170 would suddenly end at this point, leaving us to imagine the free-for-all that must have followed and to suffer the sense of anticlimax.

Claudio's hand went up. I pressed the stop button.

"'To make a prairie takes a clover and one bee / One clover and a bee. / And revery. The revery alone will do, if bees are few.'"

Dennet-Jones, paying no attention to Claudio, rushed to point out that Jaeger never answered her own question about starship anxiety and negation.

"Not explicitly," Bart protested. "But she did give an *implicit* answer."

"Excuse me?"

"She let us see the emptiness of the sky as pregnant with unactualized possibilities and ourselves as capable of loving an adventure and worlds yet unborn to which, willy-nilly, we are assigned. She reminds us that the poet celebrates the void by finding names, the painter by finding images, the musician by singing its pure affects, even the philosopher stretching language beyond all measure to think the unthinkable idea behind the words."

227

That speech did little to dissolve the consternation of our wise Elders, and some time passed before Burgess broke in, no doubt feeling compelled to say something even if it added up to nothing:

"Jaeger's prophetic call for the salvation of the soul might have some merit if there were a soul and if it wanted to be saved. But if we've reduced ourselves to animals on the way to becoming machines, then she's dreaming. People—at least those who *aren't* mystics or philosophers—will retreat into their drab little comforts and dismiss her way as madness. That may be just as well for two reasons: Most people don't have the capacity to think such lunacy, and lunacy can also be deadly!"

Then, surprise of surprises, Bart had the last word: "Living in the open or closed in ourselves, we're always dying anyway. Why live stunted? Why not live to the fullest?"

Joseph Kern sighed and rolled his eyes. "What amazes me is that a dialogue by people reputed to be learned and wise should devolve into old-time religion and the love life of the stars. But then Jaeger's imagination—and yours, Elena—exceed my feeble credulity."

At this point, when we should have been exhausted, our exchange also devolved into pandemonium. All moods and all opinions were in the air at once. Some defending "poetic license," some proposing to make philosophers of everyone, and a few sitting quietly with furrowed brows until the session broke up in a cacophony of anger and laughter.

AKIRA RETURNS

AKIRA ARRIVED IN THE shuttle bay of the Galatea as required, with the records of months of work by the explorers in hand. He was promptly escorted to the bridge where Commander Rawls and First Mate Nasser waited. Rawls ran a critical glance down the full length of his figure as though disapproving of the well-groomed, formal look of one who had just walked in from the galactic wilds. Otherwise the welcome was cordial enough as they passed into the adjacent conference room and took seats at the table, Akira on one side facing the others who, but for politeness, might have been his accusers. Rawls omitted the usual preliminary small talk and began formally:

"We've asked you here to discuss the progress of the survey. Some of our people feel that things are developing too slowly down there." After a dry, humorless chuckle, she added, "They've begun to call your people 'the immortals' in honor of the eternity it takes them to get things done. Or maybe," the remark was sharp, "because the rest of us will be dead before they make any visible progress."

Akira did not mention the fact that, from the beginning, Command had barely commented on the regular progress reports. The responses, such as they were, suggested that his communications were received perfunctorily and filed away.

Not that he minded, since neglect left the explorers free to put the well-being of future colonists ahead of technical achievements. So diplomatically, he alluded to none of that.

"I can shed light on your point later if you wish. For now, why don't we review the results of an immense amount of work by your dedicated team?"

As neither of the others replied, he projected his files on the conference room screen. "I will summarize first and then we can look more deeply into whatever topics interest you most."

Talib Nasser, Rawls' sidekick, was well-known to Akira by now. It was he who assumed the initiative as though primary responsibility for the colonial project had been delegated to him. If so, having not been advised of the fact, Akira ignored it. At the very least Nasser gave more attention to the details than Rawls, though even he seemed distracted, and neither appeared especially interested in the consultation they had required. Akira marked the fact and proceeded with the information they *should* have been interested in.

Meanwhile a series of explanations for their peculiar behavior flashed across his mind. Was theirs the bureaucratic disposition that saw only what was in front of its face? Or was it just average, everyday consciousness made dramatic by the peculiar circumstances? He was reminded that practicality does not communicate with imagination except when it's shocked out of its rut by the unexpected. At one time he and Claudio had discussed the point and Claudio had remarked, "That's related to the old problem of evil. Maybe it's why suffering is necessary." With a hearty laugh he had added, "Maybe the righteous suffer to keep them awake."

Meanwhile Akira glimpsed a third and darker possibility, one always within easy reach of the conspirator's paranoia: Perhaps Rawls and Nasser *knew* all and were laying a trap. But none of these possibilities were more than momentary flashes at the periphery of his consciousness.

The executive summary soon exhausted his hosts' attention, and Akira moved on to the architectural drawings that made a spectacular display on the big screen. The spectacle elicited a slightly more prolonged survey of the proposed habitat, though Akira saw that without experience of that rocky surface or the scorching midday air people could hardly appreciate the cloistered walks and the bubble domes imagined in Bahram's elegant designs. These space wanderers were destined to act with blind authority over the very people to whom they should have been listening.

Talib soon rose impatiently from his seat and said, "We will submit your material to our experts for evaluation."

"Excuse me," Akira responded. "I don't understand. Aren't your experts exactly the team you trained and assembled for this survey?" He held his voice to the tone of tactful cordiality, covering his disgust. "Here you have the recommendations of your authorities." The friendly directness of his glance never wandered from their faces.

As the pointless meeting ended, he was internally busy with another reality and another question. Why had he been brought here? Had the survey team been betrayed? But how? By whom? The only secrets were between him, Claudio and, to a lesser degree, Paola. Although there had been criticisms aplenty on the ground, no one had acted contrary to

instructions. Every order had been obeyed and every suggestion followed. The people in Command were hardly the
kind to object to the spirit when the letter had been promptly
obeyed, yet they were clearly on edge. Perhaps an informer
had been planted on the survey team. But to find *what* where
there was nothing to find? Two explanations remained, both
confounding credulity.

Either this was an alarming degree of intellectual sloth
among a crew with impoverished imaginations or there was
a mole in the survey party who, lacking anything substantial
to report, had been transmitting critical remarks back to the
ship, where they had raised hackles. Either possibility would
be a complicating factor, but there was no time just then to
look backward.

As Commander Rawls turned to leave the room, she said
tersely, "You will get your instructions before your return at
the end of the week." And on this ominous note the meeting
ended.

Akira left the bridge and made his way down to the residential decks. The unexpected reunion with five-year-old Yori
and his mother, Atsuko, was notable for the child's interest
in hearing all about the planet. On the day when the Galatea
made its dramatic descent Akira had taken him and a school
friend up to the observatory to see the approaching planet
through the telescopes. Yori, who had not forgotten the flat
plateau where the first explorers were to land, wanted every
detail. Akira had brought him a sedimentary rock from the
surface that, for a week and who knows how much longer,
was always in his hands. With him when he went to sleep,

next to his plate at meals, or in his pocket at the rare moments when he was not studying every striation of its surface. It was—that ordinary rock—a summons to a different life and a springboard for imagining another world.

Most of all he wanted to hear about the hills and the caves. Each afternoon when Akira came to his school to take him to the playground, he dashed into his arms and cried, "Tell about the hills, Papa. Tell what it's like there."

"Okay," Akira would answer, "but first you must tell me what you did in school today."

And so he would, mainly about that week's biology project involving insects. Then they sat on a bench while Akira described in minute detail what it was like to walk on the solid, hot plateau, feeling the scorching heat from head to foot, or to climb the hill to the north and enter the cool, dark cave where everyone slept. He took pains to convey the physical sensations of breathing the cold air at night, smelling the burning brush fire, then retreating to a warm cave and lying in total darkness on an outcropping of rock until they fell asleep.

He described the twenty young people sitting outside in the evening on the hard brow of the hill listening to the crackle of the campfire, hearing about all they had discovered that day. In every imaginable way he exerted himself to convey the physical sensations of being in a terrestrial environment. No one can foresee how such seeds planted in the child's imagination on that playground bench might develop in later years, but thus it went between son and father for a week.

On one such afternoon Yori asked, "Papa, will we all live down there some day?"

His father replied, "Yes, you may live there. But not me. My real work is always up here with the stars."

"But I can come back to see you the way you came back to see me?"

One evening Akira took him to the observatory again and trained a telescope on the planet surface. They were able to locate the very spot where the colony was to be built and, on the edge of a hill, the actual campsite where after dark the explorers sat around the fire. At the end of the week Yori clung to his father's neck and pleaded, "Take me with you. I want to see the rocks and the fire and the caves."

As a result of Akira's descriptions that week, more people than young Yori began to wish to visit the planet. The second night of his stay on board was the regular meeting of the Elders. Word had spread that he was back, but since he had spent all his time so far with his family or with his assistants in the observatory, catching up on research projects, few of us had seen him, and his appearance in the Chamber was anticipated with great interest. It was not just that we had missed him personally, though we had. For all his formality, he could bring a room to life just by entering and leave a vacuum behind when he left. But there was more. At the most critical period we had known, his absence had deprived us of eyes and ears on the bridge. For three months we had been able to learn nothing about the work of the survey party on the planet except for rumors from personal messages that we suspected were being closely monitored. We had no idea what Command might be planning next, and in this cocoon of silence our own anxiety sometimes approached the paranoid.

As he entered, Kashimoto's appearance surprised us. It was two things, really. The first was how short he was! And the second was how much his dignity contributed to our pride in the Council. He was one of those people whose physical and moral stature are hard to distinguish. By an amusing trick of memory, you expect him to be as tall as everyone else and nearly as informal, and so his presence delivered a mild shock. The erect posture and the well-groomed dark hair, beginning to grey around the edges, added distinction as he greeted the assembled company with his customary slight bow from the waist.

Clive Dennet-Jones, sitting at the opposite end of the table from the door, returned Akira's nod and, since Claudio Rucai was indisposed, addressed him in his own presumed role as spokesman. "Welcome back, Kashimoto. Please sit down and tell us about the underworld."

In his droll way, Dennet-Jones reduced the serious mood with ironic deadpan. "Since you've been gone, we've had little of what is called news to chew on. You see, you've been missed, you and your pipeline to the gods who reign on high." He raised his eyes in mock reverence toward the bridge one deck above and forward from the Council Chamber.

Akira nodded again and took his seat. He replied with a summary of progress on the ground, taking care not to imply criticism of Command or to leave any impression that relations between the technocrats and the landing party might be less than harmonious. No doubt it was gratifying to find the interest among the Elders as warm as his reception on the bridge had been chilly, and yet it must have been sobering for a man whose instinct was candor to be bridled by secrets.

235

He and Claudio had had to conceal themselves for the sake of the prospective colony, though they knew that almost every member of the Council would have agreed with them. But agreement would have come slowly—after Command had established a colonial authority—and it was too late to intervene. So on this night he reported that progress had been good and that the authorities had a scheme for locating the base of operations on the desert floor and to cover it with a kind of dome. There was another plan for laying a water pipeline north to south with a service road alongside. Then he quickly changed the subject.

"One development will greatly please you," he continued. "You all know most of the twenty people in the landing party who live and work together much of the time. Their solidarity is much like ours in this Chamber. The evenings spent together are especially pleasant and productive."

Then, as he had for little Yori, he evoked the sensations of sitting on solid earth or being underground, speculating together on every dimension of a new world and a new life. Especially the effects of the brute and irregular materiality of things so unlike the rectilinear virtual environment of a ship fabricated top to bottom.

"It's like being reborn as responsive flesh after having lived as a disembodied mind in a bottle. Sitting on a rock, usually too hot or too cold, surprises you with a primitive sense of temperature and solidity. It's like feeling 'grounded' for the first time. Considered from our hills, this ship is an insubstantial toy. A dot of light in the star-studded sky produced by a mind that had lost the sense of substance and place centuries

236

ago. It would take a poet to do it justice, but I hope the day may come soon when you have the experience. It alters the whole context of thinking. You will feel viscerally that without the brute opacity of such a place as reference point, thinking is adrift in the idealism of abstract relations. Even the relation to the stars is different. Instead of the feeling of drifting among them in a machine where motion is just a number on a screen, where here or there, fast or slow, up or down are all the same, the terrestrial platform is an anchor, a resting place, a center. From there things assume the structure of a world."

He stopped his narrative long enough to test the interest of his audience then, finding that the enthusiasm was infectious, he recurred to the young people, the same number as the Council, exploring similar topics in a similar spirit. "They may not all be aware of it just yet, but they are the nucleus of new ways of living together and of a new polity. And remember," he added with a hint of pride, "nearly all of us down there are scientists."

Several faces around the table broke out in smiles of appreciative recognition. Elena Bart interrupted with a conspiratorial giggle, "Yes, but they're *your* kind of scientists. It's what you must have been doing for half a dozen years. Creating philosopher-scientists!"

To that Akira made no reply but, seeing that they were hungry to hear more, he continued, "One person—some of you know Kwan Shi Wa, our medical officer, Yu's niece, isn't she?" Yu nodded. "Shi Wa once talked about the familiar anxieties associated with living in a machine. 'From our perch on the side of this hill,' she said, 'you can understand why life never really matures in an incubator.'

237

"Like a good physiologist, she mentioned the separation of the egg from the incubating womb, the placenta, the thrust into a cold dry world, the eventual psychic partition from the mother—every stage of development moving outward by separation. All this led her to ask, 'Would an enclosed colony be any different from a womb or a spaceship? Don't we risk emerging stillborn into this new world?'

"But Shi Wa isn't the only one to make surprising observations. One night there was an exchange between the communications officer and one of the engineers, whose assignment is to figure out how power is to be generated. The engineer observed a bit snidely that their job was to find a way to repeat the Galatea as it had repeated Ulro. Then the communications person wondered, 'Shouldn't we—or Command—try first to find out what people really want?'

"'How?' the first man asked.

"'We could just ask them.'

"The engineer laughed and said, 'If you asked, you'd get twice as many answers as there were respondents. To know what people want you must find a way to discover what they really want when they think they want something else. I'm always finding out that what I really wanted is not what I thought I wanted at all.'"

Akira was clearly amused by his kids and proud of them. He continued, "There is also general agreement that we should consult the planet itself about how to live on it as we consult one another about how we should act together. Claudio's daughter Paola has her father's way of summing things up. At the end of this discussion, she pointed out that we were opposing two things: a prefabricated culture forced on us, and a romantic primitivism that would have to rediscover fire and reinvent the plow. I can tell you that those kids aren't rejecting anything at all. Just trying to order things well."

After Akira's anecdotes, the Elders talked into the early morning hours, speculating enthusiastically about a project that in our hearts we felt was doomed. We left the Chamber convinced that nothing had been won, that the momentum behind the technocracy was too great even to hear arguments against unbridled material progress. And yet, no doubt irrationally, we felt a surge of hope.

Akira had expected to see Claudio at the Council session, but he his health had declined in recent months and he rarely went out now. So the next morning Akira went to call on him and found him propped up in bed. So he pulled a chair close and inquired about his health.

"Oh, never mind all that. Thinking about health is just an excuse for not living. I'm as well as a sick man should be near the end. What I want to hear is what's really going on down there. After all our successes, is the plot still working? We're left out of the loop, you know. We hear nothing from Command when you're not here.

"Lately I've realized that the Disruption had an effect no one recognized at the time. It closed the book on two hundred and fifty years of dual responsibility for the mission. We knew it might eventually happen, yet it happened without anyone noticing. Once Ulro Ground Control fell silent, 'might' replaced 'right' as the only reality. Except for the schools, the Council has little reason to exist. Probably not by a conscious decision from the bridge. Reality just shifted and made us irrelevant. With you gone we are like one of those Ulro retirement clubs. We can discuss the good and the true or play golf. No difference. All irrelevant."

He looked at Akira as though seeing him differently. "I see now that your position between the two cultures extended nominal cooperation for a generation. Meanwhile, our conspiracy succeeded because it had failed before it began. You and I have not spoken of this point until now. Of course the Elders retain as much public confidence as ever, but in an economy of power, moral authority is a sentimental illusion. The worst thing is that there is nothing malicious about it. For Command it's all in the day's work. No one's to blame."

Claudio stopped and rested his chin on his chest. Anyone who didn't know him would have concluded that his day had indeed passed, that he had surrendered to the inevitable. But things are never what they seem.

Akira looked away, pondering his words, not rushing. Eventually he replied very slowly, "You astonish me. I see what you think, and I see that you're right. But I disagree on one point: Our plan was not futile. Success or failure is not the measure of a good thing well done. A good act is for eternity. It shows the way. If you could see those kids on the ground, if you could listen to them for one night, you'd believe that no matter what happens next, on the backside of the Milky Way the human spirit is alive and well. That alone is success for the mission and reason for hope."

Claudio: "And what reason is that?"

"Contingency and the capacity to decide!"

Tired as he was, Claudio flashed him a roguish grin. "Fortuity, perhaps. That's a bit further from necessity." Then he dropped the philological quibble. "Have you given up at last on the principle of sufficient reason? Don't all things have their causes? Isn't that what it means to know?"

"No," Akira answered emphatically. "You have always tried to teach me that the only thing certain is that all things are contingent, that and that we are creatures of contingency. So, '*hope springs eternal*.' We devote ourselves to the good and wait faithfully for its time to come . . . without any guarantee it ever will." He got up to leave. "But I'm tiring you. I can come back tomorrow if you wish."

"Wait! Tomorrow, if it comes, also comes without a guarantee." Claudio growled and gestured for him to sit down again. "Tell me first how things really stand."

Kashimoto drew his chair a bit closer as though he imagined that what he had to say now might be overheard. "The first thing to know is that what we have always known is true: Command has no idea in mind for the colony. All they know to do is to repeat the past. Without the slightest self-consciousness, they will turn that desert plateau into an industrial complex. There's nothing devious or malicious about their ambitions. It's as far as their imaginations reach. Since we have never raised a voice against them, where would they have heard alternatives? Here's an example:

"Since water is the most precious 'natural resource,' water will drive 'development.' Soon enough they will discover the expediency of building a pipeline across several hundreds of kilometers to deliver water to the parched and barren south.

There they can build factories and transportation facilities and open mines to support an expanding planetary economy. I'm only reading between the lines of our sparse communications, but if I'm right it's back to Ulro! To support the technological fantasy that they genuinely but blindly believe is good for everybody, they'll decide to build research laboratories for biology, chemistry, and physics. Not because they're interested in 'pure science,' if there is such a thing. No more than they're interested in Italian opera or Persian poetry. This 'grand vision' will turn the New Earth into a center of production. Don't ask 'For what?' For them consciousness doesn't reach that far. 'For what?' is not a question. It's an evasion, or it's idle noise."

Claudio gave a heavy sigh before replying. "I hear the disappointment in your voice. Do the others feel as you do?"

"I can say this only to you. Our recruits are superb." He went on to describe in some detail what their days and their work and their nights were like. Then added, "One by one it's dawning on them that we may not succeed. You can tell by what's absent from their exchanges. They are not reckless, and certain topics have largely dried up. Starship Command for example."

"So the trouble begins. And trouble is why you're here!"

"That's where the trouble is sure *to begin*, and it's *probably* why I'm here."

He considered for a moment and decided once more not to mention Paola. He only added wistfully, "If there were a way to build the colony around these young people, the whole mission would be richly rewarded and our lives would have been well spent. But once again knowledge fails us."

The two friends sat on in the aura of the unknowable, trying to keep hope alive, until Akira resumed at some distance from the topic. "I wonder if you know what your greatest gift to me was. Years ago you gave me something that has become my solace."

Claudio raised a hand to protest, but he continued, "No, my friend. These months in another world have taught me that I have already had several lifetimes. That planet will never be my home. My greatest comfort, meanwhile, is what you once said. You said, 'At the end, what we can know will not sustain us. Only faith in the impossible will be sufficient. Without it we become animals or go mad.'"

"That's philosophy for a dark night. Are we facing a night that dark?"

"Yes. If I didn't know you so well, I wouldn't tell you this much truth. Surrounded with these young people full of hope and dreams, I nevertheless fear that we are staring into the abyss. For all my stoicism about faith in contingency—or 'fortuity!'—I think we face an ignoble end of our kind . . . if we can properly be called a kind."

Claudio rallied his energy to the aid of his friend. "Then it is for me to console you. If what you say is true—and I understand that it may be—still I do not want to die. I would rather see where things will go. Even at the bitterest end, if it should come to that. In the deepest misery there is an undertow of joy even in being aware of the suffering."

Akira gazed silently at him as, for weariness, he lay back again. Presently he said, "I've been lying here looking out that window for some days now, asking who those stars would

243

shine for if it weren't for us. But for us, they would be denied half their being. To be all it can be, the universe needs us human specks of intermittent consciousness to reflect it and make it resonate. So has the Galatea failed if our little colonial venture fails? From the farthest boundary of life, I say that that view is parochial. Our adventure has turned a fantasy into an eternal possibility. If you ask, to what end? I reply, ends are one of the things knowing cannot know."

That was all. The conversation ended with those words. Claudio closed his eyes and Akira slipped quietly from the room.

The next day, the day before Akira was to leave, he was summoned again to the bridge, where Commander Rawls received him alone. "After all the failures in communication, your plans have been given due consideration. It has been decided to give the project a different emphasis." She pointed at his documents neatly stacked on the conference table between them. "The decision is that your path is premature. It's too soon to worry about a full life for families, social services, education, all that. If we start there, development will take years. Survival must be assured first. So, your orders are to redirect the energies of your people accordingly. Plans for a full-scale colony must wait."

That was all. Akira gave his polite bow, gathered up the plans and restored them to his portfolio. Then with another bow and no words, he left.

A SECOND TRY

I REPEAT: THE CONVERSATIONS among the Elders are not within easy reach of everyone, often not for me. But our collective hope is that there will always be a few for whom the inquiry into living well is preferable to a life of amusement. Meanwhile, anyone who doesn't care to work a bit may skip this chapter and get on with the curious external events of our history.

One evening, during the period when everyone waited for reports from the planet surface, the atmosphere in the Council Chamber was comfortable and congenial, though the night was destined to end in controversy so bitter that our traditions could barely contain it. Here's how it happened.

We gathered, free of pressing business, and passed some time in sociable conversation. Playing the eavesdropper as usual, I listened primarily to Gwendolyn Burgess and Joseph Kern, who were standing before the great window chatting about whether technology might be altering human nature. We had all been doing more of that since Hannah Jaeger had forced us to face inside and out . . . what exactly? . . . "nothing?"

Burgess wondered, "Do you think that as products of organic evolution we're still mutating? In acquiring the aptitude for mechanical efficiency, do our older organic capacities wither away? What might we be losing?"

Rather than respond to the question directly, Kern searched for the anxiety behind it. "Why are you wondering about that?"

"Well," she continued without a hint of her ubiquitous irony, "unless something fundamental changes, the colony will be another incubator like the starship. After so many generations, the habit of depending on machinery is inevitable. Even if we wanted to, we couldn't reverse it. I just wonder if it's a good thing. Does anybody know what we're becoming?"

"Does anyone ever know what we're becoming? Actual ends rarely correspond to intended ends. That's a truth so durable it's a cliché, though we don't often stop long enough to ask if there might be other ways to approach the matter."

Burgess was not interested just then in other ways of thinking. She stopped with the effects of putting machines between us and reality. Or merging with them. "When we build instruments so complex that we can't understand and control them, do they take over and control us as our own capacities become archaic? Wishing to be more powerful, do we become weaker?"

She paused in frustration at the difficulty of articulating her anxiety. "I don't know how to do anything, because the machinery of the ship has always done everything for me. I concentrate on my work very well, but I have lost the habit of attending to things that aren't immediately useful to me. Remember how the slaves of old had to know how to do things while the masters, freed from necessity, became decadent and weak? As the machines take over, do we increase our reach and shorten our grasp until we sink into amnesia? After nine generations on the ship, we may already be a different species. How would we even know?"

"Here' s one way: When you read old fiction or watch classic Ulro films, do you feel and respond as the characters do, or are they aliens behaving absurdly? It's a test. Have the stories lost their point? If not, you're still living in the open and must be more than an organism!"

Before she could answer Ava Sarosh ambled over to them. "You two are awfully deep in some subject. May one ask what?"

Kern answered, "Burgess is wondering if we're becoming technological mutants. When Hunenko talked about the animal and the human, he promised to compare us with the cyborg, but we never let him get that far."

The bewitching eyes brightened. Sarosh looked especially exotic and dark and Persian that night as, with an unhurried shrug, she turned around to those of us who were also listening and asked, "Why not do it now? We have the time, don't we?"

The idea spread across the room, and as it met with general acceptance, Hunenko was asked to restate his point.

He responded hesitantly and mainly to Burgess, since it was her request. "It's been a while. You'll have to prime the pump. What exactly have you been wondering?"

As we all settled into our places around the table, Burgess did prime the pump, sort of: "I've especially been thinking about our androids." She threw an ironic glance at Ang Yimou, down the table to her left.

"Ang will find my method shockingly unscientific. It's all introspection arising from a curious puzzle: We build machines that behave more and more like us, even exceeding us in speed and efficiency. They perform our tasks, but they don't imitate us because they can't. So we imitate them except that, the more *they* learn to do, the more *we* forget. There's an adage about becoming what we love. Like the rest of you, I have a 'droid for my household chores, and I love the thing. The quiet hum in the night as he goes around cleaning the floors, dusting the furniture, restoring things to proper places. He's even programed to harmonize with the background drone of the ship. I love his efficiency and the sexy male voice that reminds me of my appointments or my books on the way to class, or that it's time to eat."

With a mock-adolescent snicker she added, "And the authoritative voice suggesting bed every night." There were titters at the ersatz perversity, so she adjusted her tone. "I'm not being flippant, you know. There's an erotics of the machine, too. Look at the old movie images of a certain primeval male type with his gun and his automobile. Now Hunenko, this probably falls short of what you once intended to get at under the title cyborg, but I'm grateful for these few moments in the confessional. Now all I need is absolution."

Hunenko extended his hand toward her benignantly. "Go, my child, and sin no more with your sexy machines." Then he resumed the abandoned line of thought. "I think I'll leave the erotics of androids aside and just observe that the extension of our power over nature was dehumanizing long before the industrial revolution. It was embedded like a time bomb in the metaphor of fabrication, and in the modern era, we prided ourselves on being *essentially* fabricators. To know is to make and reality is a warehouse of objects made, whether by us or by a god, to our standard of correctness."

"Always follow the metaphors!" Kern sang out gaily. "God is in the metaphors."

"Unless God *is* the metaphor," said Bart.

"Yes. I forgot." Kern nodded condescendingly. "In the beginning was the metaphor."

Playing with the idea, Rückert added, "Jaeger would say the beginning was the nothing!"

Bart: "Isn't that what I just said?"

Hunenko ignored the play and pushed ahead, knowing that he would be only half-understood but also knowing that if ideas are ever to be understood, they must first be heard. "This metaphor is as old at least as the Greeks. It's about causes. The *efficient* cause is the weaver who weaves the carpet from available *materials*, according to a *form* in her mind, and aimed at some *final* use. That paradigm never went away, especially once we resigned our status as a little lower than the angels and limited ourselves to useful labor and production."

Bart intruded with another Bartism: "So the myth of the fall returns with a vengeance! Labor resulting from being out of tune with the Real isn't redeemed by labor-saving devices. We don't get over our stories by disowning or ignoring them. Worker, redeem thyself: Build a machine, then learn to live down to it!"

The remark may have been sensible, but Hunenko was visibly annoyed. "Later still," he continued, "we recycled the metaphor of efficiency and learned to think of ourselves as not very reliable cybernetic systems. So it goes, imagination surrendering to production until *actuality* trumps *possibility* everywhere."

"Blind Argus wins again!" said Hans Rückert.

Burgess was frustrated by the density of all that and tried gently to rein Oleksiy in. "Once upon a time you set out to compare us to cyborgs. What did you mean by that word?"

He smiled at her. "Not the 'bionics' of organ replacements or prosthetics. And not robots bioengineered to replicate human functions. Mechanical imitations and enhancements of the body are as old as the first tools. The aim always was to extend our control of things. These modifications are tediously similar to the craftsman using a hammer or using spoons and forks at breakfast. They may change our dispositions and alter our habits, but the interesting idea would be a cyborg anthropology, if the phrase makes any sense."

"It doesn't." Kern persisted. "Are we still talking about the animal-human link?"

He nodded. "That, and a bit more. It all has to do with our misunderstanding ourselves as objects among other objects. Briefly, we assume a continuity across three realms: inanimate matter, the living organism, and the thinking being. A synthesis would require us to bridge two abysses that conceptually we ignore.

"First, we assume that 'dead' matter is continuous with 'life,' except that we don't know what 'life' is and never have. Transplanting one human heart for another remains in the realm of the organic, but a mechanical heart can only *imitate* organic functions."

Then, noticing a tendency in the room to squirm, he added, "The mechanical heart works very well. The result is so satisfactory that we widen rather than narrow the gap between organic and inorganic, and move blithely on. But for now let's not rush. Let's keep track of our moves. The organism is served by the instrument, but is the process reciprocal? Reversible? Can the organism be indifferently subordinated to the mechanism?"

Kern, rushing ahead: "On to the second abyss to be crossed by a leap of faith?"

"That's the fusion of the human with the organic. A modern version of the perennial puzzle between body and mind that neurology bravely addresses, arguably widening rather than reducing it. Irreversibility again. Thinking reaches the organic—as every scientist illustrates by waking up and going to the lab—-and the organic reaches thinking in the pulsions of desire. But there's light on one side of the threshold of consciousness and darkness on the other.

"In our hypothetical model—which is so real it dominates our lives—we have for centuries been building machines that imitate the cognitive results of thinking. In our enthusiasm for efficiency, we don't bother to notice that we're ruining what is called thinking. As Lefèvre once taught us, we become what we love. But I'll rest my case on a simple Ulro example: Remember the self-driving cars of the twenty-first century? They combined 'off-the-shelf' algorithms from diverse sources. No one knew what exactly was embedded in systems designed for vastly different uses. Imagine a device programed to serve people in wheelchairs. Then it turns up, unbeknownst to anyone, in an automobile that takes aim at a man in the chair crossing the street. It reacts too swiftly for any mere human to intervene, presuming that anyone even knows how to intervene without convening a conference of experts. Our 'mistakes' multiply exponentially as we correct them arithmetically. In more general terms: Instruments aren't autonomous. They exist in a continuum from a vision of a task to its recognized achievement. A device, however refined, lacks the ability to establish the continuity. An infinite number of zeros and ones remains an indifferently useful or deadly imitation."

This set off all Ang Yimou's alarms. "All you're doing is denying science and imagining a divinely installed operating system called a soul!"

"No, I'm not, Ang. This is not about science. It's not quite about technology even. It's about our self-forgetting. Perhaps when we dumped the myth of the soul, we lost sight of things that shouldn't have been forgotten."

Rojas tried to avoid letting the topic become polemical, though to my ear he only made it more obscure. "Instead of returning to the topic of mythology and losing track of the cyborg idea again, let me ask this, Hunenko: When you imply *negatively* that humans aren't really things or objects, I wonder what *positive* idea you have in mind. Do you mean that while objects exist statically present before our eyes, only we can occupy a time that spans the continuum from idea to mission accomplished?"

Burgess, who had once used the satiric phrase "the time thing" to stigmatize his ideas, had a riposte on the tip of her tongue: "You've spent too many years watching the clock, Rojas. It has warped your temporal lobes! What does time have to do with it?"

By now you know how happy I am to descend from these clouds of speculation to the people in the room. As I studied the effect of Rojas' face on the others, it provoked comparison. He was smiling affectionately at Burgess, enjoying her playfulness as much as she enjoyed having a new person to satirize. A kind of secret sensitivity, even tenderness, emanated from him much as it does from Claudio Rucai's more weathered face and gruffer manner. Both men captivate the people they're with, transforming moods by force of character. And now that I reflect on it, Rojas also reminds me of Jaeger: The high, sober forehead radiating passionate thought, if somewhat less overtly. I have never seen that trait in anyone else, present or past. There is one difference, however: Jaeger's intelligence seems actively to *penetrate* any subject she addresses, whereas he quietly *inhabits* his subject and captivates by gentle warmth and candor.

Meanwhile, back in the philosophers' cloister he was trying for a clearer explanation. "Things—objects—are limited to a present dot on a timeline: things past, things present, things still to come. The heart of the matter is that we—the very ones we want to understand—aren't like that. We're like nothing else in nature. Our natural habitat is a present instant that opens a gap in chronology without losing a limitless future and a limitless past. It's the opening that matters and makes us unique. It's not a fact to be proved. It opens our eyes to things we have always known without knowing we knew. So, Hunenko is right. Until a machine can straddle the interval between past and future and use the demonstrative pronouns Hannah Jaeger once spoke of—which has nothing to do with 'information storage' —there will be no cyborg anthropology."

With a mischievous glance at Burgess he added, "Now, for your benefit, Gwendolyn, I'll be happy to fill in a few hundred missing steps when you *have the time*." And he chuckled.

"I'll call," she answered blithely.

Hunenko tacitly acknowledged the aptness of Rojas' remarks by responding very carefully. "I agree, Nacho. You put your finger on what's essential. Androids may 'replicate' organic functions but not 'function' organically. They may 'imitate' consciousness without ever 'being' conscious, as computers could win at chess centuries ago, but they never learned to 'play.' To play one must occupy your expansive 'now' with its real—not simulated—choices, where one can choose to play by being able to choose not to play."

In truth, we had been inching up on such an idea for a long time. Even I was beginning to realize it's how I had always functioned without knowing it.

"Then it would follow," Kern said, "that the threat of some monster symbiosis of organs and cybernetics is pure fantasy. If there's anything in what you say, then while a subject may certainly imagine a hybrid of objects, the hybrid will have no access to the human." He giggled. "They can't coincide because they don't *have time*! Animal-human-cyborg is like comparing ghosts, pomegranates, and light switches."

Wang, the mild-mannered chemist with the penchant for sleeping through these conversations, was certainly not sleeping, though he may have been in the dark. Suddenly, he sat up in his chair and leaned across the table in Hunenko's direction. "In this gobbledygook about time . . . " Then he thought for a moment and retreated a little. "I don't mean it's nonsense. How would I know? It's easier to learn chemistry than to get your idea. But still, you seem to imply that the ordinary objects are abstractions."

Rückert smiled at his older colleague and took his question up very respectfully. "What's before your eyes isn't abstract unless it's seen as a generic *object*. Let's consult Galileo (or Newton) again. Say, an apple falls from a tree and lands in a meadow. Neither of these worthies cares how old or how tall or how well-shaped the tree is. No relevant concern about whether the apple is red or green or sweet or sour, nor whether the meadow is desiccated and brown or carpeted with lavender blossoms." He grinned aside. "Did they have lavender in Tuscany or in Lincolnshire?"

Then leaning forward, he met Yu's gaze with an intensity that somehow made them fellow adventurers in an urgent quest. "What matters to Galileo is the velocity of the falling object: calculation. All things of a certain kind behave alike in like circumstances. It doesn't even matter to him who takes the measurements. He limits the field to objects for the sake of certainty in small pieces and drops the remainder.

"Not only does he abstract from nature, but the experiment assaults it. I know that sounds bizarre at first, but substitute the splitting of the atom and its eventual consequences or the efforts to replicate the forces in a star on a planet, then look again. There for all to see is the gap between measuring and experiencing the world. Between the physicist's tree and the tree in the lines of the poet or in the painter's still life."

At that the young and irascible Ang Yimou slapped the table with his fist and demanded angrily, "How can you say that Galileo leaves reality out when he gets to the truth, for the first time, that the natural world is inherently mathematical?"

I can tell you that Rückert and he aren't the best of friends. Not that Ang is a hothead. Only that he knows how much is at stake in this debate. Probably knows it better than I do.

Rückert replied, "I understand that mathematics for Galileo is the key that unlocks the regularities of nature. I'm only adding, if all reality is nature, then there's a price to pay. Does lightning really travel in a straight line? Are Clouds really spheres? Galileo knows what to leave out of his calculations. He hasn't forgotten that he, his family, his home, his hopes and fears also belong to nature. Even his immortal soul, if there is such a *thing*—which, if he hadn't reined his scientific imagination in, the Church might have consigned to outer darkness. The person 'Galileo' may be concerned with concrete things in the world, but *as researcher* he leaves these prescientific sources out of account." Rückert shifted his gaze away from Ang to make the point less confrontational. "I'm not attacking the regularities of nature, only using that principle as a sufficient guide to understanding."

Bart from the prompter's box again: "Trying to keep the tree of life and the tree of knowledge in the same garden!"

Rückert stared at her, uncomprehending.

Burgess saw his response and said, "Never mind, Hans. Elena's development was arrested in Eden. She got out the gate but not much farther."

Rückert smiled and returned to Ang. "When we leave out the full play of any phenomenon, all its roles in a world, there are losses. The prescientific imaginary is where our questions and our hypotheses begin. Forgetting the imaginary has often prejudiced research."

Even the mild-mannered Yu Wang had grown impatient with these digressions. He turned the conversation back to Hunenko and said, "Getting back to cyborgs, do you allow, Hunenko, that we have been radically transformed by cybernetic systems?"

Oleksiy grinned. "That depends on what 'radical' means. If it means 'in essence'—in what marks us as human—then I am *not* saying that. There, too, we are strangely willing to forget the performances that make us *who*—not *what*—we will have been when the process can be summed up afterward. From time to time we have mentioned the paradox of the self-absorbed being who refuses to face himself. Nothing is more strange about us than our penchant for accepting one or another theory about ourselves on blind faith, as though we didn't dare rely on our role among other people in the world. For the sake of science itself, we might start by asking about the mode of the researcher's being in the world of appearances. Instead, we go about our business justifying the world by our own standards and remain strangers to ourselves!"

For obvious reasons, Rückert had gotten antsy over this direction of the discussion. "Just a minute," he said, holding up a hand in an urgent appeal for time. "There's a danger lurking here somewhere if I can find it. Maybe we're going wrong in asking for a better definition of ourselves. Even when we speak of 'living in the open' or operating in a temporal field, we're in danger of missing what we're trying to think."

He stopped for a moment, looking for an idea he couldn't get in focus. "We don't want another theory about *what* a person *is* or another redefinition of *what* we *are* or another anthropology. Do that, and we'll always find that we're not there."

"It's Macavity!" Kern cried with an enthusiasm that astonished the room.

"What?" Dennet-Jones exclaimed.

"Macavity, T. S. Eliot's mystery cat! 'You may seek him in the basement, you may look up in the air— / But I tell you once and once again, Macavity's not there!'"

He continued with irrepressible enthusiasm, "I begin to see what you're reaching for. It's the mystery of Othello's jealousy in the play! Othello can't live without the impossible certainty of Desdemona's fidelity. He wants to grasp and control her as a dependable, unchanging object. It's the role of reason in the world. The paradox is that what mesmerizes him is her unknowability. If she's free to love him, she's necessarily free not to love him, and that drives him mad. He can't bear her deviation from a predictable object, so he stops her changing by making her a corpse."

"Which is to say," Rückert answered, "we are only as we perform. That means that the next time you come looking for me, armed with some fancy definition, I won't be there. But then, neither will you, and that changes everything!"

God bless Dennet-Jones! He raised both hands and erupted, "Enough! You people have lost your way. I see from

Kern that this conceptual derangement is infectious. I demand that we adjourn until next week. In the meantime, you, Rückert, and you, Hunenko, and you, Kern, and anyone else who thinks there's sense in this logorrhea is required to undergo a seven-day regimen of mental sedatives. Then we'll reconvene and, only if you're sufficiently recovered, will we try once more to get to the subject of cyborgs."

AKIRA'S SECOND RETURN

LATE ONE AFTERNOON A shuttle arrived in the bay at the rear of the starship. A low-level officer from the bridge was waiting for Kashimoto, who had been summoned a second time to the ship on short notice. On his prior return, no one had been waiting at the quay, so here was something vaguely ominous. Still more ominous when he was immediately, word-lessly, ushered to the bridge for consultations. It's a long way from the bottom to the top of the ship and from the back to the front, a passage too long for comfortable silence between two strangers. The designated elevator car quickly moved Akira and his escort horizontally then vertically all the way forward, bypassing the public spaces.

When he arrived, Talib Nasser met him at the door and led him to the conference room. Two things made him expect the worst. First the excuse that Commander Rawls was too busy for a meeting billed "urgent." Second, Nasser's unusual cordiality. Though it would not cross Kashimoto's mind how intimidating his presence in a room can be, we know that Nasser is intimidated by people more accomplished than himself, and yet for this occasion he put on what charm he could muster. He smiled and smiled, inquired about the comfort of the explorers, about their workload, how they managed the extremities of the climate, even remarked appreciatively on Kashimoto's sacrifice in leaving his family and his research to manage the exploration. Then, all politeness, he invited him to sit at the table and even pulled out a chair for him.

The man on whom little was lost, who was as close an observer of human behavior as of the stars, had arrived with antennae fully deployed. More than a match for the transparency of Nasser's smooth veneer and pretense of concern over matters regularly reported to Command. The reception did little to reduce whatever anxiety may have been roused by the sudden order to return. Even the servility of Nasser's pulling out Kashimoto's chair then taking the seat at the head of the table was an assertion of power. But any careful observer would easily have discovered the truth of a face so false.

Akira saw and heard resentment and aggression behind the mask as Nasser announced in the most collegial tones that they would thereafter be working together. He had been assigned liaison for ground operations and, since events had reached the point where important decisions had to be made, consultations would be more frequent than in the past. Out of consideration for Akira's heavy duties, the First Mate, when he could be spared from the ship, would share the trouble of commuting back and forth. Then, with another smile, "It will mitigate the failures of communication that have occurred in the past."

In the confidence that he had skillfully managed the more delicate part of this diplomatic mission, he became businesslike. "I have the revised plan for the first phase of development of P2314. I have just posted your copy to your communications address. My feeling is that it would serve our collective understanding if you shared the text with your people when you return. We want everyone on the same page."

The text flashed on the wall screen behind him and, without turning around, he directed Akira's attention with a thumb over his shoulder. Akira's eye ran down the list of bullet items as Nasser began reading them to him like a pedagogue.

✓ Begin immediate survey of the plateau as an industrial base for all necessary support facilities:

1. permanent landing area for regular shipments of materials and workers;
2. supply depot and storage warehouse;
3. barracks for workers with full life support facilities;
4. building site for heavy machinery assembly and maintenance such as drilling, earth-moving, ground transportation;
5. facilities for moving personnel and materials around the site.

✓ Send technicians north to locate the best long-term water sources.

✓ Survey for a water supply sufficient to the industrial base either by drilling the plateau and/or constructing a pipeline from the hills to the north.

✓ Survey the right-of-way for a pipeline from the underground aquifers in the northern plateau to the base, approximate distance 325 km.

✓ Develop a plan for a road to serve the building and maintenance of said pipeline.

✓ Prepare for the steadily increasing flow of materials and labor from the ship as these plans develop.

It was a crucial moment, an epochal parting of ways, and each man had to conceal his affect as item followed item, exultation in one, apprehension in the other. I would like to have been there to see it: the weak in the position of the strong, concerned with his image and self-respect, and the strong in the position of the weak, indifferent to himself and burdened by futurity. The sheer brutality of that document and the contentious spirit in the room might have been prelude to a new Promethean struggle for the human soul.

When Nasser had finished reading the list as to a schoolchild, Akira asked a series of questions intended to help him estimate the political situation.

"May I ask why both local and distant water sources?"

Nasser, still in the full flush of success, "Our judgment is that the terrain in the mountainous north is too rugged for the permanent colony or for easy cultivation."

"What about the disregard for the planet itself? The destruction of the terrain?"

Nasser stared at him as though wondering how a distinguished scientist could be so dim. "It's our planet. We discovered it. I guess we can do what we like with it."

He stared in silence at Nasser long enough to make him uncomfortable, then said, "If we construct a north-south industrial corridor in each direction from the plateau, aren't we predetermining that the human environment will be a chaotic appendage to production? These things don't pass away. They linger indefinitely. It's almost never practical to move them or clean them up. Eventually they become wastelands, and the people who live there, generation after generation, suffer for it in a thousand ways. Once that paradigm is a reality, won't 2314 become a planetary industrial zone like the old mining camps on Ulro? What are your assessments of the quality of life there for years to come?"

Nasser was startled by such silly questions in the wake of his victory over the adversary, and he tried to brush them aside. "I don't know about the mining camps. But you don't have to worry about these things. We take good care of our people. This is the twenty-third century and it's not Ulro. That was a different world."

The fact that Nasser wasn't thinking about the issue at all led Akira to conclude that *he* wasn't the real enemy. He was just responding, exultantly, with the first cliché that came to mind, refusing to think. The interview was a chore he intended to get through as quickly as possible and get on with the important work of his day.

Akira pushed a little harder to see if the First Mate was willing to take Rawls' cause as his own. "Given your admirable concern for the workers' quality of life, what will that quality be from the moment you ferry several hundred down to build your road and pipeline?"

These questions from the man whom he had just so skillfully "set down" began to irritate him. "I don't see what you mean. They will have plenty of food, shelter, health care, protection from the elements. And no one will be forced to work against his will. Don't forget how happy they will be to get off this ship for a while. We have more volunteers than we can use."

"I'm sure you are sincere in saying that every care will be taken for the workers' welfare. I'm only worried about what your *care* means. Aren't you proposing to use the workers as raw material for the project just as you're using the planet—thoughtlessly used and used up in the service of an abstract idea of planetary development?" He made it personal deliberately, to test Nasser's commitment.

In equal degrees the Mate began to show impatience and indignation. His hands shook slightly as he fumbled with the one piece of paper on the table.

Is there a more pathetic figure than a man who represents only power facing the authority of a clear mind at work? Akira pressed a bit further, searching for, if not intelligence, then a conscience. "Your life, Talib—and those workers' lives—don't happen in the future. Life is always and only now. The quality of their lives will reside in the barracks you're proposing to build, in living in a desert that you have never set foot on, in enduring separation from their families. They will live indefinitely without access to any of the things that ennoble the human spirit, not to mention destroying the habitat that they and their descendants will be doomed to live with when it has been spoiled. How much has any of this entered into the new plan for an industrial zone?"

With each question, Nasser grew visibly more agitated. He leaned forward aggressively with both arms on the table and answered in an ambiguous voice pitched between anger and fear. "Progress takes development. You use that word as if it were an obscenity!"

Akira responded all the more quietly, "But development *for what*, Talib? What is the human face of your development?"

That seemed to complete a chiasmus between the weak and the strong: Kashimoto, defeated, spoke with the strength of prophecy, while Nasser, empowered, dropped into fuming resentment.

"You people don't get it!" he cried. "Why do you think we're doing all this? Why is there even a mission? For the survival and welfare of the species!"

By this time it was clear that Nasser was moved less by the weakness of his position than by fear of looking bad before the Commander, and by indignation at having his authority challenged. Even a little, perhaps, by fear of facing himself and the truths that were being thrust upon him.

"Didn't that help destroy Ulro?" Kashimoto continued in a voice that was almost compassionate. "Instead of engaging in a day-by-day dialogue with the planet and the whole human reality, someone is trying to engineer—or force—a future as a chain of causes and effects. Then, when the process doesn't work as intended, the fact will be labeled 'unexpected consequences' and dismissed. All I'm asking is that you—you as a responsible individual—take that result seriously in advance and expect the unexpected."

Akira sat back in his chair, perfectly at ease. He was not just wasting time, futilely trying to get a foolish man to think. There were things he needed to know. He needed a reliable view of the First Mate himself. Did he lack the capacity to grasp the subject or did he refuse out of ambition or intimidation or laziness? Was he merely following orders, or had he signed on to the technological ideal? To put it crudely, how intelligent was Nasser? As for Command in general, he needed to know whether the new plan was ideological and calculated or driven by passion and resentment. Were they united or were they divisible? And if the issues were reduced to imminent warfare, how far were they prepared to go in opposing the explorers and the Elders? And—largest question of all—when, how far, and at what cost should resolute opposition be encouraged?

When Nasser could brook the pressure no longer, he picked up the piece of paper containing the development plan and slapped it facedown on the table. Almost clenching his teeth to control himself and save face, he got up, gently replaced his chair at the table, and stood leaning with both hands on the back of the chair. Then shaking his finger almost in Akira's face, he burst out, "The trouble with you people is that you have no sense of practicality. Up here"—he meant on the bridge—"we are on the line. We have to produce results, not sit around dreaming about some fantasy 'good life.' You have your orders!" Resuming control, he walked to the door and politely held it for Kashimoto.

Akira did not move. Without so much as turning to face the man behind him, he replied in a quiet voice, "Orders or no orders, Talib, you are wrong. You are missing your only chance for a new earth." He got slowly to his feet, faced the adversary with an elegant smile, and left the room.

CYBERNETICS AND BETRAYAL

MEANWHILE, SOMETHING HAPPENED that had not happened in the history of the mission: The Council missed its next meeting. Not by plan. Nobody showed up! Well, I did. Which is how I know.

I stood around for a while, gazing into the void beyond the window, contemplating the void within, as, slowly, it began to dawn on me what had happened. In the absence of news, a kind of universal discouragement had spread among us and for one reason: Kashimoto was known to be on the ship, but none of us had seen him! That could only happen by design. Having avoided us, he would not come to the Council Chamber. That we knew. Nor would there be any message. Standing there in solitude, weighing our situation, I began to surmise why. Reliably, as I was to learn from Claudio later.

Along with everything else that happened on his second summons to the ship, Mate Nasser's repeated reference to "you people" raised an alarm in Akira that any contact with us at that juncture might compromise the landing party. But here, too, lay unintended consequences: confirmation from the best possible source that the Council was now obsolete.

Thus, a full two weeks after our last meeting, Dennet-Jones convened the next session without mention of the hiatus in the proceedings. He simply braved it with the stiff upper lip and got as far as saying, "I trust we have all recuperated from the delirium of our last meeting." Then Ava Sarosh interrupted.

She, too, avoided the proverbial elephant in the room. "Meanwhile," she said, "I have used the time to review some of the high points of our deliberations over the six years of our return journey to Planet 2314. During that period the Council has met some three hundred times, but along the way a small number of the colloquies have been converging in my mind. Tonight, I'd like briefly to recall three conversations and suggest that they may signal new directions in our thinking and hence in reality as it's available to us. If I'm not mistaken, a new historical understanding is emerging from the very contention in the starship project that makes this moment so dark."

She didn't have to tell us that her reflections had been salutary. Her face told that. It was lit by some spirit alien to the rest of us at that moment. As though she had been to the mountain and conversed with the muses or the olden-time prophets. Inspiration incarnate brought us under her spell even before she began saying what she had come to say.

"First, I want to think back six years to our review of the academy's curricula. You may remember Oleksiy Hunenko's warning at the outset against the liberal arts as anthropo-centric, as though we already knew ourselves and possessed ourselves as a well-defined species. His warning included the tempting assumption that the task of the academy was to add something *to* our students rather than summoning them *into* unimaginable ways of being that lie beyond all calculation.

"If we had begun from the notion that we knew how being human worked and needed only to add information and skills

to the blank tablets of the young, we would have lost the way
before we began. In fact we didn't take that wrong turn into
biology or the behavioral sciences. We began with grammar.
With the first reflections on language that embed us in the
words and legends that make us historical, thinking beings."

During this speech Hunenko had been looking at the
table in a dejected manner, but he suddenly responded in a
bright voice, "Thanks for the attribution, Ava, but you are
implying a far more radical understanding than I had at the
time. I was probably thinking only of language as the distinguishing function of rational animals, but you're suggesting
that it constitutes the very substance of our being. 'In the
beginning was the word'—the primal legends!"

She answered with a smile that I, at least, thought emanated
from some beatific inner radiance. "The second stop on my
little historical tour is Aurélie's memorable Klein bottle. It
was surprising at the time, but its full force was not felt in one
hearing. I'll just mention a couple of subsequent reflections.

"Though we're always saturated by some disposition or
mood, Aurélie argued that we don't have to be victimized by
an alleged competition between affects and rationality. Even
as music expands our feeling-responses to the world, it gives
form to the steams of changing mood. You'll remember that
as her 'economy of affects.' Another dimension of the Klein
bottle is the suspicion it throws on the *concept* of ourselves as
self-enclosed natural objects, distinct from the world outside.
The analogy of an indistinguishable inside-outside inspires
the idea that we don't just respond in wonder and awe, but
that we are co-constituted by the interaction.

Now let me emphasize just one more implication of that discussion. It extends far beyond sensation or 'aesthetics.' The idea undermines our myth that we are the certifying agents whose subjective conviction of truth provides the standard of all judgment. That implication was also developed long ago in Rückert's retelling of the Argus myth."

"Now it's my turn to register a disclaimer," Rückert protested, in a tone that showed brightening of the dark mood in the room. "I follow what you're saying, but at the time I didn't see that far either. I had always thought of an audience as a collection of freestanding subjects, being shaped in character by the musical performance. You're adding a more subtle—and difficult—idea that's not easy to assimilate."

"That," intervened Dennet-Jones, "is because you don't know a metaphor when you meet one. Aurélie knew that her wrong-side-out bottle was only a metaphor."

Having no time to lose trying to uproot Clive's wayward resistance, Sarosh passed on to her final remark. "The Klein bottle prepared the way for Rückert's provocative idea of the 'city without walls.' But I'm going to leave it to him to fill in the blanks."

Rückert positively leapt at the opportunity. "Your reflections have outrun me, but I see where you're headed. On your account, the polity, like human being, is not an objective thing. It's a place. A free, open place where people dwell and think and act together. The collective task of citizens, being temporal beings, is to figure out how they will do what has to be done next. Dissonances and tensions will always pop up to block their way, but they reject the idea of a sovereign power, however composed, because it would reinstitute the stasis of a 'state' and its inherent exclusion of 'the other.' For the citizens to come, the authority of 'seeing how' would not collapse into the power to command obedience. Like Aurelie's music, our city would pass through all manner of dissonances along its endless way, but never achieve a final harmonic *state*. In a symphony the final cadence may appear to be harmony achieved at last. But in fact it's the whole path traversed in the playing that lingers still in the subsequent stillness. The polity, like the music and its audience, finds its being in the passage."

"Thank you, Hans, that's exactly what the point I was reaching for."

"But," Nacho Rojas suddenly intervened. "Here's 'the time thing again'! Your chronological summary of highlights in our last six years leads us *forward* to Hannah Jaeger's climax of this line of thought 170 odd years ago."

"Whatever do you mean?" That was Dennet-Jones crying out again against offenses to common sense.

Rojas, hearing no inquiry in Dennet-Jones' question, didn't bother to reply. Hannah Jaeger summed up all we have said since about education, music, the city, and much more, long before there was any prospect of a habitable planet. Where our recent deliberations have often yielded to utility, she wasn't constrained by particular aims in view. She was challenged by human possibilities on the broadest scale, and she offered—and still offers—a glimpse of what happens when we invoke the old names and repeat the old stories. When we're set in the neighborhood of all reality, what's concealed as well as what's revealed, we are revealed to ourselves as responsive to the summons issued from those sources. Unless we retreat in terror, we are lit up in wonder by what they reveal about ourselves. The receptiveness is our freedom to see and hear in obedience to what comes from beyond us."

Elena Bart felt compelled to add her imprimatur to these obscure pronouncements. "Here's another of the analogies that Clive dearly loves. In addition to our being composed of words and narratives, we respond to—and are compounded of—all kinds of phenomena that we can't experience directly. When, for example, dark matter makes a hole in the field of our perceptions, what gives itself to us is no less real than visible things. And even better example is the 'black hole' composed by the collapse in on itself of a dying star. Its mass condenses at the center into a density so great and a gravity so strong that it swallows everything in its neighborhood, even light. Our fascination, even our awe before such wonders reveals an affective bond—a love—at the heart of our pursuit of knowledge of what's beyond our experience. If we have been slow to see these implications in our long deliberations, that's because it's all too simple for people who are accustomed to complex things like starships and the square root of -1. The summons from beyond the object-world we take as 'real,' is so close to the bone of experience that even now we can hardly bring the idea into focus."

Thus said the Bart. But I, Kahn, was busy meanwhile with a quite different impression of something down the table that was about to split this session of the Council in two.

It took no skill to see that Ang Yimou was on edge at the far limit of his self-control. What he saw as a brazen effort to restore mystery to things that had long been demystified by research provoked an eruption and a torrent of protest.

"You people . . . "—the epithet set off a Nasser-alarm in my head—"you want to bury the achievements of rational explanation and return us to the caverns of the mystery religions! I see that you want to 'take the appearances whole,' but science is more rigorous. It takes things as they really are, not as they appear to be. It explains things by their building blocks—from particles to cells to organs, from subatomic physics to chemistry to biology."

I have to interrupt to note that, however startling the outburst, it was better than dropping back into the melancholy of our last two weeks. The re-emergence of the ordinary fireworks of philosophical discussion was just a return to the comfortable bafflement of our normal way of life.

"Not at all," Rückert replied to Ang's outburst about reason and mystery. "We want to maintain rational discipline without letting the demand for certainty make us strangers to ourselves. If we disagree with you, it's only about how exactly science relates—even depends on—broader understanding of essential things. Questions of character, ethics, and politics don't yield total certainty. The doctrine of evolution was inspired by analogy with economic survival of the fittest, but it's a measure of Darwin's greatness that he neither abandoned his profound intuition nor let his economic metaphor lead him into specious conclusions.

"But we are not always so fortunate. Biology—and not only biology—has often been influenced by social ideals like adjusting organisms to their environment or preserving the purity of gene pools. Not to mention the hygienic ideals of the death camps."

"Those weren't science," Ang replied heatedly. "They were ideology!"

"Exactly!" Rückert responded more gently. "On what basis could a science decide which genetic strains should survive and which mutations should die out? Or what diseases should be cured so that everyone can be divinely normal? Or that the well-adapted has a higher value than the misfit genius? I think we would agree that these are *philosophical*, not scientific, decisions. Trouble comes in not distinguishing."

Bart tried to tie this skirmish back to Ava Sarosh's remarks. "Now *that's* interesting!" she began, as though nothing interesting had been said lately. "You're saying, Ang, that reason projects so much of reality as can be reduced to objects, that it manipulates them until they satisfy the norm of subjective of certainty. The rest of reality is jettisoned. In short, to science reality is what the gods were to the ancients: a trusted founding myth. Even an idol."

Ang fired back at Bart, "Myth is irrelevant! All this stuff is passé. Long ago biology progressed from trying to engineer organisms to describing them as information systems. Biology became cybernetics. We understand now that all things are flows of information."

"Especially starships!" said Rojas.

Rückert's smile at the remark must have struck Ang as condescending. "If we belong to the flows, who interprets the messages?"

"It isn't about interpretation!"

"But you're leaving one element out."

"What element would that be?" he sneered.

"The one that can read the information! The one who knows what, if anything, the whole system means. Somebody must be outside the system to design it and interpret it."

Rojas' intervention was not intended to raise the heat. He, if anyone present, must have been aware of how our background anxieties about the crisis of the landing party and the fate of the mission had everybody on edge and subject to intemperate remarks. At least he proceeded in his best analyst's mode to calm Ang's rising passion without compromising the issue, by means of an analogy from his own science, neurology.

Looking at Rückert rather than Ang, he said, "Here's an analogy. A camera. It can register frequencies of light and make images of visible objects. But the camera can't choose which image is worth preserving, and it can't judge the image once it's made. For both of those we need more than sensory organs and nervous systems. It's a leap of faith to think that anyone will ever be able to make a camera or a brain recognize and interpret itself. As though if you hooked me up to enough electrodes, my brain could watch itself watching itself at work in the image of a brain on the screen. An infinite series of mirrors reflecting each other could not understand what they were reflecting. They will never be able to understand what they register! When we apply the rule of empirical cause and effect, the effects must be, if not contained in their causes, then reciprocal with the causes. But where is the one neuron—or the hundred thousand neurons—that can see themselves seeing? That requires a leap more mysterious than the Holy Trinity."

In a tone of cool deliberation, Hunenko also tried to redirect the exchange. "Let's get back to cybernetics."

Ang welcomed that direction as though someone was hearing him at last, but Ava Sarosh wanted a definition. "First, I need to be told exactly what cybernetics is."

Hunenko answered. "We're talking about a universal communications framework with the human as a participating information device. The incentive is that if we can encompass everything in a single system, then we can explain reality."

For some reason Sarosh found that amusing. "Then where do we start?"

"We start with man as the animal that speaks. No 'soul,' since soul—number one—isn't a discoverable object, and—number two—doesn't fit the explanation we're looking for. So no soul. But information devices are real. We speak, and what we speak is information. We're information devices."

Ang was attentive, and his annoyance even seemed to abate a little.

"Then according to cybernetics, what is language?" Sarosh asked.

"A collection of signs for things available in the world."

"Well, thank you, Oleksiy," Kern interjected. "Since language is one of the most obscure concepts in the history of thought, it's nice to have that cleared up at last. In one simple sentence, no less!"

"Oh, it's about to get even simpler," Hunenko said, grinning only slightly. "Now you must imagine that language is essentially nothing but a sign system for communication. Never mind what your immediate experience misleads you to believe—as in conversation or philology or poetry. You are to accept the ideal of language as a system of unambiguous signs."

"Pure language!" Kern exulted. "The infamous 'weakness of language' overcome at last! Praise be to the gods of communication!"

"Versus *logos* itself!" said Bart.

This was not at all where Ang imagined the topic was headed, and he was deeply offended by the irony. "You do know that this view has been criticized as often by scientists as by philosophers?"

"I do know that." Hunenko conceded the point generously. "But it never slowed the corrosive spread of cybernetics across Ulro culture. So the human, already incarcerated in 'objectness,' has been updated to a feedback device in cyberspace. We hear it still when someone speaks of a 'failure of communication.' And note: The failure isn't mine or yours, as when I don't care enough about things to pay attention to them and name them well, nor yours for not bothering to listen to what the words say. In the switchboard of the information system, it's all formal. That has to be true by inner conviction, and accepted dogma demands it."

In all this Gwendolyn Burgess had finally gotten a response to her old question about human mutations. "So we *do* get progressively more inattentive until we lose the habit and even the capacity to listen or to speak. Then we turn that into a medical condition and go on and on repeating what 'they say.'"

Bart enjoyed the irony and kept it going by directing a mock-critique at Hunenko. "You over-subtle philosophers probably think we don't actually speak a language at all. Where there is nothing but bodies and cybernetics, even you must be able to appreciate the efficiency of all those hollow echoes of dead language passing back and forth across our switchboards."

"Another anthropology," Rückert added sadly. "The human cut to fit another different conceptual category. Meanwhile, language, pregnant with intimations of past and future, vanishes into babble, where nothing gets revealed but the nullity of language itself. Now all that is heard is 'communiqués' of fact, *showing* nothing."

At this point Ang banged both fists on the table so hard it seemed to shake the room. He leapt from his chair with a violence that sent it crashing to the floor behind him. In a near-hysterical voice he cried, "If this Council is hell-bent on sinking back into the muck of primeval superstition, then I'm through with it. I have too much work improving the human condition to waste my time on nonsense."

He stormed from the room.

We were stunned. No one said a word for a full two minutes. The Ang explosion set my own nerves ajangle. What I think I saw in that moment was how deep the rift had always been between technological and historical culture. It seemed as decisive for the future as if the starship had lost power and was left to drift until it died.

Eventually, as though nothing whatever had happened, Dennet-Jones moved the paralytic upper lip just enough to ask in a perfectly controlled voice, "So who is the cyborg?"

With a fair imitation of Clive's unruffled manner, Rückert answered, "Either the last man between the open and animal oblivion or the new man who isn't human but will never know it."

I was shocked again to see that the others were reading Ang's eulogy in this remark about the cyborg and the last man. I feared—I fear still—that the event may have also been the eulogy for the Council of Elders.

But, unwilling to be stopped even by calamity, Hunenko persisted. "Maybe not knowing will set the last man on the Ulro road to paradise: no more politics or art. No more puzzlement and discovery. No more love or friendship. The last to suffer the loss before sinking—if it's possible—into zombie or cyborg."

Bart added in a nostalgic tone, "Once we looked to the gods for security."

"But that was a cop-out too, wasn't it?" Rückert smiled broadly. "An insurance policy against the risk while we waited for a god to fix things."

Ignoring him, she added, "Unless the cure is the gift at the outer limit of the disease."

END OF A CONSPIRACY

AKIRA SPENT HIS LAST hours on board with Claudio. When they had met last, his friend remained a vigorous man in his early seventies, but a few months later, disease had aged him. Since he refused narcosis, he was confined either to the bed in one corner of his room or to a chair before the window that was more like a porthole. Small quarters for so distinguished a man, but favoritism has no place on the starship. Most of the apartments on residential decks are interior to the ship and have no exposure to the outside, but the contemplative Claudio can sit day after day and night after night gazing out into space, keeping company with "the mystery of things."

Though relatively comfortable, his, like all our cubicles, is constructed of lifeless industrial materials that resist all efforts to soften and humanize the space. It's a bit like entering one of those airlocks the technicians use for exterior repairs to the ship. You feel neither quite inside nor quite outside, but in some impossible place between finite and infinite. In his last days Claudio seems more than ever a creature of that "between." One thing, however, gives the apartment a unique ambience. It is a modest collection of treasured books along one wall, the ones we never stop rereading because they are the native food of the soul. His have been handsomely printed and bound by craftsmen who have revived these archaic skills in space.

Here Akira arrived to find his friend much weakened though possessed still of the old clarity of mind and in good spirits. But he hadn't come alone. He had brought something with him into that tranquil space that made Claudio visibly recoil as he entered. It was as though the room was hollowed out by a cloud of foreboding.

Claudio with his chair tilted back and his feet elevated in front of him took it all in. Then spoke of other things. "I want to hear about all that you and your protégés have been doing down there on your planet." And in a quieter voice, "But first, old friend, tell me about Paola." As he waited for the reply, his eyes fixed expectantly on Akira's face.

Except for two moments, once when he had recommended her for recruiting the young and later when he had warned him against including her in the landing party—except for those, he had not spoken of her in—what had it been by now—nearly a decade? Akira recognized it as the measure of his certainty that the end was near.

"She thrives," he answered. "She has found an appropriate garden spot shielded from the harsh sun and begun a farsighted project of enriching the indigenous plants with our stock. Except for the current discord with Command, she's in high spirits, happy, I believe. She's confident already that given time and patience a successful agriculture can be developed. It will take a long time, of course."

Not wishing to interrupt this paean to the person he loved most, Claudio smiled and waited for more if there was more.

"If somehow the Galatea experiment were even yet to succeed," Kashimoto continued, "no one would have been more responsible for the future of humanity than your Paola. But I must include Bahram Sarosh. They are in love, and as much in love with their new earth as with each other. You can be as proud of him as you are of your daughter."

There may have been a trace of tears in Claudio's soft voice as he replied simply, "Thank you."

In the quiet moments that followed, whatever sinister spirit their words had held at bay weighed on them. Eventually Claudio marshaled his energies and said, "Now tell me how things stand."

Akira recounted the meeting with Nasser then put the whole situation into one question: "What I need to know is this: Have we reached the end? If conditions really are reduced to either/or, as I suspect—either their ideal or ours—do we, at the extreme, submit and go underground for another three hundred or a thousand years, keeping faith with unlikely contingencies? Or do we keep the faith now at any cost?"

"At what cost? What stage has your work reached?"

"So far we have laid solid foundations for a rich life on the planet. The exploration and planning phases are essentially complete. With material and workers Bahram's first buildings could be completed quickly, and we would be ready for a first wave of colonists. It wouldn't be an easy life, but it would be a good life from the start. What's now clear is that that won't happen. Command never trusted us, and now they've decided to ignore our work and go their own way."

"Why have they changed course?"

283

"Their explanation for everything is 'failure of communications'! Which explains nothing, of course. We have sent regular
and detailed reports and fulfilled all their instructions. But they
read without imagination and see only 'information' on the
digital screens. So our prompts are taken for reality, and they
develop no intelligent questions. They hear essentially nothing
and learn still less. Now they have discovered that they don't
know what's really happening, so they're walking into our flower
bed with jackboots. They will try to use our work for their own
ends, though without us to interpret, they won't get far."

"You might resist?"

"We *could* resist. We could refuse bluntly to cooperate and
destroy our records." Akira paused as though reconsidering the
consequences. "No need for that. They wouldn't understand
anyway. Imagine some amateur striding confidently into
Paola's research garden or an engineer trying to make sense
of Bahram's detailed designs for a self-sustaining communal
life. Their failures will have been our fault, of course! To them
our work would look—does look—like no progress at all."

Claudio understood and foresaw the consequences. "What
would they do with you? With the twenty, I mean. What
would they do with our youngsters?"

When Akira hesitated to answer because the question
included Paola, Claudio continued working out the consequences for himself. "*You* would never get back. And the
others wouldn't be safe either." Each implication felt like
another drumbeat of fate. He raised himself in his chair to
something like an upright position before adding, "Rawls is
too shrewd to bring a brilliant bunch of hardened radicals

back here to stir up trouble in her pacific space village. So what will you do?"

"Stand by Paola and the others, come what may. What else can one do?"

"Then you'll go back?"

"I'll go back. Within the hour."

"Then what?"

"Then we, the twenty, have a choice to make together— the twenty and you! And you first. You have to make it today, now."

It was hardly the kind of demand one makes of a dying man, and yet it was why Akira had come. He persisted. "There are three alternatives. Out of the expediency of self-interest, we might do an about-face and actively support the industrial ambitions of Command. That would be in the knowledge that they will destroy for a very long time to come the only remaining chance for anything more than animal survival."

Claudio shook his head slowly, declining any course that would abet shortsighted practicality and technological supremacy. But there was more in it. In a single gesture he captured the spirit of lamentation for the loss of all worthy things and ended with a blank stare into pure negation.

"Or," Akira picked up the alternatives again, "we might cease our obstructive ways and give up. Command would avoid trouble at any reasonable cost." He went on to work it out. If they gave up, it would result in the explorers being split up. Some would return to the ship and be replaced by more compliant people, while others would be allowed to remain on the ground under "new management."

The alternatives came as relentlessly as a funeral march, and. Claudio's head shook more and more slowly. "No," he replied to the possibility of giving up. "Rawls would be too shrewd even for that. The mild resistance of the Elders was one thing. The dissatisfaction of a hardened and humiliated generation is another thing. Rawls would see that she was letting mutineers on board. They would talk, those kids who are kids only to us, and the most intelligent would talk persuasively. Some might do more than talk." He gave a despairing sigh. "What's your third alternative?"

"We could go on passively resisting 'progress'—essentially daring Command to do their worst." Somehow he found humor in the idea. "Maybe their first building project would be a prison for reactionary—or revolutionary—scientists. We would not get our day in court—even if there were a court. They know better than to let us become paradigms of political virtue, like Socrates or the saints. One thing is certain: No one on the ship will ever know how the crisis is resolved."

No two minds or two sensibilities ever matched more closely than these two, but Akira's descriptions, alternative after alternative, led relentlessly into futility and left Claudio nearly speechless.

He fished for some apt reply and eventually came up with this: "Which path do you think your people will choose?"

"The answer may surprise you and make you proud. I think they will take the third way. There's a kind of settled conviction that no one has dared put in words, but none of them have much hope for the colony. Having tasted terrestrial life, none would choose to return to space for the rest of their lives even if they could. Four—Paola, Bahram, Edward Hamilton, and Kwan Shi Wa—will certainly champion this option. They'd prefer to be true to themselves. No, that's not quite right. It's not to *their precious selves* that they must be true. That may have been as far as the old fool Polonius could see, but their sense of being true—we owe this bit of wisdom to you through your daughter—is keeping faith to the end with a worthy, even if impossible, future."

Claudio gave another long sigh of resignation, but in the same moment a flicker of light passed across his eyes and as quickly became a question: "If you cannot buy more time waiting for the gods to intervene"—for some reason Claudio prefers to call contingency the gods!—"if you decide on open resistance, which you can't win, then are there untried delaying tactics?"

Akira rubbed his chin. "I see what you're thinking, but what delays are there that we haven't already used, and used up?"

Claudio's flicker of light became a steady beam. "What if you raised the alarm over some environmental danger? Perhaps a communicable disease. People of a certain mindset don't notice when diseases of the spirit are destroying everything that makes life worth living. But the same people respond with terror to biological threats. At the very least it would throw them off their stride."

Akira took some time to consider the idea then smiled grimly. "That might be done, but how much time would we gain and how at this stage could we possibly use it in a way that would matter?"

"Are your survival skills such that you could, the lot of you, pack up and 'take to the hills,' move to some other part of the planet? If you could survive, you might establish some kind of life and wait. It's a fair bet that, wishing to avoid trouble, Command wouldn't pursue you far. You'd all be out of their way, and you know the technological spirit will not let the ship sit here until it rots in orbit."

Akira regarded him with quite affection and murmured, "Wait for your gods? Perhaps. I don't know. No one knows the south, but Paola and Edward Hamilton have some experience of the wilds to the north. They would know what's possible." He paused again to study the idea. "It's an interesting suggestion. Meanwhile, since I must be at the landing docks soon, help me figure out what I say to those youngsters tonight. I give them Nasser's checklist, then say what?"

It was Claudio this time who refused to be rushed. He sat thinking for several minutes before responding. At last, "You're taking this too personally, you know. You have no choice. What is said to your people tonight is said for life or death. The barest hint of concealment and you'd poison the well. Besides, this may be one of the few purely political decisions that have been made in centuries."

Even now I, Kahn, can see these two men sitting quietly together for some minutes looking away into the cosmos. They would have been thinking of a three-hundred-year mission and a still longer plot to save it, knowing intimately the inner struggle against the despair that all flesh is prone to.

When at last Akira made a gesture as though to take his leave for the last time, Claudio said, "There is a thing I must tell you before you go. You remember the chronicle of life on the ship we asked Ishmael Kahn to prepare? Since your first return I have rushed him along shamelessly. As originally conceived, the work is nearly finished. I had hoped to make a present of it, but you have come too soon. I'll find a secure way to send it later. But here's the point: Given the difficulty of the times, we can't post it on Alexandros as intended. I will have it printed privately so it may survive unread."

"Ah, that's a wrinkle I hadn't foreseen." Akira pondered a situation not discussed before. Then continued, "Maybe you should wait to see what happens to us. If things go badly, you may want to tell Kahn about the *Résistance*, beginning to end, so that story will survive too."

"Yes, my friend, but I'm afraid I don't have the time to wait. I'd have to do it now. Even so I might not last. And if things didn't go exactly by plan—when have they ever?—it could increase your risk. Yet the book must survive, on the planet *and* on the ship."

Akira answered, "I'm immensely grateful for your effort to give me a copy. And I agree that we need to get it to the ground where it can be saved for futurity. You might have my wife include it in a personal packet. Those things are never opened. No one would imagine that a thing as old-fashioned as a book could have the power to work more mischief than electronic publicity." Then with resignation, "But I'll have to leave all that to your judgment."

With that, the last meeting between the wisest men of their generation came to an end, and with it their conspiracy against the managed life. As it turned out, we were never to learn what the explorers decided that evening in their hillside conclave, because what happened next has never been explained to anyone's satisfaction.

CRISIS

I WAS SITTING AT MY desk late one night working on this Chronicle, as though it still mattered, when there came a fierce knocking at my door. Elena Bart, of all people, with a message. "It's Claudio," she said breathlessly. It's like her to respond to any unusual situation from the edge of hysteria. "I think he's dying. It's imperative that you come to him at once."

From my door to his is only one deck down and a few hundred yards along the way, but I ran the whole distance through those largely empty corridors. In the middle of this mad dash to the aid of my friend, I saw something I'd never seen before. I hesitate to give it a name, because a word with such a troubled history will be misunderstood. But the truth that came over me with the force of a last judgment was that I loved that old man as I'd never loved anyone else. As the living image of every grace of life and mind, he had been the love of my life and its guiding ideal.

When I arrived, I didn't find him at death's door as I expected. That was just Bart's anxiety speaking, but Claudio did have things to say that couldn't wait for his last days, and he had something for me to do that couldn't wait an hour.

I found him propped up on pillows but in good spirits and apparently at his ease. "Sit down," he commanded. "I

291

have a story to tell you. Something has been going on over several years now, ever since Disruption, that no one knows about. You must know it now, tonight. Disaster is at hand, and whatever happens, this story must not be lost. When you've heard it, you are to add it to your chronicle. It's a part of our history that must not be forgotten—if anyone survives to remember. Weave the story in however you can among your accounts of life on the Galatea, then make one copy in your wonderful calligraphy. But," he raised himself from the pillows and shook a finger at me, "one copy only! These are absolute conditions.

"You are to have the copy bound, and deliver it to Elena. She will have it smuggled to Kashimoto or to my daughter Paola on the ground. I'm leaving instructions for Elena. She knows nothing of any of this just yet, but she will do as I ask. Remember, one copy only, and it must leave the ship as soon as you can get it ready. Keep your working copy secure so that it can turn up on the ship when we're all gone. Whether this effort at a terrestrial settlement succeeds or fails, the ship will move on. There may be other attempts to establish colonies, and this story may help shape conditions for more propitious efforts in the future. Once you have heard, you will understand the secrecy and the haste."

Then the old man fell back into his pillows, closed his eyes, and began recounting the plot that you know already, from his first secret meeting with Akira in the observatory to the moment of this conversation. He didn't say what had happened to make the matter so urgent, but it's likely that he and Akira had devised some secret signal for emergencies.

Later when he had finished saying what he had to say and the face that had been lively at the beginning had grown haggard and worn, he stopped speaking, without dismissing me to get on with my work. I sat on digesting it all, connecting dimensionless dots between what we had known and what we had not known.

Eventually I asked, "Why did he do it?"

Claudio gave me a puzzled look.

"Why did Akira risk everything on such a dubious scheme?"

"I asked him that question when he was here last. We knew we wouldn't meet again."

He paused. Claudio has never been much given to nostalgia, but there was unguarded sorrow in his voice. "Akira said, 'Humans would seem to be among the most insignificant beings in the universe. We appear to be a statistically insignificant mutation that happened on a statistically insignificant planet on the edges of one in a hundred billion solar systems in a statistically insignificant galaxy among perhaps two trillion galaxies in the universe.' It was a kind of verbal game he enjoyed, using numbers to turn quantities into qualities. He said that measured against all that, we are rarer than the rarest particles in existence. Yet we have the totally mysterious capacity to respond to any or all of these infinite infinities."

He rested a minute or two from the exertion of speaking then went on. "But that's not all Akira said. Taken together, it was the longest speech I ever heard from him and the most eloquent. He repeated my question. 'Why do I take such a risk? Because the noble human speck betrays itself when it squanders its moment of grandeur *"sweating and whining about its condition"* or rushing about *"demented with the mania of owning things."* The first question for us is, *"To be or not to be?"* And the meaning of that question is, to love or not to love, to play or not to play, with all that offers itself to us.'"

I need hardly add that Claudio's account of that last meeting with Akira stuck me with amazement and terror, but it didn't terrorize him! Afterward I did nothing night and day but revise this manuscript as he instructed. When I finished, I rushed off to a man I know who would bind it for me without asking questions. We spent a whole night working on the task together, during which he saw nothing but the title page:

Starship Galatea
A Chronicle by I. Kahn

That done, I called Elena Bart to meet me one morning at Claudio's apartment. Not that she was needed. Probably it was an impulse to make peace with a person I had always disliked. Not recognizing my love, I had not recognized my jealousy.

An hour after we arrived Claudio sat thumbing through the pages. His beaming face during those few minutes was the only personal reward I was destined to enjoy for those years of work, but it was more than enough. Then Elena packed it up and delivered it to Akira's wife, Atsuko, and we never heard of it again.

On a Wednesday evening, soon after the book was dispatched to Akira, the Council gathered in a heightened state of anxiety. There was nothing still but ominous silence from the bridge. Then, without prologue, Commander Rawls burst breathlessly through the door, eyes aflame with what we accepted as genuine apprehension.

"I have news!" She hurled the words at us like knives. "There's a crisis on the planet." She stopped to catch a breath. "We received an urgent message yesterday afternoon. An SOS. It did not come from the team leader as it normally would but from medical officer Kwan Shi Wa. She reports that there is an illness among the explorers and that there are fatalities. She advises—essentially orders—that landing craft not approach them until they can determine the nature of the problem and assure the crew's safety. She doesn't mention Kashimoto, but her sending the message suggests that he may be ill or worse. That's all we know. But some people on the bridge suspect foul play."

Rawls stopped once more to collect herself. "Since nothing seems amiss in the atmosphere on the surface and the food supply comes entirely from here, we suspect it may be a virus or an infection, perhaps from underground. We know they sleep in a cave."

Dennet-Jones asked, "What's the basis for suspecting foul play?"

"It's a suspicion, a theory, based on the landing party having so little to show for all these months of exploration. There may have been dissension among the members that was concealed from us. Communications have never been ideal."

Ava Sarosh, whose brother has been a key player in the drama, responded with a barbed remark that would have stung had it not been delivered with such lightness: "You think they're down there in that heat enjoying a family brawl?"

There was a tone of helplessness in Rawls' reply, reminding some of us how *"uneasy lies the head that wears a crown."* Commanders, too, learn to be suspicious of everyone. "It's not that," she answered to Sarosh's gibe. "It's that they have always called the shots. From recent communications, you might think that they were a government in exile. Aside from observable movement on the surface we have no means of knowing exactly what they're doing or of controlling their activities."

Dennet-Jones continued to ask the common-sense questions. "What contingency plans are you considering?"

"For now, we wait for further word. First Mate Nasser is preparing an emergency rescue mission. If we don't hear anything within a few hours confirming the last message, we will send people in to investigate. Then we'll be governed by our own observers."

By this time several persons were getting a picture rather different from the one Rawls was painting. We knew, for example, from Ava Sarosh's private communications with her brother, that he had designed a covered village with a central square for administration and a school, industrial facilities at the perimeter, and residences between. Though her information was sketchy, it showed remarkable progress for a few short months. Rumor was that Command was dissatisfied with the explorers because they had not found a feasible right-of-way through the northern mountains for a water pipeline that Rawls and company were determined to build. It was even alleged that there were disagreements over mining and construction sites. But we knew a thing or two about Akira's way of temporizing, so even as we were concerned about the tale of the mysterious virus, we heard it with different ears. And yet it would be days before we heard more.

The situation bore the Kashimoto signature of acting while appearing to do nothing. Some of us knew that, far from nothing getting done on the ground, more would have been done than Commander Rawls might ever know.

When other news came, it was not good. This time she dispatched a messenger who, knowing nothing, could not be questioned. His instructions were to inform us that the rescue party had found several bodies outside a cave in the hills, others in the cave, and that three, including Kwan Shi Wa, were still unaccounted for. There was not one among us who was not stunned into protracted silence. Several members had children or close relatives or friends among the casualties. Under the circumstances our consciousness of the insult in the way the sketchy news was delivered dawned on us slowly. But when awareness did arrive, it spread like a poisonous wind.

After that: silence from the bridge. We received no further briefing. What we learned we learned by public announcement or by rumor, and the conviction settled in that this was the end of the Council of Elders on Starship Galatea.

ENDINGS AND BEYOND

ALL IS OVER. The explorers are dead. Akira is dead. Claudio is dead. The Elders are sidelined, and the dream of the Galatea mission is lost. At the end, words are superfluous, and yet the end is never quite the end. Endings being stubborn, contradictory things.

My posthumous book, for example. No more than a message of futility, from the dead to the dying. And yet it refuses the full stop. So I offer this brief coda to my working copy, expecting that it will suffer the same fate on the ship as the copy on the ground. My conclusion that concludes nothing is a desperate act of affirmation where nothing is left to affirm. Unless the end is not the end "after all," because the past carries the seeds of a future in its fossils and shards.

The night after we received Commander Rawls' message and for many nights thereafter, I was unable to sleep. I suspect few of the Elders slept. Some had lost children. Others, relatives. Most had lost students. The collective harm was immeasurable. The prospects for a civilized colony never were very good. Now they were ruined. Command will just have another go, and our bootless efforts will come to less than nothing once again. The endless end will have been a failure *for*—and *of*—humanity.

My personal loss is of a different kind. The single copy of my book was smuggled to trusted people on the ground who are now all dead, and my work may even be responsible for the disaster. If *Starship Galatea* was discovered by anyone in Nasser's rescue party, the revelation of the conspiracy may have caused the disaster and Command's subsequently brushing the Council aside. Contingency, all is contingency!

That's the first thing that leaves me with an attack of Jewish guilt. The other thing is the question by what right I mourn the loss of my work when others have lost flesh and blood. So I harbor my guilt and grieve my loss in solitude, hoping against hope that somehow the Chronicle may survive unseen in a dark corner of a cave to be exhumed in a distant age by some anonymous inhabitant of P2314 and serve its purpose at last. Meanwhile I wonder: Is there any harder lesson in life than learning hope when hope is futile? And yet we are such beings!

So I set about trying to make an ending, depressed as I am by "*the vanity of human wishes.*" I made a last visit to Claudio just days before he died. His losses, too, were greater far than mine. His life's work had turned to ashes. He had lost his closest friend. Lost his estranged but beloved daughter. Now he tottered on the edge of oblivion with nothing left to hope. I knew he was too frail to be burdened with my troubles, and so the only relief I sought was just to sit for a few salutary minutes in the same room with him.

When I arrived, we exchanged no greeting. Greetings are unnecessary between people who have been engaged in lifelong conversation. Sometimes we "high-verbals" barely needed words. And so at this last meeting we two conversed in silence. It was a blessing, because there are things that can only be said without words to a dying man. For example, you can't face him with an apt passage from a favorite book: *"Vanity of vanities. All is vanity."* So I kept that demon-thought to myself, sitting in dejection across his small room studying his character for the thousandth time.

I hadn't expected to find him thrown into despair, but I think I did expect to find him a bit broken by loss. What I found instead—what I was almost offended to find—was the luminous countenance of a man facing blankness with gratitude. He appeared to regret nothing and to regard the future with a kind of hope that was hope for nothing. It was as though his last day was prologue, but prologue to what?

Somehow, he found the generosity to read my thoughts in the silence of that afternoon. Eventually he put into words the dark question that I had brought into his room: "You want to ask what we have achieved, if 'achieved' is the word." He leaned his head back wearily against the chair and closed his eyes. "We have lived like the immortals, ready and waiting at the threshold of being and not being. Some among us have raged through the cosmos seeking to master and devour, but we few have prospered like the gods on our flying island. Their voyage, those others, was about ends, but we have held to what was nearest and considered means without the ends."

I dared to whisper, "Yet this is the end, and all is lost!"

Claudio opened his eyes and looked at me with the most solicitous expression I can remember. Leaning forward, he reached for both my hands and took them in his. "Thank you, my friend, for your devoted work. You have conferred immortality on the starship"—he grinned—"even if no one reads it." Then, leaning back, he added in his oblique way, "But there is a thing you don't know that is my parting gift to you. It is this: As we arrive prematurely, we die too soon. Just now we seem to be at the end. But try as you will, you can't think the end. A dash always follows. The end—dash."

"What is the dash?"

"You get as far as the twilight and find another turning point. The end always recedes from your grasp."

"So the dash is nothing."

"Not nothing. That's more than we know. Call it the vertigo of thought."

I faced this by musing aloud, "We live like the eternals and cannot find an end. Immortal then?"

"I *know* nothing of all that. Only that I cannot help peering into the dark beyond every limit. Like standing at the edge of the universe and shooting an arrow."

I must have given him a look of incomprehension, for he managed to sit up straighter in his chair as though he needed all his energy to meet the challenge. As his fingers found the tips of his thumbs in the old Buddhist mudra of discussion, he raised his trembling hands: "When you come across something as unprecedented as human being, it is not wise to press for certainty. Modesty is better. Some essential things are unthinkable. Older than knowledge."

"And yet ends come."

"The end comes."

"The end—"